THE POSTHUMOUS MEMOIRS OF
BRÁS CUBAS

A Novel by
JOAQUIM MARIA MACHADO DE ASSIS

Translated from the Portuguese by
GREGORY RABASSA

WITH A FOREWORD BY ENYLTON DE SÁ REGO

AND AN AFTERWORD BY GILBERTO PINHEIRO PASSOS

Oxford University Press
New York   Oxford

Oxford University Press

Oxford   New York
Athens   Auckland   Bangkok   Bogotá   Buenos Aires   Calcutta
Cape Town   Chennai   Dar es Salaam   Delhi   Florence   Hong Kong   Istanbul
Karachi   Kuala Lumpur   Madrid   Melbourne   Mexico City   Mumbai
Nairobi   Paris   São Paulo   Singapore   Taipei   Tokyo   Toronto   Warsaw
and associated companies in

Berlin   Ibadan

Copyright © 1997 by Oxford University Press

First Published by Oxford University Press, Inc., 1997

First issued as an Oxford University Press paperback, 1998

Oxford is a registered trademark of Oxford University Press

Library of Congress Cataloging-in-Publication Data
Machado de Assis, 1839–1908.
[Memórias póstumas de Brás Cubas. English]
The posthumous memoirs of Brás Cubas / by Joaquim Maria Machado de Assis:
translated by Gregory Rabassa: with a foreword by Enylton de Sá Rego
and an afterword by Gilberto Pinheiro Passos.
p.   cm. — (Library of Latin America)
ISBN 0-19-510170-7 (Pbk.)
I. Rabassa, Gregory. II. Title. III. Series.
PQ9697.M18M513   1997
869.3—dc20   96-44125

1 3 5 7 9 10 8 6 4 2

Printed in the United States of America

THE POSTHUMOUS MEMOIRS OF
BRÁS CUBAS

OXFORD

Contents

Series Editors' Introduction
vii

Preface
ENYLTON DE SÁ REGO
xi

The Posthumous Memoirs of Brás Cubas
JOAQUIM MARIA MACHADO DE ASSIS
I

Afterword
GILBERTO PINHEIRO PASSOS
205

Series Editors'
General Introduction

The Library of Latin America series makes available in translation major nineteenth-century authors whose work has been neglected in the English-speaking world. The titles for the translations from the Spanish and Portuguese were suggested by an editorial committee that included Jean Franco (general editor responsible for works in Spanish), Richard Graham (series editor responsible for works in Portuguese), Tulio Halperín Donghi (at the University of California, Berkeley), Iván Jaksić (at the University of Notre Dame), Naomi Lindstrom (at the University of Texas at Austin), Francine Masiello (at the University of California, Berkeley), and Eduardo Lozano of the Library at the University of Pittsburgh. The late Antonio Cornejo Polar of the University of California, Berkeley, was also one of the founding members of the committee. The translations have been funded thanks to the generosity of the Lampadia Foundation and the Andrew W. Mellon Foundation.

During the period of national formation between 1810 and into the early years of the twentieth century, the new nations of Latin America fashioned their identities, drew up constitutions, engaged in bitter struggles over territory, and debated questions of education, government, ethnicity, and culture. This was a unique period unlike the process of nation formation in Europe and one which should be more familiar than it is to students of comparative politics, history, and literature.

The image of the nation was envisioned by the lettered classes—a minority in countries in which indigenous, mestizo, black, or mulatto peasants and slaves predominated—although there were also alternative nationalisms at the grassroots level. The cultural elite were well educated in European thought and letters, but as statesmen, journalists, poets, and academics, they confronted the problem of the racial and linguistic heterogeneity of the continent and the difficulties of integrating the population into a modern nation-state. Some of the writers whose works will be translated in the Library of Latin America series played leading roles in politics. Fray Servando Teresa de Mier, a friar who translated Rousseau's *The Social Contract* and was one of the most colorful characters of the independence period, was faced with imprisonment and expulsion from Mexico for his heterodox beliefs; on his return, after independence, he was elected to the congress. Domingo Faustino Sarmiento, exiled from his native Argentina under the presidency of Rosas, wrote *Facundo: Civilización y barbarie,* a stinging denunciation of that government. He returned after Rosas' overthrow and was elected president in 1868. Andrés Bello was born in Venezuela, lived in London where he published poetry during the independence period, settled in Chile where he founded the University, wrote his grammar of the Spanish language, and drew up the country's legal code.

These post-independence intelligentsia were not simply dreaming castles in the air, but vitally contributed to the founding of nations and the shaping of culture. The advantage of hindsight may make us aware of problems they themselves did not foresee, but this should not affect our assessment of their truly astonishing energies and achievements. It is still surprising that the writing of Andrés Bello, who contributed fundamental works to so many different fields, has never been translated into English. Although there is a recent translation of Sarmiento's celebrated *Facundo,* there is no translation of his memoirs, *Recuerdos de provincia (Provincial Recollections).* The predominance of memoirs in the Library of Latin America series is no accident—many of these offer entertaining insights into a vast and complex continent.

Nor have we neglected the novel. The series includes new translations of the outstanding Brazilian writer Joaquim Maria Machado de Assis' work, including *Dom Casmurro* and *The Posthumous Memoirs of Brás Cubas.* There is no reason why other novels and writers who are not so well known outside Latin America—the Peruvian novelist Clorinda Matto de Turner's *Aves sin nido,* Nataniel Aguirre's *Juan de la Rosa,* José de Alencar's *Iracema,* Juana Manuela Gorriti's short stories—should not be read with as much interest as the political novels of Anthony Trollope.

A series on nineteenth-century Latin America cannot, however, be limited to literary genres such as the novel, the poem, and the short story. The literature of independent Latin America was eclectic and strongly influenced by the periodical press newly liberated from scrutiny by colonial authorities and the Inquisition. Newspapers were miscellanies of fiction, essays, poems, and translations from all manner of European writing. The novels written on the eve of Mexican Independence by José Joaquín Fernández de Lizardi included disquisitions on secular education and law, and denunciations of the evils of gaming and idleness. Other works, such as a well-known poem by Andrés Bello, "Ode to Tropical Agriculture," and novels such as *Amalia* by José Mármol and the Bolivian Nataniel Aguirre's *Juan de la Rosa*, were openly partisan. By the end of the century, sophisticated scholars were beginning to address the history of their countries, as did João Capistrano de Abreu in his *Capítulos de história colonial.*

It is often in memoirs such as those by Fray Servando Teresa de Mier or Sarmiento that we find the descriptions of everyday life that in Europe were incorporated into the realist novel. Latin American literature at this time was seen largely as a pedagogical tool, a "light" alternative to speeches, sermons, and philosophical tracts—though, in fact, especially in the early part of the century, even the readership for novels was quite small because of the high rate of illiteracy. Nevertheless, the vigorous orally transmitted culture of the gaucho and the urban underclasses became the linguistic repertoire of some of the most interesting nineteenth-century writers—most notably José Hernández, author of the "gauchesque" poem "Martín Fierro," which enjoyed an unparalleled popularity. But for many writers the task was not to appropriate popular language but to civilize, and their literary works were strongly influenced by the high style of political oratory.

The editorial committee has not attempted to limit its selection to the better-known writers such as Machado de Assis; it has also selected many works that have never appeared in translation or writers whose work has not been translated recently. The series now makes these works available to the English-speaking public.

Because of the preferences of funding organizations, the series initially focuses on writing from Brazil, the Southern Cone, the Andean region, and Mexico. Each of our editions will have an introduction that places the work in its appropriate context and includes explanatory notes.

We owe special thanks to Robert Glynn of the Lampadia Foundation, whose initiative gave the project a jump start, and to Richard Ekman of the Andrew W. Mellon Foundation, which also generously supported the project. We also thank the Rockefeller Foundation for funding the 1996 symposium "Culture and Nation in Iberoamerica," organized by the editorial board of the Library of Latin America. We received substantial institutional support and personal encouragement from the Institute of Latin American Studies of the University of Texas at Austin. The support of Edward Barry of Oxford University Press has been crucial, as has the advice and help of Ellen Chodosh of Oxford University Press. The first volumes of the series were published after the untimely death, on July 3, 1997, of Maria C. Bulle, who, as an associate of the Lampadia Foundation, supported the idea from its beginning.

—*Jean Franco*
—*Richard Graham*

Preface

WARNING: DEADLY HUMOR AT WORK

Dear Reader:

If you have never heard of the nineteenth-century Brazilian writer Machado de Assis, this novel will afford you a triple surprise. You will be surprised by its form, its content, and the author's strange originality behind these pages.

The form of this novel is certainly unusual. As we are told at the outset, these memoirs are posthumous, albeit not in the usual sense of having been published after the death of their author. These are posthumous memoirs in a very literal sense: Brás Cubas, the memorialist, tells us in his preface "To the Reader" that he started writing his autobiography only after he died. If you accept this quite unconventional possibility for a work of fiction, you have here an extremely uncommon form of autobiography, written from beyond the grave, with all the advantages of perfect hindsight.

Having lived his life to its very end, Brás Cubas supposedly knows the whole truth about it. Since he writes from this privileged point of view, we have the right to expect a highly organized compendium of the knowledge and wisdom acquired by Brás Cubas during his existence. If these memoirs are indeed the final confessions of a dead man, we can expect him to be deadly serious about the meaning of life. What we get instead is a digressive and fragmented account of an ordinary man's experiences, an account in which an incredibly irreverent and facetious narrator chattily addresses his readers at every step, challenging us to make our own sense of the inconsistencies of his unheroic life. From his extremely detached point of view, Brás Cubas can tell us the blunt truth about his ordinary life, unmasking in the process most conventions of appropriateness he no longer has to obey. In doing so, he compels the reader to reconsider both these social conventions and the very meaning of life. Brás Cubas is serious about life, but in a peculiarly ludicrous way: his is indeed a deadly sense of humor.

The book is broken up into 160 chapters, few containing more than three or four pages, and some made up of only one or two sentences. For example, Chapter CXXXVI in its entirety reads: "But, I'm either mistaken or I've just written a useless chapter." Fittingly, the title of this chapter is "Uselessness." Some readers will smile, finding it funny. Others will probably be annoyed, or judge the exercise clumsy and contrived, if not a good example of total uselessness, thus confirming the appropriateness of the chapter. If you are in the latter group, dear reader, your surprise will probably increase when you come upon portions of the novel containing no words at all, such as Chapter LV.

Under the title "The Old Dialogue Between Adam and Eve," a chapter is presented as a full-page conversation between a man and a woman. It starts with his asking her a question. After the give and take of a few more questions and answers, it reaches its climax with both man and woman using exclamations at the end of whatever it is they are saying to each other. Yet, the only elements we get of this verbal exchange are the question marks and the exclamation points; the whole dialogue is represented on the blank page by ellipses alone, or, graphically speaking, by suspension points. Evidently, the reader is supposed to fill in the blanks, projecting into this dialogue his or her own ideas about the tenor of Adam and Eve's intercourse. Here, as throughout this novel, the reader is invited to assume an active, creative, and critical role, a surprisingly modern approach for a novel written in the nineteenth century.

This active role is sometimes challenging. Chapter CXXXIX, "How I Didn't Get to Be Minister of State," contains only a few blank lines. The reader, probably surprised by a short, empty chapter, may decide to go on to the following chapter, CXL, "Which Explains the Previous One," only to find these opening words: "There are things that are better said in silence. Unsuccessful ambitious people will understand it." The suggestion is clear: if you want to understand the narrator's silence in Chapter CXXXIX, you will have to consider your own failures. For some readers, this may seem threatening, for we are reminded of our own frustrated ambitions for power, and nobody likes to acknowledge, however fleetingly, having ever been a loser.

These narrative tricks were uncommon in the usually romantic or realist nineteenth-century novels. Yet, they were not entirely new; English-language readers will be reminded of strategies employed by the eighteenth-century British writer Laurence Sterne in his still-hilarious *Tristram Shandy*, and the narrator Brás Cubas himself acknowledges in a foreword to the reader that he appropriated Sterne's "free-form" style for his memoirs. What is new, as he also warns the reader, is that to this usually comical form he will attach "a few fretful touches of pessimism" of his own. In an old-fashioned yet unforgettable metaphor, he tells us that he wrote his book with a playful pen, "*a pena da galhofa*," the pen of irreverent laughter—suggesting that this would certainly make his work light and funny. But he immediately adds that the ink well in which he dipped his pen contained "*a tinta da melancolia*," melancholy ink—thereby indelibly attaching to his laughter a more somber hue. This admixture of laughter and seriousness, intimately blended into the same thought or action, is an unusual and dangerous recipe for a novel: "one can readily foresee what may come of such a marriage," he concludes.

Brás Cubas is aware of the danger of mingling seriousness with amusement when vying for favorable public opinion. His book, he tells us, may have only five readers. Serious readers will probably dislike it, seeing in it only the pure fiction of a nonrealistic novel, while frivolous readers will not find in it the entertainment they crave. Thus, he adds, this book runs the risk of being deprived both of the pompous esteem of the serious and of the superficial infatuation of the frivolous. According to Brás Cubas, these are "the two main pillars" of public opinion. Some readers may be offended by his words. After all, seriousness is not always pompous, entertainment not always frivolous; and we readers, as an important part of public opinion, do not appreciate criticism from anyone, least of all a dead man.

A historical interpretation will remind us that when Machado de Assis was writing this book in Brazil in 1880 the country was still a monarchy, slavery had not yet been abolished, and only a small fraction of the population—the elite—were literate. In such an unequal society, his few potential readers would tend to go along with the mores of their times, a morality based on favoritism, patronage, and its attendant hypocrisy. In such a society, as we can easily imagine, the main practical virtues had to be social conformity and the cultivation of appearances.

So perhaps we can excuse Brás Cubas' apparent insolence on the grounds that he is criticizing others, not us.

Yet, some readers will not be convinced by this historical explanation, since our times do not seem to be that different; disrespecting public opinion remains a daring attitude. Conformity and cultivation of appearances are still considered sure recipes for success. Perception, public opinion, and "image-building" have arguably attained today the axiomatic status of political principle and even scientific dogma. By questioning accepted ideas, this book forces the perplexed reader to reexamine his or her own opinions, and ask him or herself: When I read this book, should I laugh or should I cry? With its seriocomic questioning of conventional ideas, this book is a subtle antidote to the power we ascribe to public opinion and the accompanying cultivation of appearances.

One of the conventions challenged by Brás Cubas is the traditional form of the novel itself. Nineteenth-century novels usually represent life through a convincing plot and a smooth and captivating narrative into which the reader is passively drawn and pulled along. In presenting to the reader the supposedly real-life actions and feelings of the characters, the author pretends to be absent from the text. Brás Cubas disrupts these realistic conventions with his frequent observations about his book and its style. In Chapter LXXI, for example, he makes a startling accusation: "the main defect of this book is you, reader." As if to explain his shocking statement, he adds: "You're in a hurry to grow old and the book moves slowly. You love direct and continuous narration . . . and this book and my style are like drunkards, they stagger left and right, they walk and stop, mumble, yell, cackle, shake their fists at the sky, stumble and fall . . ." Displaying once more his self-conscious and self-deprecating sense of humor, Brás Cubas is clearly warning the readers—mostly those who are used to action-packed, fast-paced plots presented in straightforward narrative—that his book is indeed very different from a traditional nineteenth-century novel. His book is intended for readers who prefer "reflection" to "anecdotes," despite Brás Cubas' ironic comment to the contrary in Chapter IV. In this sense, these posthumous memoirs are a remarkably modern book.

Other important conventions are also challenged in these memoirs. Critical readers will not miss the way in which, from the first chapter on, Brás Cubas ironically unveils the artificiality of the "pathetic fallacy"— the attribution of human feelings to inanimate nature—one of the basic artistic conventions of nineteenth-century romanticism still alive today in our culture. Describing his funeral, Brás Cubas tells us about the weather: it was raining—drizzling—and this fact of nature led one of his "last-minute faithful friends" to insert an "ingenious idea" into his eulogy, something like "nature appears to be weeping over the irreparable loss of one of the finest characters humanity has been honored with." To this flourish Brás Cubas adds, in the next paragraph: "Good and faithful friend! No, I don't regret the twenty bonds I left you."

This acerbic unmasking of the petty side of human motivations hiding behind a romantic convention does not mean, however, that these memoirs follow the other dominant schools of art in the nineteenth century, realism and naturalism. Throughout his book, Brás Cubas parodies and ridicules realistic and naturalistic narrative methods, as for example in Chapter IX, "Transition," where he starts by addressing the reader: "And now watch the skill, the art with which I make the greatest transition in this book. Watch." After a few lines of logical ratiocination, he speaks directly to the reader again: "See? Seamlessly, nothing to divert the reader's calm attention, nothing. So the book goes on like this with all of method's advantage but without method's rigidity." By poking fun at the artistic strategies and conventions of his and even in some cases of our own times, by revealing the mechanisms used by writers in the construction of their plots and narratives, Brás Cubas' voice is eminently satirical.

The reader may have already identified this detached and irreverent narrator as a satirist, but may still find it hard to pinpoint the kind of satire Brás Cubas is practicing. The two main satirical postures in our culture are well known and well established since the Romans: either the satirist is gentle and optimistic, telling the truth with a smile, like Horace, or he is austere and pessimistic, denouncing our human foibles with stern indignation, like Juvenal. Brás Cubas is neither. His self-conscious stance is always ambiguous and bittersweet, frequently parodic and self-deprecating, more akin to Woody Allen's sense of humor than to the traditional satirical personae usually associated with the two great Roman writers. Horace and Juvenal, in their different ways, had a serious common goal: they used satire to moralize. Unlike them, Brás Cubas is not a serious moralist, but a seriocomic persona; writing from beyond the grave, he places himself beyond morality. To some readers he may seem immoral. Many others, however, will see him as simply amoral, or rather as a questioner of established morality; these readers will accept the challenging reflections called forth by his constant questioning. To these readers, the strange form of this novel—the unusual form of this kind of satire—will be an invitation to a serious reexamination of the role played by chance in his and our own lives, of his and our hidden motives, of his and our own irrationality.

So my first warning to the potential readers of this book is that its form will be surprising, and may even seem offensive to a "sensitive soul" (Chapter XXXIV), if you do not accept its amusing yet often-times dangerous challenges.

The content will also come as a surprise. If we disregard the "extra-ordinary method" that allowed Brás Cubas to write his memoirs from beyond the grave, we note that the book is the story of an ordinary life.

His great-great-grandfather was an honest worker who made his fortune as a farmer. His great-grandfather inherited everything, took a law degree in Portugal and became a politician. His father was a rich, ambitious, mediocre but imaginative man: he made up an aristocratic origin for the family. Brás Cubas was born at the beginning of the nine-teenth century and grew up in a protected environment, pampered by his father. While still a teenager, he becomes involved with a courtesan who takes all she can from him. His father discovers the affair and sends him to study in Europe, from which he returns when his mother is on her deathbed. Through this last experience, he is introduced to the problem of life and death and becomes deeply depressed. He isolates himself from the world on a mountain top near Rio de Janeiro, where he discovers the voluptuousness of hypochondria and melancholy.

Brás Cubas' father pays him a visit, bringing an offer: a marriage of convenience, an arranged alliance that would bring him a successful po-litical career. After some hesitation, he accepts the deal and leaves his retreat to meet his unknown fiancée. She soon dumps him for a more ambitious and assertive rival. Years later, they become lovers. Their long-lasting liaison is almost uneventful. They are finally forced to end their relationship when her husband is appointed to a high office in a faraway province. With no great effort or emotional strain, Brás Cubas attains worldly success and old age.

At sixty-four, he has an idea that strikes him as brilliant and be-comes an obsession: the invention of an antimelancholy poultice, a cure-all designed to relieve the despondency of mankind, a panacea that would bring him wealth and fame. In his obsessive dedication to his fixed idea, he neglects his health, catches pneumonia, and dies, and with him his idea. After his death, he decides to write his memoirs, ex-posing and emphasizing his mediocrity, with the frankness which, in his opinion, is "the prime virtue of a dead man."

This is a straightforward summary of the main events in this book. Brás Cubas' narration of these same events, however, is anything but straightforward. As he has warned the reader, his book and his style, like drunkards, ramble incessantly. Moreover, he brings in an enormous number of references to other books, not always identifiable.

The reader will easily identify some of his literary allusions, such as, for example, to the New Testament (Matthew, 7:3), when he describes the impact his obsession has had on his life: "God deliver you, dear reader, from a fixed idea; better a mote in your eye, better even a beam." Most frequently, however, Brás' allusions are encyclopedic, absorbing and incorporating many great passages of Western literature and history from ancient times to his contemporaries, as if his book were in itself an intertextual library, or the result of an active dialogue with other books, an active dialogue in a very real sense, since most of these allusions to other texts are not accurate quotations. Instead, they frequently deviate slightly from the original text. Some literary critics have suggested that these deviations were the result of the alleged fact that Machado de Assis quoted from memory, not always remembering correctly the passage he was citing. The same argument—lack of memory—was used to explain Erasmus' misquotations in his *Praise of Folly* and Robert Burton's in his *Anatomy of Melancholy*, two books that belong in the same tradition of jestful encyclopedic erudition as these *Posthumous Memoirs*.

It is not known whether Machado de Assis was acquainted with Burton's book, but he certainly knew the *Praise of Folly*, since he makes Brás Cubas quote it in Chapter CXLIX, and since he even wrote a parody of it, his "Praise of Vanity." Moreover, in one of his short stories Machado de Assis justified this practice of slightly misquoting, explaining the difference between literal quotations—which simply invoke someone else's authority—and the really artistic quotations—which creatively rewrite the quoted authors.

In one of his pieces of literary criticism, Machado de Assis also discussed the subtle interplay between originality and appropriation of other texts, making use of an interesting culinary allegory: any writer has the right to look for "spices" in the work of any other writer, but the "final sauce" has to be of his or her own making. In these *Posthumous Memoirs of Brás Cubas* Machado de Assis gives a good example of the banquet he can serve to the reader. If the reader does not suffer indiges-

tion and survives this exuberant and ironic display of encyclopedic erudition, he or she will be gratified, for the result is indeed humorous.

These memoirs are humorous, but they are also serious, if we remember the seriocomic aspect of this kind of satire. Brás Cubas himself
describes his book in Chapter IV as "a supinely philosophical work, of
an unequal philosophy, now austere, now playful, something that neither builds nor destroys, neither inflames nor cools, and, yet, it is more
than a pastime and less than an apostolate." As a philosophy this does
not seem to be very powerful, but it certainly is a good definition of art
as practiced by Machado de Assis: more than mere pastime—since for
him art is a serious human activity, but not so serious as to become
preachy, since it should not be dogmatic.

Some readers will identify in Machado de Assis' unorthodox philosophy the old tradition of cynicism; others will probably see him as a
radical skeptic; others still may recognize in his novels the presence of
an old literary tradition called Menippean satire; some could even say
that his novels, written in the nineteenth century, are more modern
than many modern novels, and that they could even be considered
postmodern. Whatever classification we choose, his is indisputably a
position of unmitigated disbelief toward all philosophical systems
and categorizations, some of which he deliberately mocks through
one of this book's characters, the philosophizing Quincas Borba. His
medium, however, is not the well-reasoned philosophical or scientific
treatise, but the lighter form of the novel. Since any novel presupposes
a social context, other readers will probably enjoy what has been called
Machado's deceptive realism, a kind of realism that allegorically describes, in a very devious and disguised way, the social realities of nineteenth-century Brazil, or, in a still more indirect way, the reality of our
own times.

But who was this Machado de Assis, this strange nineteenth-century Brazilian writer? As I promised in my opening lines, this is the last
surprise to the readers—the last, that is, before the best surprise, the
book itself.

Machado de Assis was born in 1839, in Rio de Janeiro. His father, a
poor house painter, was the son of freed slaves. His mother was a servant from the Azores who worked in a wealthy household on the out-
skirts of the city. She died when her son was nine years old. Machado's
father was remarried to a poor black woman, and then died a few years
later. Machado de Assis, therefore, grew up a poor, mulatto orphan, the
grandson of slaves in a country where slavery would continue officially

to exist until he was fifty years old. He had no formal education and probably never attended school.

Machado also had some other problems: he was frail and shy, terribly myopic. He almost went blind at forty, and he stuttered and was epileptic. Despite all these social and personal disadvantages, he acquired French and English, read voraciously in several languages, worked as a typesetter and journalist and from his youth onward dedicated his life to literature. At thirty-one, he married a Portuguese woman five years his senior. She died in 1904 and he, four years later. As founder and president of the Brazilian Academy of Letters, he was recognized as the most important and famous writer of his time. He wrote nine novels, a few plays and volumes of poetry, some literary criticism, many journalistic columns, and also published a few excellent translations from French and English.

Some literary critics, both in Brazil and abroad, have tried to explain Machado's production in terms of his biological and psychological history. Some have suggested that he wrote in a fragmented style because he stuttered. Others have focused on the influence of his epilepsy and his eye problems on his approach to life and literature. Others still have suggested that his racial origins determined the content of his literary production.

This search for an ultimate scientific cause for Machado's literary genius is ironic, given his radically skeptical views of all-encompassing explanations of human behavior, especially those of the reductionist kind. Whatever the reason for his greatness, it is surprising that a man who was born in poverty, had no formal education, and faced so many physical and social disadvantages was able to become such an impressive writer. His novels—and most of all these *Posthumous Memoirs of Brás Cubas*—have been admired, studied, analyzed, and even carefully dissected by many critics, some very sympathetic and some less so. But even those who are not amused by his style and his message do not deny his importance for Brazilian and world literature.

But I fear this introduction is becoming too long. As Brás Cubas himself says in his first words to the reader, "the best prologue is the one that says the fewest things or which tells them in an obscure and truncated way . . . The work itself is everything."

So you have been warned, dear potential reader of this book: enjoy it, but beware, because there is in it some deadly humor at work.

—*Enylton de Sá Rego*

THE POSTHUMOUS MEMOIRS OF
BRÁS CUBAS

To the Worm
Who
Gnawed the Cold Flesh
of My Corpse
I Dedicate
These Posthumous Memoirs
As a Nostalgic Remembrance

Prologue to the Third Edition

The first edition of these *Posthumous Memoirs of Brás Cubas* came in sections in the *Revista Brasileira* during the 1880s. When they were put into book form later on I corrected the text in several places. Now that I have had to review it for the third edition, I have emended yet a few more things and eliminated two or three dozen lines. Revised in this way, this work which seems to have garnered some acceptance on the part of the public, is published once again.

Capistrano de Abreu, taking note of the publication of the book, asked "Is *The Posthumous Memoirs of Brás Cubas* a novel?" Macedo Soares in a letter that he wrote me around that time recalled fondly the *Travels in My Land* [of Almeida Garrett]. To the first the late Brás Cubas has already replied (as the reader has seen and will see in the prologue by him that opens the book) yes and no, that it was a novel for some and wasn't for others. As for the second, this is how the decedent has explained it: "It's a question of a scattered work where I, Brás Cubas, have adopted the free form of a Sterne or a Xavier de Maistre. I'm not sure, but I may have put a few fretful touches of pessimism into it." All those people traveled: Xavier de Maistre around his room, Garrett in his land, Sterne in other people's lands. It might be said of Brás Cubas that he traveled around life.

What makes my Brás Cubas a singular author is what he calls "a few fretful touches of pessimism." There is in the soul of this book, for all of its merry appearance, a harsh and bitter feeling that is a far piece from its models. It's a goblet that may carry a similar design but contains a different wine. I shall say no more so as not to get into any criticism of a dead man who painted himself and others according to what seemed best and most authentic to him.

—*Machado de Assis*

To the Reader

That Stendhal should have confessed to have written one of his books for a hundred readers is something that brings on wonder and concern. Something that will not cause wonder and probably no concern is whether this other book will have Stendhal's hundred readers, or fifty, or twenty, or even ten. Ten? Five, perhaps. The truth is that it's a question of a scattered work where I, Brás Cubas, have adopted the free-form of a Sterne or a Xavier de Maistre. I'm not sure, but I may have put a few fretful touches of pessimism into it. It's possible. The work of a dead man. I wrote it with a playful pen and melancholy ink and it isn't hard to foresee what can come out of that marriage. I might add that serious people will find some semblance of a normal novel, while frivolous people won't find their usual one here. There it stands, deprived of the esteem of the serious and the love of the frivolous, the two main pillars of opinion.

Nonetheless, I hope to entice sympathetic opinion and the first trick is to avoid any explicit and long prologue. The best prologue is the one that says the fewest things or which tells them in an obscure and truncated way. Consequently, I shall not recount the extraordinary process through which I undertook the composition of these *Memoirs*, put together here in the other world. It would have been interesting but excessively long and also unnecessary for an understanding of the work.

The work itself is everything: if it pleases you, dear reader, I shall be well paid for the task; if it doesn't please you, I'll pay you with a snap of the finger and goodbye.

—Brás Cubas

I

The Author's Demise

For some time I debated over whether I should start these memoirs at the beginning or at the end, that is, whether I should put my birth or my death in first place. Since common usage would call for beginning with birth, two considerations led me to adopt a different method: the first is that I am not exactly a writer who is dead but a dead man who is a writer, for whom the grave was a second cradle; the second is that the writing would be more distinctive and novel in that way. Moses, who also wrote about his death, didn't place it at the opening but at the close: a radical difference between this book and the Pentateuch.

With that said, I expired at two o'clock on a Friday afternoon in the month of August, 1869, at my beautiful suburban place in Catumbi. I was sixty-four intense and prosperous years old, I was a bachelor, I had wealth of around three hundred *contos*, and I was accompanied to the cemetery by eleven friends. Eleven friends! The fact is, there hadn't been any cards or announcements. On top of that it was raining—drizzling—a thin, sad, constant rain, so constant and so sad that it led one of those last-minute faithful friends to insert this ingenious idea into the speech he was making at the edge of my grave: "You who knew him, gentlemen, can say with me that nature appears to be weeping over the irreparable loss of one of the finest characters humanity has been honored with. This somber air, these drops from heaven, those dark clouds that cover the blue like funeral crepe, all of it is the cruel and terrible grief that gnaws at nature and at my deepest insides; all that is sublime praise for our illustrious deceased."

Good and faithful friend! No, I don't regret the twenty bonds I left you. And that was how I reached the closure of my days. That was how I set out for Hamlet's undiscovered country without the anxieties or doubts of the young prince, but, rather, slow and lumbering, like someone leaving the spectacle late. Late and bored. Some nine or ten people had seen me leave, among them three ladies: my sister Sabina, married to Cotrim—their daughter, a lily of the valley,—and . . . Be patient! In just a little while I'll tell you who the third lady was. Be content with knowing that the unnamed one, even though not a relative, suffered more than the relatives did. It's true. She suffered more. I'm not saying that she wailed, I'm not saying that she rolled on the ground in convulsions, or that my passing was a highly dramatic thing . . . An old bachelor who expires at the age of sixty-four doesn't seem to gather up all the elements of a tragedy in himself. And even if that were the case, what least suited that unnamed lady was to show such feelings. Standing by the head of the bed, her eyes cloudy, her mouth half open, the sad lady had a hard time believing my extinction.

"Dead! Dead!" she kept saying to herself.

And her imagination, like the storks that an illustrious traveler watched taking flight from the Ilissus on their way to African shores without the hindrance of ruins and times—that lady's imagination also flew over the present rubble to the shores of a youthful Africa . . . Let it go. We'll get there later on. We'll go there when I get my early years back. Now I want to die peacefully, methodically, listening to the ladies sobbing, the men talking softly, the rain drumming on the caladium leaves of my suburban home, and the strident sound of a knife a grinder is sharpening outside by a harness-maker's door. I swear to you that the orchestra of death was not at all as sad as it might have seemed. From a certain point on it even got to be delightful. Life was thrashing about in my chest with the surging of an ocean wave. My consciousness was evaporating. I was descending into physical and moral immobility and my body was turning into a plant, a stone, mud, nothing at all.

I died of pneumonia, yet if I tell my reader that it wasn't so much the pneumonia that caused my death but a magnificent and useful idea he might not believe me and, nevertheless, it's the truth. Let me explain briefly. You can judge for yourself.

I I

The Poultice

As it so happened, one day in the morning while I was strolling about my place an idea started to hang from the trapeze I have in my brain. Once hanging there it began to wave its arms and legs and execute the most daring antics of a tightrope-walker that anyone could imagine. I let myself stand there contemplating it. Suddenly it took a great leap, extended its arms and legs until it took on the shape of an X: decipher me or I'll devour you.

That idea was nothing less than the invention of a sublime remedy, an antihypochondriacal poultice, destined to alleviate our melancholy humanity. In the patent application that I drew up afterward I brought that truly Christian product to the government's attention. I didn't hide from friends, however, the pecuniary rewards that would of needs result from the distribution of a product with such far-reaching and profound effects. But now that I'm on the other side of life I can confess everything: what mainly influenced me was the pleasure I would have seeing in print in newspapers, on store counters, in pamphlets, on street corners, and, finally, on boxes of the medicine these three words: *Brás Cubas Poultice*. Why deny it? I had a passion for ballyhoo, the limelight, fireworks. More modest people will censure me perhaps for this defect. I'm confident, however, that clever people will recognize this talent of mine. So my idea had two faces, like a medal, one turned toward the public and the other toward me. On one side philanthropy and profit, on the other a thirst for fame. Let us say: —love of glory.

An uncle of mine, a canon with full prebend, liked to say that love of temporal glory was the perdition of souls, who should covet only eternal glory. To which another uncle, an officer in one of those old infantry regiments called *terços*, would retort that love of glory was the most truly human thing there was in a man and, consequently, his most genuine attribute.

Let the reader decide between the military man and the canon. I'm going back to the poultice.

III

Genealogy

N ow that I've mentioned my two uncles, let me make a short genealogical outline here.

The founder of my family was a certain Damião Cubas, who flourished in the first half of the eighteenth century. He was a cooper by trade, a native of Rio de Janeiro, where he would have died in penury and obscurity had he limited himself to the work of barrel making. But he didn't. He became a farmer. He planted, harvested, and exchanged his produce for good, honest silver *patacas* until he died, leaving a nice fat inheritance to a son, the licentiate Luís Cubas. It was with this young man that my series of grandfathers really begins—the grandfathers my family always admitted to—because Damião Cubas was, after all, a cooper, and perhaps even a bad cooper, while Luís Cubas studied at Coimbra, was conspicuous in affairs of state, and was a personal friend of the viceroy, Count da Cunha.

Since the surname Cubas, meaning kegs, smelled too much of cooperage, my father, Damião's great-grandson, alleged that the aforesaid surname had been given to a knight, a hero of the African campaigns, as a reward for a deed he brought off: the capture of three hundred barrels from the Moors. My father was a man of imagination; he flew out of the cooperage on the wings of a pun. He was a good character, my father, a worthy and loyal man like few others. He had a touch of the fibber about him, it's true, but who in this world doesn't have a bit of that? It should be noted that he never had recourse to invention except after an attempt at falsification. At first he had the family branch off from that famous namesake of mine, Captain-Major Brás Cubas, who founded the town of São Vicente, where he died in 1592, and that's why he named me Brás. The captain-major's family refuted him, however, and that was when he imagined the three hundred Moorish kegs.

A few members of my family are still alive, my niece Venância, for example, the lily of the valley, which is the flower for ladies of her time. Her father, Cotrim, is still alive, a fellow who . . . But let's not get ahead of events. Let's finish with our poultice once and for all.

I V

The Idée Fixe

M y idea, after so many leaps and bounds, had become an *idée fixe*. God save you, dear reader, from an *idée fixe*, better a speck, a mote in the eye. Look at Cavour: It was the *idée fixe* of Italian unity that killed him. It's true that Bismarck didn't die, but we should be warned that nature is terribly fickle and history eternally meretricious. For example, Suetonius gave us a Claudius who was a simpleton—or "a pumpkinhead" as Seneca called him—and a Titus who deserved being the delight of all Rome. In modern times a professor came along and found a way of demonstrating that of the two Caesars the delight, the real delight, was Seneca's "pumpkinhead." And you Madame Lucrezia, flower of the Borgias, if a poet painted you as the Catholic Messalina, along came an incredulous Gregorovius who did a great deal to quench that quality and even if you didn't come out a lily, you weren't a smelly fen either. I'll take my position between the poet and the savant.

So, long live history, voluble history, which is good at anything, and, getting back to the *idée fixe*, let me say that it's what produces strong men and madmen. A mobile idea, vague or changeable, is what produces a Claudius—according to the formula of Suetonius.

My idea was fixed, fixed like . . . I can't think of anything fixed enough in this world: maybe the moon, maybe the pyramids of Egypt, maybe the dead German Diet. Let the reader find the comparison that fits best, let him find it and not stand there with his nose out of joint just because we haven't got to the narrative part of these memoirs. We'll get there. I think he prefers anecdotes to reflections, like other readers, his confrères, and I think he's right. So let's get on with it. It must be said, however, that this book is written with apathy, with the apathy of a man now freed of the brevity of the century, a supinely philosophical work, of an unequal philosophy, now austere, now playful, something that neither builds nor destroys, neither inflames nor cools, and, yet, it is more than a pastime and less than an apostolate.

Let's go. Straighten out your nose and let's get back to the poultice. Let's leave history with its whims of an elegant lady. Neither of us fought the battle of Salamina or wrote the Augsburg Confession. For my part, if I can ever remember Cromwell it's only because of the idea that His Highness, with the same hand that locked up Parliament might have imposed the Brás Cubas poultice on the English. Don't laugh at that joint victory of pharmaceutics and puritanism. Who isn't aware that beneath every great, public, showy flag quite often there are several other modestly private banners that are unfurled and waving in the shadow of the first, and ever so many times outlive it? To make a poor comparison, it's like the rabble huddled in the shadow of a feudal castle, and when the latter fell, the riffraff remained. The fact is they became big shots and castellans . . . No, that's not a good comparison.

V

In Which a Lady's Ear Appears

When I was busy preparing and refining my invention, however, I was caught in a strong draft. I fell ill right after and I didn't take care of myself. I had the poultice on my brain. I was carrying with me the *idée fixe* of the mad and the strong. I could see myself from a distance rising up from the mob-ridden earth and ascending to heaven like an immortal eagle, and before such a grand spectacle no man can feel the pain that's jabbing at him. The next day I was worse. I finally did something about it, but in an incomplete way, with no method or attention or follow-through. Such was the origin of the illness that brought me to eternity. You already know that I died on a Friday, an unlucky day, and I think I've shown that it was my invention that killed me. There are less lucid and no less winning demonstrations.

It might not have been impossible, however, for me to have climbed to the heights of a century and figure in the pages of newspapers among the great. I was healthy and robust. Let it be imagined that, instead of laying down the bases for a pharmaceutical invention, I was trying to bring together the elements of a political institution or a religious refor-

mation. The current of air came and efficiently conquered human calculations and there went everything. That's the way man's fate goes.

With that reflection I took leave of the woman, I won't say the most
discreet, but certainly the most beautiful among her contemporaries,
the one whose imagination, like the storks on the Ilissus . . . She was
fifty-four then, she was a ruin, a splendid ruin. Let the reader imagine
that we had been in love, she and I, many years before and that, one day,
when I was already ill, I see her appear in the door of my bedroom.

V I

Chimène, Qui L'eût Dit?
Rodrigue, Qui L'eût Cru?

I see her appear in the door of my bedroom—pale, upset, dressed in
black—and remain there for a minute without the courage to come
in, or held back by the presence of the man who was with me. From the
bed where I was lying I contemplated her all that time, neglecting to say
anything to her or make any gesture. We hadn't seen each other for two
years and I saw her now not as she was but as she had been, as we both
had been, because some mysterious Hezekiah had made the sun turn
back to the days of our youth. The sun turned back, I shook off all my
miseries, and this handful of dust that death was about to scatter into
the eternity of nothingness was stronger than time, who is the minister
of death. No water from Iuventus could match simple nostalgia in that.

Believe me, remembering is the least evil. No one should trust present happiness, there's a drop of Cain's drivel in it. With the passing of
time and the end of rapture, then, yes, then perhaps it's possible really
to enjoy, because between these two illusions the better one is the one
that's enjoyed without pain.

The evocation didn't last long. Reality took over immediately. The
present expelled the past. Perhaps I'll explain to the reader in some corner

of this book my theory of human editions. What matters now is that Virgília—her name was Virgília—entered the room with a firm step, with the gravity that her clothes and the years gave her, and came over to my bed. The outsider got up and left. He was a fellow who would visit me every day and talk about exchange rates, colonization, and the need for developing railroads, nothing of greater interest to a dying man. He left. Virgília stood there. For some time we remained looking at each other without uttering a word. What was there to say? Of two great lovers, two great passions, there was nothing left twenty years later. There were only two withered hearts devastated by life and glutted with it; I don't know whether in equal doses, but glutted nonetheless. Virgília now had the beauty of age, an austere, maternal look. She was less thin than when I saw here the last time at a Saint John's festival in Tijuca and, as she was someone who had a great deal of resistance, only now were a few silver threads beginning to mingle with her dark hair.

"Are you making the rounds visiting dying men?" I asked her. "Come now, dying men!" Virgília answered with a pout. And then, after squeezing my hands, "I'm making the rounds to see if I can get lazy loafers back out onto the street."

It didn't have the teary caress of other times, but her voice was friendly and sweet. She sat down. I was alone in the house except for a male nurse. We could talk to each other without any danger. Virgília gave me lots of news from the world outside, narrating it with humor, with a certain touch of a wicked tongue, which was the salt of her talk. I, ready to leave the world, felt a satanic pleasure in making fun of it all, in persuading myself that I wasn't leaving anything worthwhile.

"What kind of ideas are those?" Virgília interrupted me, a little annoyed. "Look, I'm not going to come back. Dying! We all have to die. It's enough just being alive."

And looking at the clock:

"Good heavens! It's three o'clock. I've got to go."

"So soon?"

"Yes. I'll come back tomorrow or sometime later."

"I don't know if you're doing the proper thing," I replied. "The patient is an old bachelor and the house has no women in it . . ."

"What about your sister?"

"She's going to come and spend a few days here, but she can't get here until Saturday."

Virgília thought for a moment, straightened up, and said gravely:

"I'm an old woman! Nobody pays any attention to me anymore. But just to put an end to any doubts I'll come with Nhonhô."

Nhonhô was a lawyer, the only child from her marriage, who at the age of five had been the unwitting accomplice in our love affair. They came together two days later and I must confess that when I saw them there in my bedroom I was taken by a reticence that prevented me from replying immediately to the lad's affable words. Virgília sensed this and told her son:

"Nhonhô, don't pay any attention to that big trickster there. He doesn't want to talk so he can make you think that he's at death's door."

Her son smiled. I think I smiled, too, and everything ended up as a big joke. Virgília was serene and smiling. She had the look of immaculate life. No suspect look, no gesture that might have given anything away, a balance in word and spirit, control over herself, all of which seemed—and perhaps was—strange. As by chance we touched upon an illicit love affair, half-secret, half-known, I saw her speak a disdainful word and a bit indignantly about the woman involved, a friend of hers besides. Her son felt satisfied when he heard that strong and fitting word and I asked myself what the hawks might have said about us humans if Buffon had been born a hawk . . .

It was the start of my delirium.

V I I

Delirium

As far as I know, no one has ever spoken about his own delirium. I'm doing just that and science will thank me for it. If the reader isn't given to the contemplation of these mental phenomena, he may skip this chapter and go straight to the narrative. But if he has the slightest bit of curiosity, I can tell him now that it's interesting to know what went on in my head for some twenty or thirty minutes.

At the very first I took on the figure of a Chinese barber, potbellied, dexterous, who was giving a close shave to a mandarin, who paid me for my work with pinches and sweets: the whims of a mandarin.

Right after that I felt myself transformed into Aquinas' *Summa Theologica*, printed in one volume and morocco-bound, with silver clasps and illustrations. This was an idea that gave my body a most complete immobility and even now I can remember that with my hands as the book's clasps crossed over my stomach, someone was uncrossing them (Virgília most certainly) because that position gave her the image of a dead person.

Finally, restored to human form, I saw a hippopotamus come and carry me off. I let myself go, silent, I don't know whether out of fear or trust, but after a short while the running became so dizzying that I dared question him and in some way told him that the trip didn't seem to be going anywhere.

"You're wrong," the animal replied, "we're going to the origin of the centuries."

I suggested that it must be very far away, but the hippopotamus either didn't understand me or didn't hear me, unless he was pretending one of those things, and when I asked him, since he could talk, if he were a descendant of Achilles' horse or Balaam's ass, he answered me with a gesture peculiar to those two quadrupeds, he flapped his ears. For my part, I closed my eyes and let myself go where chance would take me. I must confess now, however, that I felt some sort of prick of curiosity to find out where the origin of the centuries was, if it was as mysterious as the origin of the Nile, and, most of all, whether the consummation of those same centuries was really worth anything: the reflections of a sick mind. Since I was going along with my eyes closed I couldn't see the road. I can only remember that a feeling of cold grew stronger as the journey went on and that a time came when it seemed to me that we were entering the region of perpetual ice. In fact, I opened my eyes and saw that my animal was galloping across a white plain of snow, here and there a mountain of snow, vegetation of snow, and several large animals of snow. Everything snow. A sun of snow was coming out to freeze us. I tried to speak but all I could manage was to grunt this anxious question:

"Where are we?"

"We just passed Eden."

"Fine. Let's stop at Abraham's tent."

"But we're traveling backward!" my mount retorted mockingly.

I was vexed and confused. The trip was beginning to seem tiresome and reckless, the cold was uncomfortable, the ride furious, and the result impalpable. And afterward—the cogitations of a sick man—if we did reach the indicated goal, it wasn't impossible that the centuries, annoyed at having their origin infringed upon, would squash me between their fingers, which must have been as age-old as they. While I was thinking along those lines we were gobbling up the road and the plain flew under our feet until the animal became fatigued and I was able to look more calmly at my surroundings. Only look: I saw nothing except the vast whiteness of the snow, which by now had invaded the sky itself, blue up till then. Here and there a plant or two might appear, huge and brutish, the broad leaves waving in the wind. The silence of that region was like a tomb. It could be said that the life of things had become stupidity for man.

Had it fallen out of the air? Detached itself from the earth? I don't know. I do know that a huge shape, the figure of a woman, appeared to me then, staring at me with eyes that blazed like the sun. Everything about that figure had the vastness of wild forms and everything was beyond the comprehension of human gaze because the outlines were lost in the surroundings and what looked thick was often diaphanous. Stupefied, I didn't say a word, I couldn't even let out a cry, but after a time, which was brief, I asked who she was and what her name was: the curiosity of delirium.

"Call me Nature or Pandora. I am your mother and your enemy."

When I heard that last word I drew back a little, overcome by fear. The figure let out a guffaw, which produced the effect of a typhoon around us; plants twisted and a long moan broke the silence of external things.

"Don't be frightened," she said, "my enmity doesn't kill, it's confirmed most of all by life. You're alive: that's the only torment I want."

"I'm alive?" I asked, digging my nails into my hands as if to certify my existence.

"Yes, worm, you're alive. Don't worry about losing those rags that are your pride, you're still going to taste the bread of pain and the wine of misery for a few hours. You're alive. Right now while you're going crazy, you're alive, and if your consciousness gets an instant of wisdom, you'll say you want to live."

Saying that, the vision reached out her arm, grabbed me by the hair, and lifted me up as if I were a feather. Only then did I manage to get a close look at her face, which was enormous. Nothing more serene; no violent contortion, no expression of hatred or ferocity. The only expression, general, complete, was that of selfish impassivity, that of eternal deafness, that of an immovable will. Wrath, if she had any, was buried in her heart. At the same time, in that face of glacial expression there was a look of youth and a blend of strength and vitality before which I felt the weakest and most decrepit of creatures.

"Did you understand me?" she asked me after some time of mutual contemplation.

"No," I answered, "nor do I want to understand you. You're an absurdity, you're a fable. I'm dreaming most certainly or if it's true that I went mad, you're nothing but the conception of a lunatic. I mean a hollow thing that absent reason can't control or touch. You Nature? The Nature I know is only mother and not enemy. She doesn't make life a torment, nor does she, like you, carry a face that's as indifferent as the tomb. And why Pandora?"

"Because I carry good and evil in my bag and the greatest thing of all, hope, the consolation of mankind. Are you trembling?"

"Yes, your gaze bewitches me."

"I should think so. I'm not only life, I'm also death, and you're about to give me back what I loaned you. You great lascivious man, the voluptuosity of nothingness awaits you."

When that word, "nothingness," echoed like a thunderclap in that huge valley, it was like the last sound that would reach my ears. I seemed to feel my own sudden decomposition. Then I faced her with pleading eyes and asked for a few more years.

"You miserable little minute!" she exclaimed. "What do you want a few more instants of life for? To devour and be devoured afterward? Haven't you had enough spectacle and struggle? You've had more than enough of what I presented you with that's the least base or the least painful: the dawn of day, the melancholy of afternoon, the stillness of night, the aspects of the land, sleep, which when all's said and done is the greatest benefit my hands can give. What more do you want, you sublime idiot?"

"Just to live, that's all I ask of you. Who put this love of life in my heart if not you? And since I love life why must you hurt yourself by killing me?"

"Because I no longer need you. The minute that passes doesn't matter to time, only the minute that's coming. The minute that's coming is strong, merry, it thinks it carries eternity in itself and it carries death, and it perishes just like the other one, but time carries on. Selfishness, you say? Yes, selfishness, I have no other law. Selfishness, preservation. The jaguar kills the calf because the jaguar's reasoning is that it must live, and if the calf is tender, so much the better: that's the universal law. Come up and have a look."

Saying that, she carried me up to the top of a mountain. I cast my eyes down one of the slopes and for a long time, in the distance, through the mist I contemplated a strange and singular thing. Just imagine, reader, a reduction of the centuries and a parade of all of them, all races, all passions, the tumult of empires, the war of appetites and hates, the reciprocal destruction of creatures and things. Such was that spectacle, a harsh and curious spectacle. The history of man and the earth had an intensity in that way that neither science nor imagination could give it, because science is slower and imagination is vaguer, while what I was seeing there was the living condensation of all ages. In order to describe it one would have to make a lightning bolt stand still. The centuries were filing by in a maelstrom and yet, because the eyes of delirium are different, I saw everything that was passing before me—torments and delights—from that thing called glory to the other one called misery, and I saw love multiplying misery and I saw misery intensifying weakness. Along came greed that devours, wrath that inflames, envy that drools, and the hoe and the pen, damp with sweat and ambition, hunger, vanity, melancholy, wealth, love, and all of them shaking man like a rattle until they destroyed him like a rag. They were different forms of an illness that sometimes gnaws at the entrails, sometimes at thoughts, and in its Harlequin costume eternally stalks the human species. Pain relents sometimes, but it gives way to indifference, which is a dreamless sleep, or to pleasure, which is a bastard pain. Then man, whipped and rebellious, ran ahead of the fatality of things after a nebulous and dodging figure made of remnants, one remnant of the impalpable, another of the improbable, another of the invisible, all sewn together with a precarious stitch by the needle of imagination. And that figure—nothing less than the chimera of happiness—either runs away from him perpetually or lets itself be caught by the hem, and man would clutch it to his breast, and then she would laugh, mockingly, and disappear like an illusion.

As I contemplated such calamity I was unable to hold back a cry of anguish that Nature or Pandora heard without protest or laughter. And, I don't know by what law of cerebral upset, I was the one who started to laugh—an arrhythmic and idiotic laugh.

"You're right," I said, "this is amusing and worth something—monotonous maybe, but worth something. When Job cursed the day he was conceived it was because he wanted to see the spectacle from up here on top. Come on, Pandora, open up your womb and digest me. It's amusing, but digest me."

Her answer was to force me to look down below and watch the centuries that were still passing, swift and turbulent, the generations that were superimposed on generations, some sad like the Hebrews of the Captivity, others merry like Commodus' profligates, and all of them punctual for the tomb. I tried to flee but a mysterious force held back my feet. Then I said to myself: "Fine, the centuries keep passing, mine will arrive and it will pass, too, right down to the last one, which will decipher eternity for me." And I fixed my gaze on them and continued watching the ages, which kept coming and passing, calm and resolute now. I don't know, but I may even have been happy. Happy perhaps. Each century brought its portion of light and shadow, apathy and combat, truth and error, and its cortège of systems, new ideas, new illusions. In each of them the greenery of a springtime was bursting forth, and then they would yellow, to be rejuvenated later on. So in that way life had the regularity of a calendar, history and civilization were being made, and man, naked and unarmed, armed himself and dressed; built hovel and palace, a crude village and Thebes of a Thousand Gates; created science that scrutinizes and art that elevates; made himself orator, mechanic, philosopher, covered the face of the globe; descended into the bowels of the Earth; climbed up to the sphere of the clouds, collaborating in that way in the mysterious work with which he mitigated the necessities of life and the melancholy of abandonment. My gaze, bored and distracted, finally saw the present century arrive, and behind it the future ones. It came along agile, dexterous, vibrant, self-confident, a little diffuse, bold, knowledgeable, but in the end as miserable as the ones before, and so it passed, and that was how the others passed, with the same rapidity and the same monotony. I redoubled my attention, sharpened my sight. I was finally going to see the last—the last! But by then the speed of the march was such that it went beyond all comprehension. At its base a lightning flash would have been a century. Maybe that was why objects began to change. Some grew, others shrank, others were lost in their background. A mist covered everything—except the hippopotamus who had brought me there and who, likewise, began to grow smaller, and smaller, and smaller, until he reached the size of a cat. In fact he was a cat. I took a good look at him.

It was my cat, Sultão, who was playing by the door of the room with a ball of paper.

V I I I

Reason Versus Folly

The reader has already come to see that it was Reason returning home and inviting Folly to leave, proclaiming with perfect right Tartuffe's words:

La maison est à moi, c'est à vous d'en sortir.

But it's an old quirk of Folly's to develop a love of other people's houses, so that no sooner is she mistress of one than it's difficult to make her clear out. It's a quirk. There's no getting rid of her. She was hardened to shame a long time ago. Now, if we take note of the huge number of houses she occupies—some permanently, others during their periods of calm—we will conclude that this affable wanderer is the terror of householders. In our case there was almost a commotion at the door to my brain because the intruder didn't want to relinquish the house and the owner wouldn't give up her intention of taking what was hers. In the end Folly contented herself with a small corner of the attic.

"No, ma'am," Reason replied. "I'm tired of letting you have attics, sick and tired. What you're after is to move quietly from attic to dining room, from there to the living room and everywhere else."

"All right, just let me stay a little while longer. I'm on the trail of a mystery . . ."

"What mystery?"

"Two of them," Folly corrected. "That of life and that of death. I'm only asking you for ten minutes."

Reason began to laugh.

"You'll always be the same . . . always the same . . . always the same . . ."

And so saying Reason grabbed Folly by the wrists and dragged her outside. Then she went in and closed the door. Folly still moaned some entreaties, growled some curses, but she soon gave up, stuck out her tongue as a jeer, and went on her way . . .

I X

Transition

A nd now watch the skill, the art with which I make the greatest transition in this book. Watch. My delirium began in Virgília's presence. Virgília was the great sin of my youth. There's no youth without childhood, childhood presumes birth, and here is how we come, effortlessly, to that day of October 20, 1805, on which I was born. See? Seamlessly, nothing to divert the reader's calm attention, nothing. So the book goes on like this with all of method's advantages but without method's rigidity. It was about time. Because this business of method, being something indispensable, is better still if it comes without a necktie or suspenders, but, rather, a little cool and loose, like someone who doesn't care about the woman next door or the policeman on the block. It's like eloquence, because there's one kind that's genuine and vibrant, with a natural and fascinating art, and another that's stiff, sticky, and stale. Let's get along to October 20th.

X

On that Day

On that day the family tree of the Cubases blossomed with a delicate flower. I was born. I was received in the arms of Pascoela, the celebrated midwife from Minho, who boasted of having opened the door to the world for a whole generation of aristocrats. It's possible that my father had heard that declaration, but I think that paternal feeling was what induced him to show her his gratification with two half-doubloons. Washed and swathed, I immediately became the hero of our house. Everybody predicted for me what best fitted his taste. My Uncle João, the former infantry officer, saw a certain Bonapartean look in me, which made my father nauseous when he heard it. My Uncle Ildefonso, a simple priest at the time, sensed a canon in me.

"A canon's what he's going to be, and I say no more so that it won't look like pride, but I wouldn't be the least bit surprised if God has destined him for a bishopric . . . That's right, a bishopric. It's not impossible. What do you say, brother Bento?"

My father replied to all that I would be whatever God wished me to be and he lifted me up into the air as if he intended to show me to the city and to the world. He was asking everybody if I looked like him, if I was intelligent, handsome . . .

I tell these things haphazardly, according to what I heard years later. I'm ignorant of the greater part of the details of that famous day. I do know that the neighborhood came or sent greetings to the newborn and for the first week there were a lot of visitors to our house. There wasn't a single sedan chair that wasn't in use. There were a lot of frock coats and breeches in circulation. If I don't mention the caresses, kisses, admiration, and blessings it's because if I did the chapter would never end and I must end it.

Note: I can't say anything about my baptism because nobody has spoken to me in that regard unless to say that it was one of the grandest affairs of the following year, 1806. I was baptized in São Domingos church one Tuesday in March, a clear day, bright and pure, with Colonel Rodrigues de Matos and his wife as godparents. They were both descendants of old northern families and truly an honor to the blood that flowed in their veins, which in times past had been shed in the war against Holland. I think the names of both were the first things I learned and I must have repeated them quite graciously or revealed some precocious talent because there was no stranger before whom I wasn't obliged to recite them.

"Young man, tell these gentlemen your godfather's name."

"My godfather? He's the Honorable Colonel Paulo Vaz Lobo César de Andrade e Sousa Rodrigues de Matos. My godmother is the Honorable Dona Maria Luisa de Macedo Resende e Sousa Rodrigues de Matos."

"Your boy is a sharp one," the listeners would exclaim.

"Very sharp," my father would agree, and his eyes dripped with pride and he would lay his hand on my head, stare at me for a long time lovingly, bursting with pride.

Note: I began to walk. I don't know exactly when, but ahead of time. Perhaps in order to speed up nature they had me hold onto chairs, held me by the diaper, gave me a wooden cart. "By yourself, by yourself, little master, by yourself, by yourself," the nursemaid would say to me. And, attracted by the tin rattle that my mother shook in front of me, I would head toward her, fall this way, fall that way, and I was walking, probably not too well, but I was walking, and I kept on walking.

X I

The Child Is Father to the Man

I grew. My family had no part in that. I grew naturally, the way magnolias and cats do. Cats may be less sly and magnolias are certainly less restless than I was in my childhood. The poet said that the child is father to the man. If that's true, let's have a look at some of the markings of the child.

From the age of five I'd earned the nickname of "Devil Child," and I really was just that. I was one of the most malevolent children of my time, evasive, nosey, mischievous, and willful. For example, one day I split open the head of a slave because she'd refused to give me a spoonful of the cocoanut confection she was making and, not content with that evil deed, I threw a handful of ashes into the bowl and, not satisfied with that mischief, I ran to tell my mother that the slave was the one who'd ruined the dish out of spite. And I was only six years old. Prudêncio, a black houseboy, was my horse every day. He'd get down on his hands and knees, take a cord in his mouth as a bridle, and I'd climb onto his back with a switch in my hand. I would whip him, make him do a thousand turns, left and right, and he would obey—sometimes moaning—but he would obey without saying a word or, at most, an— "Ouch, little master!"—to which I would retort, "Shut your mouth, animal!" Hiding visitors' hats, pinning paper tails on dignified people, pulling pigtails, pinching matrons on the arm, and many other deeds of that sort were the sign of a restive nature, but I have to believe that they were also the expressions of a robust spirit, because my father held me in great admiration, and if at times he scolded me in the presence of people, he did it as a mere formality. In private he would give me kisses.

You mustn't conclude that I spent the rest of my life cracking people's skulls or hiding their hats, but opinionated, selfish, and somewhat contemptuous of people, that I was. If I didn't spend my time hiding their hats, I did pull their pigtails on occasion.

I also took a liking to the contemplation of human injustice. I tended to mitigate it, explain it, classify it into sections, understand it not according to a rigid pattern but in light of circumstance and place. My mother indoctrinated me in her own way, made me learn certain precepts and prayers by heart. But I felt that, more than by the prayers, I was governed by nerves and blood, and the Golden Rule lost its living spirit and became a hollow formula. In the morning before porridge and at night before bed, I would beg God's forgiveness the same as I forgave my debtors. But between morning and night I would be involved in some terrible bit of mischief and my father, after the uproar had passed, would pat me on the cheek and exclaim, laughing: "Oh, you little devil! You little devil!"

Yes, my father adored me. My mother was a weak woman with not much brain and lots of heart, quite credulous, sincerely pious—homespun in spite of being pretty and modest in spite of being well-off, afraid of thunder and of her husband. Her husband was her god on Earth. My upbringing was born of the collaboration of those two people and although there was some good about it, in general it was corrupt, incomplete, and in some ways negative. My uncle the canon would sometimes remark to his brother about it, telling him that he was giving me more freedom than education and more affection than correction, but my father would answer that he was applying a system to my education that was completely superior to the usual system and in that way, while not confusing his brother, he was duping himself.

Along with communication with education there was also outside example, the domestic milieu. We've seen the parents, now let's have a look at the uncles and the aunt. One of them, João, was a man with a loose tongue, a dashing life, and picaresque conversation. From the age of eleven on I was admitted to his anecdotes, true or otherwise, all contaminated with obscenity or filth. He didn't respect my adolescence any more than he respected his brother's cassock, with the difference that the latter would flee as soon as some scabrous subject was touched upon. Not I. I allowed myself to stay without understanding anything at first, later understanding, and finally finding him amusing. After a time the one who sought him out was I and he liked me a lot, gave me candy, took me for walks. At home, when he would come to spend a few days, it happened quite often that I would find him in the rear of the house in the laundry chatting with the slave girls who were washing clothes. That's where he'd string together stories, comments, questions, and there'd be an explosion of laughter that nobody could hear because the laundry was too far away from the house. The black women, with clothes around their middle, their dresses hiked up a little, some inside the tank, others outside, leaning over the articles of clothing, beating them, soaping them, twisting them, went on listening to Uncle João's jokes and commenting on them from time to time, saying:

"Get thee behind me, Satan! This Master João is the devil himself!"

My uncle the canon was quite different. He was full of austerity and purity. Those traits weren't elevating a superior spirit, however, but only compensating for a mediocre one. He was not a man who saw the substantive side of the church. He saw the superficial side; hierarchy, preeminences, vestments, genuflections. He was closer to sacristy than to altar. A slip in ritual would arouse him more than an infraction of the commandments. Now, after so many years away from it, I'm not sure whether or not he could easily understand a passage from Tertullian or expound without hesitation the story of the Nicene symbol. But no one at high mass knew better than he the number and type of bows to be made to the officiant. Being canon was the only ambition in his life. And he said with all his heart that it was the only honor to which he could aspire. Pious, austere in his habits, precise in his observance of the rules, limp, timid, subordinate, he possessed some few virtues in which he was exemplary, but he was absolutely lacking in the strength to instill them or impose them on others.

I won't say anything about my maternal aunt, Dona Emerenciana, or add that she was the person who had the most authority over me. That made her quite different from the others, but she only lived with us a short time, a couple of years. Other relatives and a few close friends aren't worth mentioning. We had no life in common, only intermittently and with great spans of separation. What is important is the general description of the domestic milieu and that has been shown here—vulgarity of character, love of gaudy appearance and clamor, a slackness of will, the rule of whim, and more. Out of that earth and that manure this flower was born.

X I I

An Episode in 1814

B ut I don't want to go ahead without giving a quick rundown of a stirring episode in 1814. I was nine years old.

When I was born Napoleon was already basking in all the splendor of his power and his glory. He was emperor and had completely conquered men's admiration. My father, who, on the strength of having persuaded others of our nobility had ended up persuading himself, kept on feeding a completely mental hatred of him. That was the motive for some angry disputes in our house because my Uncle João—I don't know whether out of a spirit of class or sympathy for his profession— pardoned in the despot what he admired in the general. My priest uncle was inflexible in his opposition to the Corsican and my other relatives were divided. That was the basis of the controversy and the rows.

When the news of Napoleon's first fall reached Rio de Janeiro, there was naturally great shock in our house, but no gibes or taunts. The losers, witnessing the public rejoicing, considered it more decorous to remain silent. Some even went so far as to clap hands. The populace, cordially happy, didn't skimp on their affection for the royal family. There were torches, salvos, *Te-Deums*, parades, and cheers. I went about those days with a new rapier my godfather had given me on Saint Anthony's Day and, quite frankly, I was more interested in the rapier than in Bonaparte's fall. I've never forgotten that. I've never stopped thinking to myself that my rapier has always been greater than Napoleon's sword. And please note that I heard a lot of speeches when I was alive, read a lot of controversial pages with big ideas and bigger words, but—I don't know why—behind all the applause they drew from my mouth, some-times that voice of experience would echo:

"Come on, all you care about is your rapier."

My family wasn't satisfied with having an anonymous share of the public celebration. They found it opportune and indispensable to celebrate the overthrow of the emperor with a banquet, and such a banquet that the sound of the acclamations would reach the ears of His Highness or, at least, those of his ministers. No sooner said than done. All the old silver inherited from my grandfather Luís Cubas was taken down. The tablecloths from Flanders were unpacked, the large pitchers from India. A barrow was slaughtered. Compotes and quince marmalades were ordered from the nuns of Ajuda. Everything was washed, scoured, and polished: parlors, stairs, candlesticks, wall brackets, lamp chimneys, all items of classic luxury.

At the given hour a very select society gathered: the district judge, three or four military officers, some businessmen and lawyers, several government officials, some with their wives and daughters, some without them, but all with a common desire to stuff a turkey with Bonaparte's memory. It wasn't a banquet but a *Te-Deum*. That was more or less what one of the lawyers present, Dr. Vilaça, said. He was a famous glosser who added the tidbit of the muses to the dishes of the house. I remember as if it were yesterday, I remember seeing him rise up with his long hair gathered in a pigtail, silk tailcoat, an emerald on his finger, and ask my priest uncle to repeat a maxim, and when the maxim was repeated, he fastened his eyes on the head of a lady, coughed, lifted his right hand, clenched except for his forefinger which pointed to the ceiling, and, posed and composed like that, he gave back the word with a gloss. Not just one gloss, but three. Then he swore to his gods that it would never end. He would ask for a maxim, would be given one, would quickly gloss it, and then ask for another, and another, to the point that one of the ladies present couldn't keep her admiration silent.

"You say that," Vilaça modestly replied, "because you never heard Bocage in Lisbon at the end of the century as I did. That was something! The ease! And such lines of poetry! We had battles that went on glossing for an hour or two in the midst of applause and bravos in Nicola's bar. Bocage had a tremendous talent! That was what I was told a few days ago by Her Grace the Duchess of Cadaval . . ."

And those last three words, expressed quite emphatically, produced a flutter of admiration and amazement in all assembled because so cordial and so simple a man, in addition to competing with poets, was close to duchesses! A Bocage and a Cadaval! Contact with such a man made the ladies feel superrefined. The males looked on him with respect, some with envy, no few with disbelief. He, meanwhile, went along piling adjective on adjective, adverb on adverb, listing everything that rhymed with *tyrant* and *usurper*. It was dessert time. No one was thinking anymore about eating. During the intervals in the glosses a merry murmur went about, the chatter of full stomachs. The eyes, sluggish and moist or lively and warm, lounged or leaped about the table loaded with sweets and fruit—pineapple wedges here, melon slices there, the crystal dessert dishes displaying the thinly shredded cocoanut sweets, yellow as an egg yolk—or the molasses, thick and dark, not far from the cheese. From time to time a full, jovial, unbuttoned laugh—a family laugh—would come along to break the political gravity of the banquet. In the midst of the great and common interest, the small and private ones were also moving about. The girls spoke about the *modinhas* they were going to sing to the accompaniment of the harpsichord, the minuets, the English airs. Nor was there any lack of a matron who promised to perform an eight-beat dance just to show them how she had enjoyed herself in the good old days of childhood. One fellow, next to me, was passing on to another a recent report on the new slaves who were on their way according to letters he'd received from Luanda, one letter in which his nephew told him that he'd already made a deal for about forty head, and another in which . . . He had them right there in his pocket but he couldn't read them on that occasion. What he guaranteed is that from this one shipment we can count on some hundred and twenty slaves at least.

"Shh . . . shh . . . shh . . .," Vilaça was saying, clapping his hands. The noise quickly stopped, like a pause with an orchestra, and all eyes turned to the glosser. Those farther off cupped their ears in order not to lose a single word. Most of them, even before the gloss, had already given a chuckle of approval, mild and sincere.

As for me, there I was, solitary and out of it, making eyes at a certain dessert that was my passion. I was happy with the end of each gloss, hoping that it would be the last, but it wasn't, and the dessert remained intact. No one had thought to say the first word. My father, at the head of the table, was savoring the joy of the guests with deep swallows, he had eyes only for the jolly fat faces, the dishes, the flowers. He was delighted with the familiarity that bound the most distant spirits together, the influence of a good dinner. I could see that because I dragged my eyes away from the compote to him and then from him back to the compote, as if begging him to serve me some. But it was in vain. He didn't see anything; he was seeing himself. And the glosses went on one after the other like sheets of water, obliging me to withdraw the desire and the plea. I was as patient as I could be, but I couldn't be for long. I asked for some dessert in a low voice. Finally I roared, bellowed, stamped my feet. My father, who would have given me the sun if I'd asked for it, called to a slave to serve me the sweet, but it was too late. Aunt Emerenciana pulled me out of my chair and turned me over to a slave girl in spite of my shouts and shoves.

The glosser's crime had been only that: delaying the compote and bringing about my exclusion. But that was sufficient for me to think about revenge, whatever it might be, that would be huge and exemplary, which would make him look ridiculous in some way. Since Dr. Vilaça was a serious man, mannerly and calm, forty-seven years old, married and a father, I wasn't content with a paper tail or his pigtail. It had to be something worse. I began scrutinizing him for the rest of the afternoon, following him around the grounds, where they'd all gone to stroll. I saw him chatting with Dona Eusébia, Sergeant-Major Domingues' sister, a big robust maiden lady, who, if she wasn't pretty, wasn't ugly either.

"I'm very angry with you," she was telling him.

"Why?"

"Because . . . I don't know why . . . because it's my fate . . . sometimes I think dying is better . . ."

They'd gone behind a little thicket. It was twilight. I followed them. There was a spark of wine and sensuality in Vilaça's eyes.

"Let go of me," she said.

"Nobody can see us. Dying, my angel? What kind of an idea is that? You know that I would die, too . . . What am I saying? . . . I die every day, from passion, from longing . . ."

Dona Eusébia put her handkerchief to her eyes. The glosser was digging in his memory for some literary fragment and he found this one, which I later discovered was from an opera by Antônio José da Silva, the Jew:

"Don't weep my love, don't wish for the day to break with two dawns."

He said that and pulled her toward him. She resisted some but let herself go. Their faces came together and I heard the smack, very light, of a kiss, the most timid of kisses.

"Dr. Vilaça kissed Dona Eusébia!" I bellowed, running through the yard.

Those words of mine were an explosion. Stupefaction immobilized everyone. Eyes looked out all over. Smiles were exchanged, furtive whispers. Mothers dragged their daughters off with the pretext of the dew. My father pulled my ears, faking it but really annoyed at my indiscretion. The next day at lunch, however, recalling the incident, he tweaked my nose, laughing: "Oh, you little devil! You little devil!"

X I I I

A Leap

L et's put our feet together now and leap over school, the irksome school where I learned to read, write, count, whack noggins, get mine whacked, and make mischief, sometimes up on the hills, sometimes on the beaches, wherever it was convenient for loafers.

They were bitter times. There were the scoldings, the punishments, the arduous long lessons and little else, very little and very slight. The only really bad part was the whacking of the palms with a ruler, and even then . . . Oh, ruler, terror of my boyhood, you who were the *compelle intrare* with which an old teacher, bony and bald, instilled in my brain the alphabet, prosody, syntax, and everything else he knew, blessed ruler, so cursed by moderns, if only I could have remained under your yoke with my beardless soul, my ignorance, and my rapier, that rapier from 1814, so superior to Napoleon's sword! What was it that my old primary teacher wanted, after all? Memorization and behavior in the classroom. Nothing more, nothing less than what life, the final class, wants, with the difference that if you put fear into me, you never put anger. I can still see you now, coming into the room with your white leather slippers, cape, handkerchief in hand, bald head on display, chin clean-shaven. I see you sit down, snort, grunt, take an initial pinch of snuff, and then call us to order for the lesson. And you did that for twenty-three years, quiet, obscure, punctual, stuck in a little house on the Rua do Piolho, not bothering the world with your mediocrity, until one day you took the great dive into the shadows and nobody wept for you except an old black man—no one, not even I, who owe you the rudiments of writing.

The teacher's name was Ludgero. Let me write his full name on this page: Ludgero Barata—a disastrous name whose second part means cockroach and that gave the boys an eternal basis for crude jokes. One of us, Quincas Borba, was cruel to the poor man at that time. Two or three times a week he would put a dead roach into his pants pocket—wide trousers tied with a cord—or in the desk drawer, or by his inkwell. If he found it during school hours he would leap up, pass his flaming eyes over us, call us by our last names: we were parasites, ignoramuses, brats, scoundrels . . . Some trembled, others snorted. Quincas Borba, however, allowed himself to remain quiet, his eyes staring into space.

A delight, Quincas Borba. Never in my childhood, never in my whole life did I find a funnier, more inventive, more mischievous boy. He was a delight not only in school but all over the city. His mother, a widow of certain means, worshiped her son and would bring him to school pampered, well dressed, all decked out, with a striking houseboy following, a houseboy who would let us play hooky, go hunt for birds' nests or lizards on Livramento and Conceição hills, or simply roam the streets on the loose like two idle loafers. And as emperor! It was a pleasure to see Quincas Borba play the emperor during the festival of the Holy Spirit. In our children's games he would always choose the role of king, minister, general, someone supreme, whoever he might be. The rascal had poise and gravity, a certain magnificence in his stance, in his walk. Who would have said that . . . Let's hold back our pen, let's not get ahead of events. Let's take a leap to 1822, the date of our political independence and of my first personal captivity.

X I V

The First Kiss

I was seventeen. My upper lip was beginning to sprout as I strove to grow a mustache. My eyes, lively and resolute, were my really masculine feature. Since I showed a certain haughtiness it was hard to tell whether I was a child with the arrogance of a man or a man with the look of a boy. In short, I was a handsome young fellow, handsome and bold, who was entering life in boots and spurs, a whip in his hand and blood in his veins, mounted on a nervous, robust, swift steed, like the steeds in ancient ballads, for whom romanticism went looking in medieval castles, only to run into him on the streets of our century. The worst is that the romantics wore the fellow out so much that it became necessary to lay him aside, where realism came to find him, eaten by leprosy and worms, and, out of compassion, they bore him off for their books.

Yes, I was that handsome, graceful, well-to-do young fellow, and it's easy to imagine how more than one lady lowered her pensive brow before me or lifted her covetous eyes up to me. Of them all, however, the one who captivated me immediately was a . . . a . . . I don't know if I should say it. This book is chaste, at least in its intention. In its intention it is ever so chaste. But out with it, either you say everything or nothing. The one who captivated me was a Spanish woman, Marcela, "beautiful Marcela," as the boys of those times called her. And the boys were right. She was the daughter of a gardener from Asturias. She told me so herself during a day of sincerity, because the accepted version was that she'd been born to a lawyer from Madrid, a victim of the French invasion, wounded, jailed, and shot when she was only twelve years old. *Cosas de España.* Whatever her father was, however, lawyer or gardener, the truth is that Marcela didn't have any rustic innocence and hardly understood the morality of the law. She was a good girl, cheerful, without scruples, a little hampered by the austerity of the times, which wouldn't allow her to haul her flightiness and her gossip games through the streets, fond of luxury, impatient, a friend of money and young men. That year she was madly in love with a certain Xavier, a wealthy and tubercular fellow—a pearl.

I saw her for the first time on the Rossio Grande, the night of fire-works celebrating the declaration of independence, a springtime festival, the dawn of the public soul. We were a couple of youths, the people and I. We were coming out of childhood with all the ecstasy of youth. I saw her get out of a sedan chair, graceful and eye-catching, a slim, swaying body, elegant—something I'd never found in chaste women. "Follow me," she said to her page. And I followed her, as much a page as the other, as if the order had been given to me. I let myself go, in love, vibrant, full of the first inklings of a dawn. Along the way they called out to her, "Beautiful Marcela!" I remembered that I'd heard that name from my Uncle João and I stood there, I must confess, I stood there stupefied.

Three days later my uncle asked in secret if I wanted to have dinner with some "girls" in Cajueiros. We went. It was Marcela's house. Xavier, along with all his tubercles, presided over the nocturnal banquet at which I ate little or nothing because I only had eyes for the lady of the house. The Spanish woman was so elegant! There were more than half a dozen women—all in the amorous profession—and pretty, lively, but the Spaniard . . . The enthusiasm, a few swallows of wine, an imperious temperament, hotheaded—all of that led me to do a singular thing. On leaving, at the street door, I told my uncle to wait a moment and I went back up the steps.

"Did you forget something?" Marcela asked, standing on the landing.

"My handkerchief."

She went to open the way back to the parlor for me. I grasped her hands, pulled her toward me, and gave her a kiss. I don't know whether she said anything, cried out, or called anyone. I don't know anything. I do know that I went back down the steps as swift as a typhoon and as unsteady as a drunkard.

X V

Marcela

It took me thirty days to get from the Rossio Grande to Marcela's heart, no longer riding the courser of blind desire but the ass of patience, crafty and stubborn at the same time, for there are really two ways of enticing a woman's will: the violent way like Europa's bull and the insinuative way like Leda's swan or Danaë's shower of gold—three inventions of Father Zeus, which, being out of fashion, have been replaced by the horse and the ass. I won't mention the plots I wove or the bribes or the alternation of confidence and fear or the wasted waiting or any other of those preliminary things. I can tell you that the ass was the equal of the courser—an ass like Sancho's, a philosopher, really, who bore me to her house at the end of the period mentioned above. I dismounted, patted him on the haunch, and sent him off to forage.

Oh, first agitation of my youth, how sweet you were to me! That was what the effect of the first sunlight must have been like in biblical creation. Just imagine the effect of the first sun beating down on the face of a world in bloom. Because it was the same thing, dear reader, and if you have ever counted eighteen years, you must certainly remember that it was exactly like that.

Our passion, or union, or whatever name it went by, because I don't hold much with names, had two phases: the consular phase and the imperial phase. During the first, which was short, Xavier and I ruled without his ever thinking he was sharing the government of Rome with me. But when credulity could no longer resist evidence, Xavier lowered his standards and I gathered all power into my hands. It was the Caesarean phase. It was my universe, but, alas, it wasn't free. I had to gather money together, multiply it, invent it. First I exploited my father's largesse. He would give me anything I asked for without scolding, without delay, without coldness. He told everybody that I was young and that he'd been young once himself. But the abuse reached such extremes that he put restrictions on his liberality, then more, then still more. Then I went to my mother and induced her to turn something my way, which she did in secret. It wasn't much. Then I laid hands on a final recourse: I got to sacking my father's legacy, signing notes that I would redeem one day at usurious rates.

"Really," Marcela would tell me when I brought her something in silk, some piece of jewelry, "really, you're trying to start a fight with me . . . Because this is something that . . . such an expensive gift . . ."

And if it was a jewel, she said that as she examined it between her fingers, looking for the best light, trying it on, laughing, and kissing me with an impetuous and sincere obstinacy, but protesting, though happiness was pouring out of her eyes and I felt happy seeing her like that. She liked our ancient gold doubloons very much and I would bring her as many as I could get hold of. Marcela would put them all together in a little iron box whose key was kept where no one ever knew. She hid it because she was afraid of the slaves. The house in which she lived in Cajueiros belonged to her. The carved jacaranda furniture was solid and good as were all the other items, mirrors, pitchers, a silver plate—a beautiful plate from India that an appeals judge had given her. You devilish plate, you always got on my nerves. I told its owner herself many times. I didn't hide from her the annoyance that these and other spoils from her loves of other times brought on in me. She would listen to me and laugh, with an innocent look—innocence and something else that I didn't understand too well at the time, but now, recalling the case, I think it was a mixed laugh, as if it were coming from a creature born to a witch of Shakespeare's by a seraph of Klopstock's. I don't know if I'm explaining myself. So it happened one day when I was unable to give her a certain necklace she'd seen at a jeweler's she retorted that it was all a game, that our love didn't need such a vulgar stimulant.

"I'll never forgive you if you get that awful idea of me," she concluded, threatening me with her finger.

And then, quick like a bird, she opened her hands, grasped my face in them, pulled me to her, and put on a funny expression, the mummery of a child. Afterward, reclining on the settee, she continued talking about it with simplicity and frankness. She'd never wanted people to buy her affection. She'd sold the appearances of it many times, but the reality she saved for the few. Duarte, for example, Second Lieutenant Duarte, whom she'd really loved two years before. Only after a struggle had he been able to give her something of value, as had happened with me. She would only willingly accept keepsakes with a low price tag, like the gold cross he'd given her once as a present.

"This cross . . ."

She said that putting her hand into her bosom and taking out a delicate gold cross attached to a blue ribbon and tied around her neck.

"But that cross," I observed, "didn't you tell me it was your father who . . ."

Marcela shook her head with a look of pity.

"Couldn't you tell that it was a lie, that I told you that in order not to upset you? Come here, *chiquito*, don't be so mistrustful with me . . . I was in love with somebody else. What difference does it make? It's all over. Someday, when we break up . . ."

"Don't say that!" I roared.

"Everything comes to an end! Someday . . ."

She couldn't go on. A sob was strangling her voice. She held out her hands, took mine, snuggled me against her breast, and whispered softly in my ear, "Never, never, my love!" I thanked her, teary-eyed. The next day I brought her the necklace I'd refused to get.

"For you to remember me with when we've broken up," I said.

Marcela at first maintained an indignant silence. Then she made a grand gesture: she made as if to throw the necklace into the street. I held back her arm, kept begging her not to do such an awful thing to me, to keep the jewel. She smiled and kept it.

In the meantime she was rewarding me abundantly for my sacrifices. She would ferret out my most hidden thoughts. There was no desire of mine that she wouldn't hasten to fulfill with all her heart, without any effort, by some kind of law of awareness of the needs of the heart. The desires were never reasonable, but pure whims, some childish wish to see her dress in a certain way, with such and such accessories, this dress and not that one, to go for a walk or something like that, and she would accede to everything, smiling and chattering.

"You're a regular expert," she would tell me.

And she would go put on the dress, the lace, the earrings with bewitching obedience.

X V I

An Immoral Reflection

An immoral reflection occurs to me, one which at the same time is a correction of style. I think I said in Chapter XIV that Marcela was dying with love for Xavier. She wasn't dying, she was living. Living isn't the same as dying. That is attested to by all the jewelers in this world, people held in great esteem for their grammar. My good jewelers, what would become of love were it not for your trinkets and your credit? A third or a fifth at least of the universal trade in hearts. This is the immoral reflection I was trying to make and which is really more obscure than immoral because what I'm trying to say isn't easily understood. What I'm trying to say is that the most beautiful head in the world will be no less beautiful if ringed by a diadem of fine stones, neither less beautiful nor less loved. Marcela, for example, who was quite pretty, Marcela loved me . . .

X V I I

Of the Trapeze and Other Things

. . . Marcela loved me for fifteen months and eleven *contos*, no more, no less. My father, as soon as he got wind of the eleven *contos*, was really taken by surprise. He thought the case was reaching beyond the bounds of a juvenile caprice.

"This time," he said, "you're going to Europe. You're going to study at a university, probably Coimbra. I want you to be a serious man, not a loafer and a thief." And since I showed an expression of surprise, "Thief, yes sir. A son who does this to me is nothing but . . ."

He took from his pocket my I.O.U.s that he had already redeemed and waved them in my face. "Do you see these, you rascal? Is this how a young man is supposed to protect his family name? Do you think my grandfathers and I earned our money in gambling houses or drifting about in the streets? You playboy! This time either you take account of yourself or you'll be left with nothing."

He was furious, but with a tempered and short fury. I listened to him in silence and didn't oppose the trip in any way as I'd done at other times. I was pondering the idea of taking Marcela with me. I went to see her. I explained the crisis and made my proposal. Marcela listened to me with her eyes in the air, without responding immediately. As I insisted, she told me that she would stay, that she couldn't go to Europe.

"Why not?"

"I can't," she said with a sorrowful look. "I can't breathe that air while I think of my poor father, killed by Napoleon."

"Which one, the gardener or the lawyer?"

Marcela furrowed her brow, hummed a *sequidilha*, then complained about the heat and sent for a glass of pineapple wine. A slave girl brought it on a silver tray, which was part of my eleven *contos*. Marcela politely offered me the refreshment. My answer was to strike the glass and the tray. The liquid spilled into her lap and the black girl cried out. I roared at her to get out. When we were alone I poured out all the despair in my heart. I told her that she was a monster, that she'd never loved me, that she'd let me drop down to the bottom without even the excuse of sincerity. I called her all sorts of ugly names, making wild gestures. Marcela kept herself seated, tapping her teeth with her nails, cold as a piece of marble. I had an urge to strangle her, humiliate her at least, make her crawl at my feet. Perhaps I would have, but my actions took the opposite turn: It was I who threw myself at her feet, contrite and supplicant. I kissed them, I remembered those months of our happiness alone together, I repeated our pet names from past times to her, sitting on the floor with my head between her knees, squeezing her hands, gasping, delirious, I begged her, tearfully, not to abandon me . . . Marcela sat looking at me for a few seconds, both of us silent, until she pushed me away softly and with an annoyed air.

"Stop annoying me," she said.

She got up, shook her dress, still wet, and went to her bedroom. "No," I shouted. "You're not going in there . . . I don't want you to . . ." I went to reach out my hands to her. It was too late, she'd gone in and locked the door.

I ran out, crazy. I spent two fatal hours wandering through the most distant and deserted neighborhoods, where it would have been hard to find me. I went along gnawing on my despair with a kind of morbid gluttony. I brought back the days, the hours, the instants of delirium, and now I was gratified in believing that they were eternal, that all of this was a nightmare. Deceiving myself now, I tried to push them away like a useless burden. Then I resolved to embark immediately in order to cut my life into two halves, and I pleased myself with the idea that Marcela, learning of my departure, would be tormented by longing and remorse. Since she'd been madly in love with me, she would have to feel something, some kind of remembrance, like that of Lieutenant Duarte . . . At that point the fangs of jealousy buried themselves in my heart. All of nature roared that I had to take Marcela with me.

"By force . . ., by force . . .," I kept saying, hitting the air with my fist.

Finally I got an idea that would save things . . . Oh! trapeze of my sins, trapeze of abstruse notions! The saving idea worked out on it like the one about the poultice (Chapter II). It was nothing less than bewitching her, bewitching her greatly, dazzling her, pulling her along. It reminded me to ask her by more concrete means than entreaty. I didn't measure the consequences: I had recourse to one last loan. I went to the Rua dos Ouvires, bought the finest piece of jewelry in the city, three large diamonds inlaid on an ivory comb. I ran to Marcela's house.

Marcela was lying in a hammock with a soft and weary expression, one leg hanging down, showing her little foot clad in a silk stocking, her hair loose and flowing, her look quiet and dreamy.

"Come with me," I said. "I'll get the money . . . we've got lots of money, you can have anything you want . . . Look, take it."

And I showed her the comb with the diamonds. Marcela gave a slight start, raised up halfway, and, leaning on an elbow looked at the comb for a few short seconds. Then she withdrew her eyes, got control of herself. I thrust my hands into her hair, drew it together, quickly wove into braids, improvised a hairdo that wasn't very neat, and topped it off with the comb and the diamonds. I drew back, went closer again, adjusted the braids, lowered the comb on one side, tried to find some kind of symmetry in that disorder, all with the careful touch and care of a mother.

"There," I said.

"Lunatic!" was her first response.

The second was to pull me to her and reward my sacrifice with a kiss, the most ardent ever. Then she took off the comb, admired the material and the craftsmanship for a long time, looking at me every so often and nodding her head with a scolding look.

"What am I going to do with you!" she said.

"Are you coming with me?"

Marcela thought for a moment. I didn't like the expression with which her eyes passed from me to the wall and from the wall to the jewel. But that bad impression vanished completely when she answered resolutely:

"I'll go. When do you sail?"

"Two or three days from now."

"I'll go."

I thanked her on my knees. I'd found the Marcela of my early days and I told her that. She smiled and went to put the jewel away while I went down the stairs.

X V I I I

A Vision in the Hall

At the bottom of the stairs, at the rear of the dark hall, I stopped for a few seconds to catch my breath, to touch myself, to call forth scattered ideas, to see myself in the midst of ever so many deep and contrary feelings once more. I thought I was happy. The diamonds, true, were corrupting my happiness a bit, but no less true was the fact that a pretty lady was quite capable of loving the Greeks and their gifts. And, after all, I trusted my good Marcela. She may have had defects, but she loved me . . .

"An angel!" I murmured, looking at the hall ceiling.

And there, like mockery, I saw Marcela's gaze, the gaze that a short time before had given me a shade of mistrust, gleaming over a nose that was Bakbarah's nose and mine at the same time. Poor lover from *The Arabian Nights*! I could see you right there, running along the gallery after the vizier's wife, she beckoning to you with possession and you running, running, up to the long tree-lined drive from where you came out onto the street where all the harness-makers jeered at you and thrashed you. Then it seemed to me that Marcela's hallway was the drive and the street was in Baghdad. As a matter of fact, looking toward the door I saw three harness-makers on the sidewalk, one in a cassock, another in livery, another in civilian clothes, as all three entered the hallway, took me by the arms, put me into a carriage, my father on the right, my canon uncle on the left, the one in livery on the driver's seat, and from there they took me to the house of a police official, from where I was transported to a ship that was to leave for Lisbon. You can imagine my resistance, but all resistance was useless.

Three days later I left the harbor behind, downcast and silent. I was-n't even weeping. I had an *idée fixe* . . . Damned *idées fixes!* The one on that occasion was to dive into the ocean repeating Marcela's name.

X I X

On Board

We were eleven passengers: a crazy man accompanied by his wife, two youths going on an excursion, four businessmen, and two servants. My father entrusted me to all of them, starting with the ship's captain, who had much of his own to look after as well because, on top of everything else, he was carrying his wife, who was in the last stages of tuberculosis.

I don't know whether the captain suspected anything of my lugubri-ous project or whether my father had put him on the alert, but I do know that he never took his eyes off me, called to me everywhere. When he couldn't be with me he brought me to his wife. The woman was almost always on a low couch, coughing a lot, and promising to show me the sights in Lisbon. She wasn't thin, she was transparent. It was impossible to know why she didn't die from one moment to the next. The captain pretended not to believe in her approaching death, perhaps to deceive himself. I didn't know or think anything. What did the fate of a tubercular woman in the middle of the ocean matter to me? The world for me was Marcela.

Once, after a week had passed, I thought it a propitious time to die. I went cautiously up on deck, but I found the captain standing beside the rail with his eyes fixed on the horizon.

"Expecting a storm?" I asked.

"No," he replied, shivering. "No, I was only admiring the splendor of the night. Take a look. It's celestial!"

The style didn't fit the person, rather crude and a stranger to recherché expressions. I stared at him. He seemed to be savoring my surprise. After a few seconds he took my hand and pointed to the moon, asking me why I wasn't writing an ode to the night. I replied that I wasn't a poet. The captain snorted something, took two steps, put his hand in his pocket, took out a piece of crumpled paper, and then, by the light of a lantern, he read a Horacian ode on the freedom of maritime life. It was his poetry.

"What do you think?"

I can't remember what I told him, but I do remember that he took my hand with a great deal of strength and a great amount of thanks. Right after that he recited two sonnets for me. He was going to recite another when they came to get him for his wife. "I'll be right there," he said and he recited the third sonnet for me, slowly, with love.

I was left alone, but the captain's muse had swept away all evil thoughts from my spirit. I preferred going to sleep, which is an interim way of dying. The following day we awakened in the midst of a storm that put fear into everyone except the madman. He started leaping about saying that his daughter was sending for him in a brougham. The death of a daughter had been the cause of his madness. No, I'll never forget the hideous figure of the poor man in the midst of the tumult of the people and the howls of the hurricane, humming and dancing, his eyes bulging from his pale face, his hair bristly and long. Sometimes he would stop, lift up his bony hands, make crosses with his fingers, then a checkerboard, then some rings, and he laughed a lot, desperately. His wife could no longer take care of him; given over to the terror of death, she was praying to all the saints in heaven for herself. Finally the storm abated. I must confess that it was an excellent diversion from the tempest in my heart. I, who'd thought about going to meet death, didn't dare look it in the eye when it came to meet me.

The captain asked me if I'd been afraid, if I'd felt threatened, if I hadn't found the spectacle sublime. All of that with the interest of a friend. Naturally, the conversation turned to life at sea. The captain asked me if I liked piscatorial idylls. I answered ingenuously that I didn't know what they were.

"You'll see," he replied.

And he recited a little poem for me, then another—an eclogue— and finally five sonnets, with which he capped literary confidence for that day. The following day, before reciting anything, the captain explained to me that only because of the gravest reasons had he embraced the maritime profession, because his grandmother had wanted him to be a priest and, indeed, he'd had some schooling in Latin. He didn't get to be a priest but he never stopped being a poet, which was his natural vocation. In order to prove it he immediately recited for me, in person, a hundred lines. I noticed one phenomenon: the gestures he used were such that they made me laugh once. But the captain, as he recited, looked so deep inside himself that he didn't see or hear anything.

The days passed, and the waves, and the poetry, and with them the life of his wife was also passing. She wasn't for long. One day, right after lunch, the captain told me that the sick woman might not last the week.

"So soon!" I exclaimed.

"She had a very bad night."

I went to see her. She was almost moribund, really, but she still talked about resting in Lisbon a few days before going to Coimbra with me, because it was her proposal to take me to the university. I left her, disconsolate, and went to find her husband, who was looking at the waves as they came to die against the hull of the ship, and I tried to console him. He thanked me, told me the tale of their love, praised his wife's fidelity and dedication, remembered the verses he'd written for her, recited them to me. At that point they came from her to get him. We both ran. It was a crisis. That day and the following one were cruel. The third was the day of her death. I fled from the sight, it was repugnant to me. A half hour later I found the captain sitting on a pile of hawsers, his head in his hands. I said some things to comfort him.

"She died like a saint," he answered. And so those words wouldn't be taken as a sign of weakness, he immediately stood up, shook his head, and peered at the horizon with a long, profound expression. "Let's go," he continued, "let's consign her to the grave that's never opened again."

Indeed, a few hours later her corpse was cast into the sea with the customary ceremony. Sadness had shriveled all the faces. That of the widower had the look of a hillock struck by a great bolt of lightning. Deep silence. The wave opened its womb, received the remains, closed—a slight ripple—and the ship went on. I let myself linger at the stern for a few minutes with my eyes on that uncertain spot in the sea where one of us had been left behind . . . I went off to find the captain, to distract him.

"Thank you," he told me, understanding my intent. "You must believe that I'll never forget her good care. God is the one who'll pay her for it. Poor Leocádia! Think of us in heaven."

He wiped an inconvenient tear with his sleeve. I tried to find a way out in poetry, which was his passion. I spoke to him about the verses he'd read to me and offered to get them published. The captain's eyes lighted up a little. "They might take them," he said. "But, I don't know, they're rather weak verses." I swore to him that they were not. I asked him to put them together and give them to me before we landed.

"Poor Leocádia!" he murmured without answering my request. "A corpse . . . the sea . . . the sky . . . the ship . . ."

The next day he came to read me a newly composed elegy in which the circumstances of the death and burial of his wife were memorialized. He read it to me with a truly emotional voice and his hand trembled. At the end he asked if the poem was worthy of the treasure he'd lost.

"Yes," I answered.

"It may not have style," he pondered after an instant, "but no one can deny me feeling, unless that very feeling is harmful to the perfection . . ."

"I don't think so. I think it's a perfect poem."

"Yes, I think that . . . The poem of a sailor."

"Of a sailor poet."

He shrugged his shoulders, looked at the piece of paper, and recited the composition again, but this time without trembling, stressing the literary intent, giving emphasis to the imagery and melody to the lines. At the end he confessed to me that it was his most accomplished piece of work. I said that it was. He shook my hand and predicted a great future for me.

X X

I Am Graduated

A great future! With that word pounding in my ears I turned my eyes back to the distance, to the mysterious and uncertain horizon. One idea drove out another, ambition was displacing Marcela. Great future? Maybe a naturalist, a literary man, an archeologist, a banker, a politician, or even a bishop—let it be a bishop—as long as it meant responsibility, preeminence, a fine reputation, a superior position. Ambition, since it was an eagle, had broken the shell of its egg on that occasion and removed the cover from that tawny, penetrating eye. Farewell, love! Farewell, Marcela! Days of delirium, priceless jewels, ungoverned life, farewell! Here I come for toil and glory. I leave you with the short pants of childhood.

And that was how I disembarked in Lisbon and continued on to Coimbra. The university was waiting for me with its difficult subjects. I studied them in a very mediocre way, but even so I didn't lose my law degree. They gave it to me with all the solemnity of the occasion, following years of custom, a beautiful ceremony that filled me with pride and nostalgia—mostly nostalgia. In Coimbra I'd earned a great reputation as a carouser. I was a profligate, superficial, riotous, and petulant student, given to larks, following romanticism in practice and liberalism in theory, living with a pure faith in dark eyes and written constitutions. On the day that the university certified me, on parchment, a knowledge that was far from rooted in my brain, I must confess I thought myself hoodwinked in some way, even though I was proud. Let me explain: the diploma was a certificate of emancipation. It gave me freedom, but it also gave me responsibility. I put it away, I left the banks of the Mondego and came away rather disconsolate but already feeling a drive, a curiosity, a desire to elbow others aside, to influence, to enjoy, to live—to prolong the university for my whole life forward . . .

X X I

The Muleteer

Going on, then, the donkey I was riding balked. I whipped him and he gave two bucks, then three more, and finally another one that shook me out of the saddle so disastrously that my left foot got stuck in the stirrup. I tried to hold on to the beast's belly, but by then, spooked, he took off down the road. I'm not telling it right: he tried to take off and did take a couple of bounds, but a muleteer who happened to be there ran up in time to grab the reins and hold him, not without some effort and danger. With the animal under control, he untangled me from the stirrup and stood me on my feet.

"Lucky you were to escape, sir," the muleteer said.

And he was right. If the donkey had run away I really would have got bruised and I'm not sure but that death might have been the outcome of the disaster. Head split open, a congestion, some kind of internal injury, all my budding knowledge leaving me. The muleteer may have saved my life. I was sure of it. I felt it in the blood that was pounding through my heart. Good muleteer! While I was taking account of myself, he was carefully adjusting the donkey's harness with great skill and zeal. I decided to give him three gold coins from the five I was carrying with me. Not because it was the price of my life—that was inestimable—but because it was just recompense for the dedication with which he'd saved me. All settled, I'd give him the three coins.

"All ready," he said, handing me the reins to my mount.

"Not quite yet," I answered. "Let me wait a bit. I'm still not myself."

"Come, now, sir!"

"Well, isn't it a fact that I was almost killed?"

"If the donkey had run off, maybe so, but with the help of the Lord you can see that nothing happened, sir."

I went to the saddlebags, took out an old waistcoat in the pocket of which I was carrying the five gold coins, but during that interval I'd got to thinking that maybe the gratuity was excessive, that two coins might be sufficient. Maybe one. As a matter of fact, one coin was enough to make him quiver with joy. I examined his clothing. He was a poor devil who'd never seen a gold coin. One coin, therefore. I took it out, saw it glitter in the sunlight. The muleteer didn't see it because I had my back turned, but he may have suspected something. He began talking to the donkey in a meaningful way. He was giving it advice, telling it to watch out, that the "good doctor" might punish it. A paternal monologue. Good Lord! I even heard the smack of a kiss. It was the muleteer kissing it on the head.

"Hurray!" I exclaimed.

"Begging your pardon, sir, but the devilish creature was looking at us with such charm . . ."

I laughed, hesitated, put a silver *cruzado* in his hand, mounted the donkey, and went off at a slow trot, a little bothered, I should really say a little uncertain of the effect of the piece of silver. But a few yards away I looked back and the muleteer was bowing deeply to me as an obvious sign of contentment. I noted that it must have been just that. I'd paid him well; maybe I'd paid him too much. I put my fingers into the pocket of the waistcoat I was wearing and I felt some copper coins. They were the *vinténs* I should have given the muleteer instead of the silver *cruzado*. Because, after all, he didn't have any recompense or reward in mind. He'd followed a natural impulse, his temperament, the habits of his trade. Furthermore, the circumstance of his being right there, not ahead and not behind, but precisely at the point of the disaster, seemed to be the simple instrument of Providence. And, in one way or another, the merit of the act was positively nonexistent. I became disconsolate with that reflection. I called myself prodigal. I added the *cruzado* to my past dissipations. I felt (why not come right out with it?), I felt remorse.

XXII

Return to Rio

Blasted donkey, you made me lose the thread of my reflections! Right now I'm not going to say what I went through from there to Lisbon or what I did in Lisbon, on the Peninsula, or in other places in

Europe, the old Europe that seemed to be rejuvenating at that time. No, I'm not going to say that I was present at the dawn of Romanticism, that I, too, went off to write poetry to that effect in the bosom of Italy. I'm not going to say a thing. I would have to write a travel diary and not memoirs like these, where only the substance of life will enter.

After some years of wandering I heeded my father's entreaties: "Come home," he said in his last letter, "if you don't come quickly you'll find your mother dead!" That last word was a blow to me. I loved my mother very much. I still had the last blessing she'd given me on board the ship before my eyes. "My poor child, I'll never see you again!" the unfortunate lady had sobbed, clutching me to her breast. And those words echoed in my ears now like a prophecy fulfilled.

Let it be noted that I was in Venice, still redolent with the verses of Lord Byron. There I was, sunk deep in dreams, reliving the past, thinking that I was in the Most Serene Republic. It's true. It occurred to me once to ask the innkeeper if the doge would take his walk that day. "What doge, *signor mio?*" I came back to my senses, but I didn't confess the illusion. I told him that my question was a kind of South American charade. He acted as if he understood and added that he liked South American charades a lot. He was an innkeeper. Well, I left all that, innkeeper, doge, Bridge of Sighs, gondolas, poetry of the lord, ladies of the Rialto, I left it all and took off like a shot in the direction of Rio de Janeiro.

I came . . . But no, let's not lengthen this chapter. Sometimes I forget myself when I'm writing and the pen just goes along eating up paper to my great harm, because I'm an author. Long chapters are better suited for logy readers and we're not an *in-folio* public but an *in-12* one, not much text, wide margins, elegant type, gold trim, and ornamental designs . . . designs above all . . . No, let's not lengthen the chapter.

X X I I I

Sad, But Short

I came. I won't deny that when I caught sight of my native city I had a new sensation. It was not the effect of my political homeland, it was that of the place of my childhood, the street, the tower, the fountain on the corner, the woman in a shawl, the black street sweeper, the things and scenes of boyhood engraved in my memory. Nothing less than a rebirth. The spirit, like a bird, didn't take into consideration the flow of years, it fluttered toward the original spring and went to drink its cool, pure waters, still not mingled with the torrent of life.

If you take careful note you'll see a commonplace there. Another commonplace, sadly common, was the family's consternation. My father embraced me in tears. "Your mother isn't going to live," he told me. Indeed, it wasn't the rheumatism that was killing her anymore, it was a stomach cancer. The poor thing was suffering cruelly because cancer is indifferent to a person's virtues. My sister Sabina, married by then to Cotrim, was on the point of dropping from fatigue. Poor girl! She got only three hours of sleep a night, no more. Even Uncle João was downcast and sad. Dona Eusébia and some other ladies were there, too, no less sad and no less dedicated.

"My son!"

The pain held back its pincers for a moment. A smile lighted the face of the sick woman over whom death was beating its eternal wings. It was less a face than a skull. Its beauty had passed like a bright day. The bones, which never grow thin, were left. I could hardly recognize her. It had been eight or nine years since we'd seen each other. Kneeling by the foot of the bed with her hands in mine, I remained mute and still, not daring to speak because every word would have been a sob and we were afraid to tell her of the end. Vain fear! She knew that she was close to the end. She told me so. We found out the next morning.

Her agony was long, long and cruel with a meticulous, cold, repetitious cruelty that filled me with pain and bewilderment. It was the first time I'd seen someone die. I'd only known death by hearsay. At most I'd seen it, petrified already, in the face of some corpse I accompanied to the cemetery, or I carried the idea of it wrapped up in the rhetorical amplifications of professors of ancient matters—the treacherous death of Caesar, the austere death of Socrates, the proud death of Cato. But that duel between to be and not to be, death in action, painful, contracted, convulsive, without any political or philosophical apparatus, the death of a loved one, that was the first time I'd faced it. I didn't weep. I remember that I hadn't wept during the whole spectacle. My eyes were dull, my throat tight, my awareness open-mouthed. Why? A creature so docile, so tender, so saintly, who'd never caused a tear of displeasure to fall, a loving mother, and immaculate wife, why did she have to die like that, handled, bitten by the teeth of a pitiless illness? I must confess that it all seemed obscure to me, incongruous, insane . . .

A sad chapter. Let's pass on to a happier one.

X X I V

Short, But Happy

I was prostrate. And this in spite of the fact that I was a faithful compendium of triviality and presumption at that time. The problem of life and death had never weighed on my brain. Never until that day had I peered into the abyss of the Inexplicable. I lacked the essential thing, which is a stimulus, a sudden impulse . . .

To tell you the truth, I mirrored the opinions of a hairdresser I'd met in Modena who was distinguished by having absolutely none. He was the flower of hairdressers. No matter how long the operation on the coiffure took, he never got angry. He would intersperse the combing with lots of maxims and jests, full of a certain malice, a zest . . . He had no other philosophy. Nor did I. I'm not saying that the university hadn't taught me some philosophical truths. But I'd only memorized the formulas, the vocabulary, the skeleton. I treated them as I had Latin: I put three lines from Virgil in my pocket, two from Horace, and a dozen moral and political locutions for the needs of conversation. I treated them the way I treated history and jurisprudence. I picked up the phraseology of all things, the shell, the decoration . . .

Perhaps I'm startling the reader with the frankness with which I'm exposing and emphasizing my mediocrity. Be aware that frankness is the prime virtue of a dead man. In life the gaze of public opinion, the contrast of interests, the struggle of greed all oblige people to keep quiet about their dirty linen, to disguise the rips and stitches, not to extend to the world the revelations they make to their conscience. And the best part of the obligation comes when, by deceiving others, a man deceives himself, because in such a case he saves himself vexation, which is a painful feeling, and hypocrisy, which is a vile vice. But in death, what a difference! What a release! What freedom! Oh, how people can shake off their coverings, leave their spangles in the gutter, unbutton themselves, unpaint themselves, undecorate themselves, confess flatly what they were and what they've stopped being! Because, in short, there aren't any more neighbors or friends or enemies or acquaintances or strangers. There's no more audience. The gaze of public opinion, that sharp and judgmental gaze, loses its virtue the moment we tread the territory of death. I'm not saying that it doesn't reach here and examine and judge us, but we don't care about the examination or the judgment. My dear living gentlemen and ladies, there's nothing as incommensurable as the disdain of the deceased.

X X V

In Tijuca

Drat! My pen got away from me there and slipped into the emphatic. Let's be simple, as simple as the life I led in Tijuca during the first weeks after my mother's death.

On the seventh day, when the funeral mass was over, I gathered together a shotgun, some books, clothing, cigars, a houseboy—the Prudêncio of Chapter XI—and went off to establish myself in an old house we owned. My father made an effort to make me change my mind, but I couldn't and didn't want to obey him. Sabina wanted me to go live with her for a while—two weeks at least. My brother-in-law was on the point of carrying me off forcibly. He was a good lad, that Cotrim. He'd gone from profligacy to circumspection. Now he was a food merchant, toiling from morning till night with perseverance. In the evening, sitting by the window and twirling his sideburns, that was all he had on his mind. He loved his wife and the son they had at that time who died a few years later. People said he was tightfisted.

I had given up everything. I was in a state of shock. I think it was around that time that hypochondria began to bloom in me, that yellow, solitary, morbid flower with an intoxicating and subtle odor. " 'Tis good to be sad and say nothing!" When those words of Shakespeare's caught my attention I must confess that I felt an echo in myself, a delightful echo. I remember that I felt an echo in myself, a delightful echo. I remember that I was sitting under a tamarind tree with the poet's book in my hands and my spirit was even more downcast than the character's,— or crestfallen, as we say of sad hens. I clutched my taciturn grief to my breast with a singular sensation, something that could be called the sensuality of boredom. The sensuality of boredom: memorize that expression, reader, keep it, examine it, and if you can't get to understand it you may conclude that you're ignorant of one of the most subtle sensations of this world and that time.

Sometimes I would go hunting, at other times sleep, and at others read—I read a lot—other times, well, I did nothing. I let myself ramble from idea to idea, from imagination to imagination, like a vagrant or hungry butterfly. The hours dripped away, one by one, the sun set, the shadows of night veiled the mountain and the city. No one came to visit me. I had expressly asked to be left alone. One day, two days, three days, a whole week spent like that without saying a word was enough for me to shake off Tijuca and rejoin the bustle. Indeed, at the end of a week I'd had more than enough of solitude. My grief had abated. My spirits were no longer satisfied with only shotgun and books or with the view of the woods and the sky. Youth was reacting, it was necessary to live. I packed away the problem of life and death, the poet's hypochondriacs, the shirts, the meditations, the neckties in a trunk and I was about to close it when the black boy Prudêncio told me that the day before a person of my acquaintance had moved into a purple house a couple of hundred steps away from ours.

"Who?"

"Does Little Master remember Dona Eusébia maybe?"

"I remember . . . Is it she?"

"She and her daughter. They got in yesterday morning."

The episode from 1814 came to me immediately and I felt annoyed. But I called my attention to the fact that events proved me right. Actually, it had been impossible to prevent the intimate relations between Vilaça and the sergeant-major's sister. Even before I sailed there was already a mysterious wagging of tongues about the birth of a girl. My Uncle João wrote me later that Vilaça, when he died, had left a good legacy to Dona Eusébia, something that caused a lot of talk in the neighborhood. Uncle João himself, greedy when it came to scandal, didn't talk about anything else in the letter—several pages long, by the by. Events had proved me right. Even though they had, however, 1814 was a long way back and with it Vilaça's mischief and the kiss in the shrubbery. Finally, no close relations existed between her and me. I made that reflection to myself and finished closing the trunk.

"Isn't the Little Master going to visit Missy Dona Eusébia?" Prudêncio asked me. "She was the one who dressed the body of my departed mistress."

I remembered that I'd seen her among other ladies on the occasion of the death and the burial. I didn't know, however, that she'd lent my mother that final kindness. The houseboy's reflection was reasonable. I owed her a visit. I decided to do it at once and then leave.

XXVI

The Author Hesitates

S uddenly I heard a voice. "Hello, my boy, this is no life for you!" It was my father, who was coming with two proposals in his pocket. I sat down on the trunk and welcomed him without any fuss. He stood looking at me for a few moments and then extended his hand in an emotional gesture.

"My son, make adjustment to the will of God."

"I've already adjusted," was my answer, and I kissed his hand.

He hadn't had lunch. We lunched together. Neither of us mentioned the sad reason for my withdrawal. Only once did we talk about it, in passing, when my father brought the conversation around to the Regency. It was then that he mentioned the letter of condolence that one of the Regents had sent him. He had the letter with him, already rather wrinkled, perhaps from having been read to so many other people. I think he said it was one of the Regents. He read it to me twice.

"I've already gone to thank him for that mark of consideration," my father said, "and I think you should go, too . . ."

"I?"

"You. He's an important man. He takes the place of the Emperor these days. Besides, I've brought an idea with me, a plan, or . . . yes, I'll tell you everything. I've got two plans: a position as deputy and a marriage."

My father said that slowly, pausing, and not in the same tone of voice but giving the words a form and placement with an end to digging them deeper into my spirit. The proposals, however, went so much against my latest feelings that I really didn't get to understand them. My father didn't flag and he repeated them, stressing the position and the bride.

"Do you accept?"

"I don't understand politics," I said after an instant. "As for the bride . . ., let me live like the bear I am."

"But bears get married," he replied.

"Then bring me a she-bear. How about the Ursa Major?"

My father laughed and after laughing went back to speaking seriously. A political career was essential for me, he said, for twenty or more reasons, which he put forth with singular volubility, illustrating them with examples of people we knew. As for the bride, all I had to do was see her. If I saw her, I would immediately go ask her father for her hand, immediately, without waiting a single day. In that way first he tried fascination, then persuasion, then intimation. I gave no answer, sharpening the tip of a toothpick or making little balls of bread crumbs, smiling or reflecting. And, to say it outright, neither docile nor rebellious concerning the proposals. I felt confused. One part of me said yes, that a beautiful wife and a political position were possessions worthy of appreciation. Another said no, and my mother's death appeared to me as an example of the fragility of things, of affections, of family . . .

"I'm not leaving here without a final answer," my father said. "Fi-nal an-swer!" he repeated, drumming out the syllables with his finger.

He drank the last drops of his coffee, relaxed, started talking about everything, the senate, the chamber, the Regency, the restoration, Evaristo, a coach he intended to buy, our house in Matacavalos . . . I remained at a corner of the table writing crazily on a piece of paper with the stub of a pencil. I was tracing a word, a phrase, a line of poetry, a nose, a triangle, and I kept repeating them over and over, without any order, at random, like this:

arma virumque cano

A
Arma virumque cano

arma virumque cano
arma virumque

arma virumque cano
virumque

All of it mechanically and, nonetheless, there was a certain logic, a certain deduction. For example, it was the *virumque* that made me get to the name of the poet himself, because of the first syllable. I was going to write *virumque*—and *Virgil* came out, then I continued:

Vir   Virgil
        Virgil   Virgil
                Virgil

                                                      Virgil

My father, a little put off by that indifference, stood up, came over to me, cast his eyes onto the paper . . .

"Virgil!" he exclaimed. "That's it, my boy. Your bride just happens to be named Virgília."

X X V I I

Virgília?

Virgília? But, then, was it the same lady who some years later . . . ?
The very same. It was precisely the lady who was to be present
during my last days in 1869 and who before, long before, had played an
ample part in my most intimate sensations. At that time she was only
fifteen or sixteen years old. She was possibly the most daring creature of
our race and, certainly, the most willful. I shan't say that she was already
first in beauty, ahead of the other girls of the time, because this isn't a
novel, where the author gilds reality and closes his eyes to freckles and
pimples. But I won't say either that any freckle or pimple blemished her
face, no. She was pretty, fresh, she came from the hands of nature full of
that sorcery, uncertain and eternal, that an individual passes to another
individual for the secret ends of creation. That was Virgília, and she was
fair, very fair, ostentatious, ignorant, childish, full of mysterious drives, a
lot of indolence, and some devoutness—devoutness or maybe fear. I
think fear.

There in a few lines the reader has the physical and moral portrait of
the person who was to influence my life later on. She was all that at sixteen. You who read me, if you're still alive when these pages come to
life—you who read me, beloved Virgília, have you noticed the difference between the language of today and the one I first used when I saw
you? Believe me, it was just as sincere then as now. Death didn't make
me sour, or unjust.

"But," you're probably saying, "how can you discern the truth of
those times like that and express it after so many years?"

Ah! So indiscreet! Ah! So ignorant! But it's precisely that which has
made us lords of the earth; it's that power of restoring the past to touch
the instability of our impressions and the vanity of our affections. Let
Pascal say that man is a thinking reed. No. He's a thinking erratum,
that's what he is. Every season of life is an edition that corrects the one
before and which will also be corrected itself until the definitive edition,
which the publisher gives to the worms gratis.

X X V I I I

Provided That . . .

"Virgília?" I interrupted. "Yes, sir. That's the name of the bride. An angel, you ninny, an angel without wings. Picture a girl like that, this tall, a lively scamp, and a pair of eyes . . . Dutra's daughter . . ."

"What Dutra is that?"

"Councilor Dutra. You don't know him, lots of political influence. All right, do you accept?"

I didn't answer right off. I stared at my shoetops for a few seconds. Then I declared that I was willing to think both things over, the candidacy and the marriage, provided that . . .

"Provided that what?"

"Provided that I'm not obliged to accept both things. I think that I can be a married man and a public man separately . . ."

"All public men have to be married," my father interrupted sententiously. "But do what you will. It's all right with me. I'm sure that seeing will be believing! Besides, bride and parliament are the same thing . . . that is, not . . . you'll find out later . . . Go ahead. I accept the delay, provided that . . ."

"Provided that what?" I interrupted, imitating his voice.

"Oh, you rascal! Provided that you don't let yourself sit there useless, obscure, and sad. I didn't put out money, care, drive not to see you shine the way you should and as suits you and all of us. Our name has to continue; continue it and make it shine even more. Look, I'm sixty, but if it were necessary to start life over I wouldn't hesitate a single minute. Fear obscurity, Brás, flee from the negligible. Men are worth something in different ways, and the surest one of all is being worthy in the opinion of other men. Don't squander the advantages of your position, your means . . ."

And the magician went ahead waving a rattle in front of me as they used to do when I was little in order to make me walk more quickly, and the flower of hypochondria retreated into its bud to leave another flower less yellow and not at all morbid—the love of fame, the Brás Cubas poultice.

XXIX

The Visit

My father had won. I was prepared to accept diploma and marriage, Virgília and the Chamber of Deputies. "The two Virgílias," he said with a show of political tenderness. I accepted them. My father gave me two strong hugs. It was his own blood that he was finally recognizing.

"Are you coming back down with me?"

"I'll go down tomorrow. First I'm going to pay a visit to Dona Eusébia . . ."

My father wrinkled his nose but didn't say anything. He said goodbye and went back down. The afternoon of that same day I went to visit Dona Eusébia. I found her scolding a black gardener, but she left off everything to come and talk to me, with a bustle and such sincere pleasure that I immediately lost my shyness. I think she even put her pair of robust arms around me. She had me sit down by her feet on the veranda in the midst of many exclamations of contentment.

"Just look at you, Brazinho! A man! Who would have said years back . . . A great big man! And handsome, I'll say! You don't remember me too well, do you?"

I said that I did, that it was impossible to forget such a familiar friend of our house. Dona Eusébia began to talk about my mother with great longing, with so much longing that she immediately got to me and I grew sad. She perceived it in my eyes and changed the topic. She asked me to tell her about my travels, my studies, my love affairs . . . yes, my love affairs, too. She confessed to me that she was an old gadabout. At that point I remembered the episode of 1814, her, Vilaça, the shrubbery, the kiss, my shout. And as I was recalling it I heard the creak of a door, a rustle of skirts, and this word:

"Mama . . ., Mama . . ."

X X X

The Flower from the Shrubbery

T he voice and skirts belonged to a young brunette who stopped in the doorway for a few seconds on seeing a stranger. A short, constrained silence followed. Dona Eusébia broke it with a frankness and resolve.

"Come here, Eugênia," she said, "say hello to Dr. Brás Cubas, Mr. Cubas' son. He's back from Europe."

And turning to me:

"My daughter, Eugênia."

Eugênia, the flower from the shrubbery, barely responded to the courteous bow I gave her. She looked at me, surprised and bashful, and slowly, slowly came forward to her mother's chair. Her mother fixed one of the braids of her hair whose end had become undone. "Oh, you scamp!" she said. "You can't imagine, doctor, what it's like . . ." And she kissed her with such great tenderness that it moved me a bit. It reminded me of my mother and—I'll say it right out—I had an itch to be a father.

"Scamp?" I said. "But isn't she beyond that age now? It would look that way."

"How old would you say she is?"

"Seventeen."

"One less."

"Sixteen. Well, then, she's a young lady."

Eugênia couldn't hide the satisfaction she felt with those words of mine, but she immediately got hold of herself and was the same as before—stiff, cold, mute. As a matter of fact she looked even more womanly than she was. She could have been a child playing at being a young lady but, quiet, impassive like that, she had the composure of a married woman. That circumstance may have diminished her virginal grace a bit. We quickly became familiar. Her mother sang her praises and I listened to them willingly and she was smiling, her eyes sparkling as if inside her brain a little butterfly with golden wings and diamond eyes were flying . . .

I say inside because what was fluttering outside was a black butterfly that had come onto the veranda all of a sudden and began to flap its wings around Dona Eusébia. Dona Eusébia cried out, stood up, swore with some disconnected words: "Away with you! . . . Get away, you devilish thing! . . . Holy Mother Virgin! . . ."

"Don't be afraid," I said and, taking out my handkerchief, I shooed the butterfly away. Dona Eusébia sat down again, puffing, a little embarrassed. Her daughter, pale with fear, perhaps, concealed that impression with great willpower. I shook hands with them and left, laughing to myself at the two women's superstition, a philosophical, disinterested, superior laugh. In the afternoon I saw Dona Eusébia's daughter pass by on horseback, followed by a houseboy. She waved to me with her whip. I must confess that I flattered myself with the idea that a few steps farther on she would look back, but she didn't turn her head.

X X X I

The Black Butterfly

T he next day as I was getting ready to go back down a butterfly entered my bedroom, a butterfly as black as the other one and much larger. I remembered the episode of the day before and laughed. I immediately began to think about Dona Eusébia's daughter, the fright she'd had and the dignity that she managed to maintain in spite of it all. The butterfly, after fluttering all about me, alighted on my head. I shook it off. It went on to land on the counterpane and because I chased it off again, it left there and settled on an old portrait of my father. It was as black as night. The soft movement with which it began to move its wings after alighting had a certain mocking way about it that bothered me a great deal. I turned my back, left the room, but when I returned a few minutes later and found it in the same spot I felt a nervous shock. I laid hands on a towel, struck it, and it fell.

It didn't fall down dead. It was still twisting its body and moving its antennae. I regretted what I'd done, took it in the palm of my hand, and went over to put it down on the window sill. It was too late. The poor thing expired after a few seconds. I was a little upset, bothered.

"Why the devil wasn't it blue?" I said to myself.

And that reflection—one of the most profound that has been made since butterflies were invented—consoled me for the evil deed and reconciled me with myself. I let myself contemplate the corpse with a certain sympathy, I must confess. I imagined that it had come out of the woods, having had breakfast, and that it was happy. The morning was beautiful. It came out of there, modest and black, having fun butterflying under the broad cupola of a blue sky, which is always blue for all wings. It came through my window and found me. I suppose it had never seen a man before. It didn't know, therefore, what a man was. It executed infinite turns around my body and saw that I moved, that I had eyes, arms, legs, a divine look, colossal stature. Then it said to itself: "This is probably the inventor of butterflies." The idea subjugated it, terrified it, but fear, which is also suggestive, hinted to it that the best way to please its creator was to kiss him on the forehead, and it kissed me on the forehead. When I drove it away, it went to land on the counterpane. There it saw my father's picture and it's quite possible that it discovered a half-truth there, to wit, that this was the father of the inventor of butterflies, and it flew over to beg his mercy.

Then the blow of a towel put an end to the adventure. The blue immensity was of no use to it, nor the joy of the flowers, nor the splendor of the green leaves against a face towel, a foot of raw linen. See how fine it is to be superior to butterflies! Because, it's proper to say so, had it been blue, or orange, its life wouldn't have been any more secure. It was quite possible that I would have run it through with a pin for the pleasure of my eyes. It wasn't. That last idea gave me back my consolation. I put my middle finger against my thumb, gave a flick, and the corpse fell into the garden. It was time. The provident ants were already arriving . . . No, I go back to the first idea: I think it would have been better had it been born blue.

XXXII

Lame from Birth

I went on from there to finish my preparations for the trip. I'm not going to delay it any more. I'm going down immediately. I'm going down even if some circumspect reader holds me back to ask if the last chapter is only a disagreeable incident or whether I'd been made a fool of . . . Alas, I didn't count on Dona Eusébia. I was all ready when she came into the house. She was coming to invite me to postpone my descent and come have dinner with her that day. I worked hard at turning her down, but she insisted so much, so very much, ever so much that I couldn't help accepting. Besides, I owed her those amends. I went.

Eugênia didn't put on her adornments for me that day. I think they'd been for me—unless she went around like that a lot of times. Not even the gold earrings she'd worn the day before were hanging from her ears now, two delicately shaped ears on the head of a nymph. A simple white muslin dress without any decorations, having a mother-of-pearl button at the neck instead of a brooch and another button at the wrists, closing the sleeves, without a shadow of a bracelet.

That was how she was in body and no less in spirit. Clear ideas, simple manners, a certain natural grace, the air of a lady, and, I don't know, perhaps something else. Yes, a mouth exactly like her mother's, which recalled the episode in 1814 for me and then I had an urge to gloss the same verse for the daughter . . .

"Now let me show you the property," the mother said as we finished the last sip of coffee.

We went out onto the veranda, from there to the grounds, and it was then that I noticed something. Eugênia was limping slightly, so slightly that I asked her if she'd hurt her foot. Her mother fell silent. The daughter answered without hesitation.

"No, sir, I've been lame from birth."

I cursed myself to every hell there was. I called myself clumsy, rude. Really, the simple possibility of her being lame was enough not to ask anything. Then I remember the first time I'd seen her—the day before—the girl had approached her mother's chair slowly, and on that same day I'd found her already at the dinner table. It might have been to hide the defect. But what was her reason for confessing it now? I looked at her and noted that she was sad.

I tried to get rid of the remains of my blunder—it wasn't difficult, because the mother was, as she'd confessed, an old carouser and she quickly started a conversation with me. We looked over the whole property, trees, flowers, duck pond, laundry tank, an infinity of things that she kept showing me and commenting on while I, surreptitiously, scrutinized Eugênia's eyes . . .

I give my word that Eugênia's look didn't limp but was straight, perfectly healthy. It came from a pair of dark and tranquil eyes. I think that they were lowered two or three times, a little cloudy, but only two or three times. In general they looked at me with frankness, without timidity or false modesty.

X X X I I I

Fortunate Are They
Who Don't Descend

T he worst of it was that she was lame. Such lucid eyes, such a fresh mouth, such ladylike composure—and lame! That contrast could lead one to believe that nature is sometimes a great mocker. Why pretty if lame? Why lame if pretty? That was the question I kept asking myself on my way back home at night without hitting upon the solution to the enigma. The best thing to do when an enigma is unresolved is to toss it out the window. That was what I did. I laid hand onto another towel and drove off that other black butterfly fluttering in my bran. I felt relieved and went to bed. But dreams, which are a loophole in the spirit, let the bug back in and I spent the whole night delving into the mystery without explaining it.

It was raining that morning and I postponed my descent. But the next day the morning was clear and blue and in spite of that I let myself stay, the same on the third day, the fourth, right to the end of the week. Beautiful, cool, inviting mornings. Down below, the family, the bride, parliament were calling me and I was unable to attend to anything, bewitched at the feet of my Crippled Venus. Bewitched is just a way of enhancing style. There was no bewitchment but, rather, pleasure, a certain physical and moral satisfaction. I loved her, true. At the feet of that so artless creature, a spurious, lame daughter, the product of love and disdain, at her feet I felt good, and she, I think, felt even better at my feet. And all that in Tijuca. A simple eclogue. Dona Eusébia kept watch over us, but not so very much. She tempered necessity with expedience. The daughter, in that first explosion of nature, gave me her soul in bloom.

"Are you going back down tomorrow?" she asked on Saturday.

"I'm planning to."

"Don't."

I didn't go back down and I added a verse to the Gospel: "Blessed are they who do not descend for theirs is the first kiss of young girls." Indeed, Eugênia's first kiss came on a Sunday—the first, which no other male had taken from her, and it wasn't stolen or snatched, but innocently offered, the way an honest debtor pays a debt. Poor Eugênia! If you only knew what ideas were drifting out of my mind on that occasion! You, quivering with excitement, your arms on my shoulders, contemplating your welcome spouse in me, and I, my eyes on 1814, on the shrubbery, on Vilaça, and suspecting that you couldn't lie to your blood, to your origins . . .

Dona Eusébia entered unexpectedly, but not so suddenly as to catch us at each other's feet. I went to the window. Eugênia sat down to adjust one of her braids. Such delightful pretense! Such infinitely delicate skills! Such profound Tartuffeanism! And all of it natural, alive, unstudied, as natural as appetite, as natural as sleep. So much the better! Dona Eusébia didn't suspect anything.

X X X I V

For a Sensitive Soul

There among the five or six people reading me is some sensitive soul who must surely be a bit upset with the previous chapter and who begins to tremble over Eugênia's fate and, perhaps . . . yes, perhaps deep down inside is calling me a cynic. I, a cynic, sensitive soul? By Diana's thigh, that insult deserves being washed away in blood, if blood can wash anything away in this world. No, sensitive soul, I'm not a cynic, I was a man. My brain was a stage on which plays of all kinds were presented: sacred dramas, austere, scrupulous, elegant comedies, wild farces, short skits, buffoonery, pandemonium, sensitive soul, a hodge-podge of things and people in which you could see everything, from the rose of Smyrna to the rue in your own backyard, from Cleopatra's magnificent bed to the corner of the beach where the beggar shivers in his sleep. Crossing it are thoughts of varied types and shapes. There wasn't only the atmosphere of water and hummingbird there, there was also that of snail and toad. Take back the expression, then, sensitive soul, control your nerves, clean your glasses—because this is sometimes due to glasses—and let's be done with this flower from the shrubbery.

X X X V

The Road to Damascus

It so happened that a week later, as if I were on the road to Damascus, I heard a mysterious voice that whispered the words of the Scripture (Acts, 9:6) to me: "*Arise, and go into the city.*" That voice was coming from myself and it had a double origin: the pity that rendered me helpless before the innocence of the little one, and the terror of really falling in love with her and marrying her. A lame woman! As for that being the reason for my descent, there's no doubt that she thought so and she told me. It was on the veranda on a Monday afternoon when I told her I would be going back down the next morning. "Goodbye," she sighed, holding out her hand with simplicity. "You're doing the right thing." And since I didn't say anything, she went on. "You're doing the right thing in running away from the ridiculous idea of marrying me." I was going to tell her, no. She withdrew slowly, swallowing her tears. I caught up with her after a few steps and swore to her by all the saints in heaven that I was obliged to go back down, but that I hadn't stopped loving her and very much. All cold hyperbole, which she listened to without saying anything.

"Do you believe me?" I finally asked.

"No, and I say you're doing the right thing."

I tried to hold her back, but the look she gave me was no longer a plea but a command. I went down from Tijuca the next morning a little embittered but also a little satisfied. I went along saying to myself that it was right to obey my father, that it was fitting to take up a political career . . . that the constitution . . . that my bride . . . that my horse . . .

X X X V I

On Boots

M y father, who hadn't been expecting me, embraced me, full of tenderness and thanks. "Is it true, then?" he said. "Can I finally . . . ?"

I left him with that reticence and went to take off my boots, which were tight. Once relieved, I took a deep breath and stretched out while my feet and all that extended up from them went into relative bliss. Then I pondered the fact that tight boots are one of the best bits of good fortune on earth, because by making one's feet hurt they give occasion to the pleasure of taking them off. Punish your feet, wretch, then unpunish them and there you have cheap happiness, at the mercy of shoemakers and worthy of Epicurus. While that idea was working out on my famous trapeze, I cast my eyes up toward Tijuca and saw the little cripple disappearing over the horizon of the past and I felt that my heart wouldn't be long in taking off its boots either. And they were taken off by lechery. Four or five days later I was savoring that quick, ineffable, and irrepressible moment of pleasure that follows a sharp pain, a preoccupation, an indisposition . . . From that I inferred that life is the most ingenious of phenomena because hunger only becomes sharp with an aim to bring on the occasion for eating, and that life only invented calluses because they perfect earthly happiness. In all truth I can tell you that all of human wisdom isn't worth a pair of short boots.

You, my Eugênia, never took them off. You went along the road of life limping from your leg and from love, sad as a pauper's burial, solitary, silent, laborious, until you, too, came to this other shore . . . What I don't know is whether your existence was quite necessary for the century. Who knows? Maybe one less walk-on would make the human tragedy a failure.

X X X V I I

Finally!

Finally! Here's Virgília. Before going to Councilor Dutra's house I asked my father if there was any commitment of marriage.

"No commitment. Some time back, while speaking to him about you, I confessed my desire to see you a deputy. And I spoke in such a way that he promised to do something and I think he will. As for the bride—that's the name I give to a lovely creature who's a jewel, a flower, a star, something rare . . . She's his daughter. I imagined that if you married her you'd get to be a deputy quicker."

"Is that all?"

"That's all."

From there we went to Dutra's house. The man was a delight, smiling, jovial, patriotic, a bit irritated by public ills but not despairing about curing them quickly. He thought my candidacy was legitimate. It was best, however, to wait a few months. And then he introduced me to his wife—an estimable lady—and his daughter, who in no way belied my father's panegyric. I swear to you, in no way. Reread Chapter XXVII. I, who had an idea regarding the little one, stared at her in a certain way. She, who I'm not sure had one or not, didn't stare at me any differently. And that first look was purely and simply conjugal. At the end of a month we were close.

X X X V I I I

The Fourth Edition

"Come dine with us tomorrow," Dutra told me one night. I accepted the invitation. The next day I told the carriage to wait for me on the Largo São Francisco de Paula and I went to take a stroll. Do you still remember my theory of human editions? Well, know, then, that at that time I was in my fourth edition, revised and corrected, but still contaminated with careless errors and incorrect usage. A defect that, on the other hand, was compensated for by the type, which was elegant, and the binding, which was deluxe. After my stroll, as I went along the Rua dos Ouvires I looked at my watch and the crystal fell to the sidewalk. I went into the first shop at hand. It was a cubicle, little more—dusty and dark.

In the rear, behind the counter, a woman was sitting and her yellow, pockmarked face wasn't visible at first sight. But as soon as it was it became a curious spectacle. She couldn't have been ugly, on the contrary, it was obvious that she'd been pretty, quite pretty. But the illness and a precocious old age had destroyed the flower of her beauty. The smallpox had been terrible. The marks, large and plentiful, formed bumps and notches up and down her face and they gave the feeling of thick sand-paper, enormously thick. The eyes were the best part of the figure and yet they had a singular and repugnant expression that changed, how-ever, as soon as I began to speak. As for her hair, it was gray and almost as dusty as the doorway to the shop. A diamond gleamed on one of the fingers of her left hand. Can you believe it, you future generations? That woman was Marcela.

I didn't recognize her right away. It was difficult. She, however, rec-ognized me as soon as I spoke to her. Her eyes sparkled and changed their usual expression for another, half sweet and half sad. I caught a movement by her as if to hide or flee. It was the instinct of vanity, which only lasted for an instant. Marcela settled down and smiled.

"Do you want to buy something?" she asked, holding out her hand to me.

I didn't answer. Marcela understood the cause of my silence (it wasn't difficult) and only hesitated, I think, in deciding which was stronger, the fright of the present or the memory of the past. She brought me a chair and with the counter between us spoke to me at length about her-self, the life she'd led, the tears I'd caused her to shed, the longing, the disasters, finally the smallpox that had scarred her face, and time, which the illness had helped in bringing on her early decline. The truth is that she did have a decrepit soul. She'd sold everything, almost everything. A man who'd loved her in times past and died in her arms had left her that jewelry store but, to make misfortune complete, there weren't many customers coming to the shop now—maybe because of the odd situa-tion that it was run by a woman. She immediately asked me to tell her about my life. I didn't spend much time telling it. It was neither long nor interesting.

"Did you get married?" Marcela asked after my narration.

"Not yet," I replied drily.

Marcela cast her eyes out onto the street with the weakness of some-one reflecting or remembering. I let myself go into the past then and in the midst of memories and nostalgia asked myself whatever could have been the reason for my having been so foolish. This one certainly wasn't the Marcela of 1822, but was the beauty of times gone by worth a third of my sacrifices? That was what I was seeking to find out by interrogat-ing Marcela's face. The face told me no. At the same time the eyes were telling me that back then, the same as today, the flame of greed burned in them. Mine hadn't been able to see it in her. They were the eyes of the first edition.

"So why did you come in here? Did you see me from the street?" she asked, coming out of that kind of torpor.

"No, I thought I was coming into a watchmaker's shop. I wanted to buy a crystal for this watch. I'll go somewhere else. You'll have to excuse me, I'm in a hurry."

Marcela smiled sadly. The truth is that I felt distressed and annoyed at the same time and I was anxious to get myself out of that place. Marcela, however, called a black boy, gave him the watch, and, in spite of my objections, sent him to a shop in the neighborhood to buy the crystal. There was no way out. I sat down again. Then she said that she wanted the protection of people she knew in times gone by. She thought that sooner or later it would be natural for me to get married and swore to me that she would get me fine jewelry at a cheap price. She didn't say *cheap price*, but she used a delicate and transparent metaphor. I began to suspect that she hadn't suffered any disaster (except for the illness), that she had her money safely put away, and that she was bargaining with the sole aim of satisfying her passion for profit, which was the worm that gnawed at her existence. That was exactly what I was told later.

X X X I X

The Neighbor

While I was reflecting on that to myself, a short fellow, hatless and leading a girl of four by the hand, entered the shop.

"How'd the morning go today?" he asked Marcela.

"So, so. Come here, Maricota."

The fellow picked up the child by the arms and passed her over the counter.

"Go ahead," he said. "Ask Dona Marcela how she spent the night. She was anxious to come here, but her mother hadn't been able to dress her . . . So, Maricota? Ask her for her blessing . . . Watch out for the switch! That's the way . . . You can't imagine what she's like at home. She talks about you all the time, and here she acts like a dummy. Just yesterday . . . Shall I tell her, Maricota?"

"No, don't tell her, Papa."

"Was it something naughty, then?" Marcela asked, patting the girl's face.

"I'll tell you. Her mother has taught her to say an Our Father and a Hail Mary every night to Our Lady, but yesterday the little one asked me in a very timid voice . . . can you imagine what? . . . If it would be all right to offer them to Saint Marcela."

"Poor thing!" Marcela said, kissing her.

"It's a love affair, a passion, you can't imagine . . . Her mother says she's bewitched . . ."

The fellow told many other things, all very pleasant, until he left, taking the girl, but not before casting a curious or suspicious glance in my direction. I asked Marcela who he was.

"He's a watchmaker in the neighborhood, a good person. His wife, too. And the daughter is a charm, don't you think? She seems to like me a lot . . . They're good people."

As she spoke those words there seemed to be a quiver of joy in Marcela's voice. And on her face something that spread a wave of happiness across it . . .

X L

In the Carriage

At that point the black boy came in carrying the watch with a new crystal. It was about time. It was already beginning to bother me being there. I gave the boy a small silver coin, told Marcela that I'd come back on another occasion, and went out with long strides. To tell the truth, I must confess that my heart was pounding a little. But it was a kind of death knell. My spirit was bound by opposing impressions.

Remember that the day had dawned happily for me. My father had repeated in advance for me at breakfast the first speech I would make in the Chamber of Deputies. We were laughing a lot and the sun was, too, brilliant as on the most beautiful days in the world, the same way that Virgília should laugh when I told her about our breakfast fantasies. All is going well when I lose the crystal to my watch, go into the first shop at hand, and, behold, the past rises up before me, lacerates and kisses me, interrogates me with a face scarred by nostalgia and smallpox . . .

I left it behind and hurriedly got into the carriage, which was waiting for me on the Largo São Francisco de Paula, and I ordered the coachman to drive fast. The coachman whipped up the animals and the carriage began to shake me up. The springs groaned, the wheels cut rapidly through the mud that the recent rain had left, and yet it all seemed stock-still to me. Isn't there a kind of lukewarm wind that blows sometimes, not strong or harsh, but a little sultry, which doesn't blow the hat off your head or swirl women's skirts up, and yet is or seems to be worse than the one that does both those things because it lowers, weakens, kind of dissolves the spirit? Well, I had that wind with me, and, certain that it was blowing on me because I found myself in a kind of gorge between the past and the present, I was longing to come out onto the plain of the future. The worst of it was that the carriage wasn't moving.

"João," I shouted to the coachman, "Is this carriage moving or not?"

"Oh, Little Master! We're parked by the Councilor's door already."

X L I

The Hallucination

He was right. I hurried in. I found Virgília anxious, in a bad mood, frowning. Her mother, who was deaf, was with her in the living room. After the greetings, the girl told me dryly:

"We expected you sooner."

I defended myself as best I could. I mentioned a balky horse, a friend who'd held me up. All of a sudden my voice died on my lips, I was paralyzed with wonder. Virgília . . . could that girl be Virgília? I took a good look at her and the feeling was so painful that I took a step back and turned my eyes away. I looked at her again. The smallpox had eaten at her face. Her skin, so delicate and pink and pure before, just a day ago, looked yellow to me now, stigmatized by the same lash that had devastated the Spanish woman's face. Her eyes, which used to be lively, were dull, her lips were sad and she had a weary air about her. I took a good look, took her hand and softly drew her toward me. I hadn't been deceived, they were pockmarks. I think I took on an expression of revulsion.

Virgília drew away from me and went to sit down on the sofa. I spent some time looking at my shoetops. Should I leave or stay? I rejected the first suggestion, which was quite absurd, and walked over to Virgília, who was sitting there without saying a word. I looked in vain for some vestige of the illness on her face. There was none. It was the usual delicate and white skin.

"Haven't you ever seen me before?" Virgília asked, noticing that I was staring at her intently.

"Never so pretty."

I sat down while Virgília, silent, clicked her fingernails. There was a pause of a few seconds. I spoke to her about things that had nothing to do with the incident. She didn't say anything in response nor did she look at me. Except for the clicking of her nails she was the statue of Silence. Only once did she set her eyes on me, but far above me, raising the left corner of her mouth, knitting her brows to the point of bringing them together. That whole combination of things gave her face an intermediate expression, somewhere between comic and tragic.

There was a certain affection in that disdain. It was a kind of contrived expression. She was suffering inside, and quite a bit—it was either real suffering or just annoyance. And because pain that's covered up hurts all the more, quite probably Virgília was suffering twice over what she really should have been suffering. I think that's called metaphysics.

X L I I

What Aristotle Left Out

A nother thing that seems metaphysical to me is this: put a ball into motion, for example. It rolls, touches another ball, transmits the impulse, and there you have the second ball rolling like the first. Let us suppose that the first ball is called . . . Marcela—and it's only a supposition. The second Brás Cubas—the third Virgília. Put the case that Marcela, receiving a flick from the past, rolls until she touches Brás Cubas—who, reacting to the impelling force, begins to roll, too, until he runs up against Virgília, who had nothing to do with the first ball. And there you have now, by the simple transmission of a force, two social extremes come into contact and something is established that we can call . . . the solidarity of human aversion. How is it that Aristotle left that chapter out?

X L I I I

A Marchioness, Because I Shall Be Marquis

V irgília was positively a mischief-maker, an angelic mischief-maker, but one all the same, then . . .

Then Lobo Neves appeared, a man who was no slimmer than I, nor more elegant, nor better read, nor more pleasant, and yet it was he who snatched Virgília and the candidacy away from me in a matter of a few weeks and with truly Caesarian drive. There was no anger preceding it, no family dispute at all. Dutra came to tell me one day that I should wait for another opportunity because Lobo Neves' candidacy was backed by people of great influence. I gave in. Such was the start of my defeat. A week later Virgília asked Lobo Neves, smiling, when he was going to be a cabinet minister.

"As far as I'm concerned, right now, according to others, a year from now."

"Promise me that you'll make me a baroness someday?"

"A marchioness, because I shall be a marquis."

From that moment on I was lost. Virgília compared the eagle to the peacock and chose the eagle, leaving the peacock with his surprise, his spite, and the three or four kisses she'd given him. Maybe five kisses. But even if there'd been ten, they wouldn't have meant anything. A man's lip isn't like the hoof of Atilla's horse, which sterilized the ground it trod. Quite the opposite.

X L I V

A Cubas

My father was astounded at the outcome and I'd like to think that there was nothing else that caused his death. So many were the castles that he'd built, ever so many the dreams, that he couldn't bear to see them demolished without suffering a great shock to his organism. At first he refused to believe it. A Cubas! A twig of the illustrious tree of the Cubases! And he said that with such conviction that I, aware by then of our cooperage, forgot the fickle lady for a moment to think only about that phenomenon, not strange, but curious: imagination raised up to certitude.

"A Cubas!" he repeated to me the next morning at breakfast.

It wasn't a joyful breakfast. I myself was dropping from lack of sleep. I'd stayed awake a good part of the night. Because of love? Impossible. One doesn't love the same woman twice, and I, who would love that one some time later, wasn't held at that time by any other bond than a passing fantasy, a certain obedience to my own fatuousness. And that was enough to explain my wakefulness. It was spite, a sharp little spite with the prick of a pin, which disappeared with cigars, pounding fists, scattered reading, until dawn broke, the most tranquil of dawns.

But I was young, I had the cure in myself. It was my father who couldn't bear the blow so easily. When I think about it, it might be that he didn't die precisely because of the disaster, but the disaster surely complicated his final ailments. He died four months latter—disheartened, sad, and with an intense and continuous preoccupation, something like remorse, a fatal disenchantment that went along with his rheumatism and coughing. He had a half hour of joy all the same. It was when one of the ministers came to call. I saw that he had—I remember it well—I saw that he had the pleased smile of other days and a concentration of light in his eyes that was, so to speak, the last flash of an expiring soul. But the sadness returned immediately, the sadness or dying without seeing me in some high position as befitted me.

"A Cubas!"

He died a few days after the minister's visit one morning in May, between his two children, Sabina and me, along with Uncle Ildefonso and my brother-in-law. He died in spite of the physicians' science or our love or our care, which was great, or anything else. He was to die and he died.

XLV

Notes

Sobs, tears, the house all prepared, black velvet over the doorways, a man who came to dress the corpse, another who took measurements for the coffin, bier, candle holders, invitations, guests slowly entering, stepping softly, shaking hands with the family, some sad, all serious and silent, priest and sacristan, prayers, the sprinkling of holy water, nailing shut the coffin, six people lifting it and carrying it down the steps in spite of the cries, sobs, the new tears on the part of the family, and going up to the hearse, placing it on top and tying it down, the hearse rolling along, and the carriages, one by one . . . What looks like a simple inventory here are notes I'd taken for a sad and banal chapter that I won't write.

X L V I

The Inheritance

L et the reader have a look at us now, a week after my father's death—my sister sitting on a sofa—Cotrim a little in front of her, leaning against a sideboard, his arms folded and nibbling on his mustache—I walking back and forth staring at the floor. Deep mourning. Profound silence.

"But, after all," Cotrim was saying, "this house can't be worth much more than thirty *contos*. Let's make it thirty-five . . ."

"It's worth fifty," I figured. "Sabina knows it cost fifty-eight . . ."

"It could have cost sixty," Cotrim replied, "but it doesn't follow that it was worth it, much less that it's worth it today. You know that houses have gone down in price over the years. Look, if this one is worth the fifty *contos*, how much do you think the one you want for yourself, the country house, is worth?"

"Let's not talk about that. It's an old house."

"Old?" Sabina exclaimed, lifting her hands to the ceiling.

"Do you think it's new? I bet you do."

"Come on, brother, let's stop this," Sabina said, getting up from the sofa. "We can work everything out in a friendly fashion, smoothly. For example, Cotrim won't take the slaves, only the coachman and Paulo . . ."

"Not the coachman," I hastened to add. "I'm getting the carriage and I'm not going to buy another driver."

"Well, I'll stick with Paulo and Prudêncio."

"Prudêncio is free."

"Free?"

"Since two years ago."

"Free? How could your father have managed things here without telling anyone? That's great! What about the silver? . . . I don't imagine he freed the silver, did he?"

We'd spoken about the silver, the old silver from the time of Dom José I, the most important part of the inheritance, for its workmanship, for its antiquity, for the origins of its ownership. My father had said that the Count da Cunha, when he was Viceroy of Brazil, had given it to my great-grandfather Luís Cubas, as a present.

"About the silver," Cotrim went on, "I wouldn't bring it up if it weren't for your sister's wish to keep it. And I think she's right. Sabina's a married woman and she needs a fine setting, a presentable one. You're a bachelor, you don't entertain, you don't . . ."

"But I might get married."

"What for?" Sabina interrupted.

That question was so sublime that for a few moments it made me forget all about my interests. I smiled, took Sabina's hand, patted her palm lightly, all with such a delicate appearance that Cotrim interpreted the gesture as one of acquiescence and he thanked me.

"What's that?" I retorted. "I haven't given up anything and I'm not going to."

"You're not going to?"

I nodded.

"Let it pass, Cotrim," my sister said to her husband. "Let's see if he wants the clothes on our backs, too. That's all that's missing."

"Nothing more is missing. You want the carriage, you want the coachman, you want the silver, you want everything. Look, it would be quicker if you took us to court and proved with witnesses that Sabina isn't your sister, that I'm not your brother-in-law, and that God isn't God. Do that and you won't lose anything, not even a little teaspoon. Come now, my friend, try something else!"

He was so irritated that I no less that I thought of suggesting a means for conciliation: dividing up the silver. He laughed and asked me who would get the teapot and who would get the sugar bowl. And, after that question, he declared that we would have an opportunity to liquidate our demands in court at least. In the meantime Sabina had gone to the window that looked out onto the grounds—and after a moment she turned and proposed giving up Paulo and the other black on the condition that she get the silver. I was going to say that I didn't want that, but Cotrim got ahead of me and said the same thing.

"Never! I won't give any charitable donations," he said.

We dined sadly. My uncle the canon appeared after dinner and witnessed yet another small altercation.

"My children," he said. "Remember that my brother left a loaf large enough to be divided up for everyone."

But Cotrim said, "I know, I know. But the question doesn't concern the bread, it concerns the butter. I can't swallow dry bread."

The division was finally made but peace wasn't. And I can tell you that, even so, it was very difficult for me to break with Sabina. We'd been such good friends! Childhood games, childhood furies, the laughter and sadness of adult life, so many times we'd divided that loaf of joy and misery like brother and sister, like the good brother and sister we were. But we'd broken up. Just like Marcela's beauty, which had vanished with the smallpox.

X L V I I

The Recluse

Marcela, Sabina, Virgília . . . here I am putting together all the contrasts as if those names and people were only stages of my inner affections. Be sorry for bad habits, put on a stylish necktie, a less-stained waistcoat, and then, yes, come with me, enter this house, stretch out on this hammock that cradled me for the better part of two years, from the inventory of my father's estate until 1842. Come. If you smell some dressing-table perfume, don't think I had it sprinkled for my pleasure. It's the vestige of N. or Z. or U.—because all those capital letters cradle their elegant abjection there. But, if in addition to the perfume you want some thing else, keep that wish to yourself, because I don't keep portraits or letters or diaries. The excitement itself has vanished and left me with the initials.

I lived half like a recluse, attending, after long intervals, some ball or theater or a lecture, but I spent most of the time by myself. I was living, letting myself float on the ebb and tide of events and days, sometimes lively, sometimes apathetic, somewhere between ambitious and disheartened. I was writing politics and making literature. I sent articles and poems to newspapers and I managed to attain a certain reputation as a polemicist and poet. When I thought of Lobo Neves, who was already a deputy, and Virgília, a future marchioness, I asked myself whether I wouldn't have been a better deputy and a better marquis than Lobo Neves—I, who was worth more, much more, than he—and I said that looking at the tip of my nose . . .

X L V I I I

A Cousin of Virgília's

"**D**o you know who got in from São Paulo yesterday?" Luís Dutra asked me one night.

Luís Dutra was a cousin of Virgília's who was also an intimate of the muses. His poetry was more pleasing and was worth more than mine, but he had a need for the approval of some in order to confirm the applause of others. Since he was bashful he never asked anyone, but he enjoyed hearing some word of appreciation. Then he would gather new strength and plunge into the work like an adolescent.

Poor Luís Dutra! As soon as he published something he would run to my place and start hovering around me on the lookout for an opinion, a word, a gesture that would approve his recent production, and I would speak to him of a thousand different things—the latest ball in Catete, salon discussions, carriages, horses—about everything except his poetry or prose. He would respond with animation at first, then more sluggishly, turning the gist of the conversation toward his matter. He would open a book, ask me if I'd done any new work, and I would answer yes or no and turn the direction away and there he was behind me, until he would be completely balked and go away sad. My intent was to make him doubt himself, dishearten him, eliminate him. And all of that looking at the tip of my nose . . .

X L I X

The Tip of My Nose

Nose, conscience without remorse, you were very helpful to me in life . . . Have you ever meditated sometime on the purpose of the nose, dear reader? Dr. Pangloss' explanation is that the nose was created for the use of eyeglasses—and I must confess that such an explanation, up till a certain time, seemed to be the definitive one for me. But it happened one day while ruminating on those and other obscure philosophical points that I hit upon the only true and definitive explanation.

All I needed, really, was to follow the habits of a fakir. As the reader knows, a fakir spends long hours looking at the tip of his nose with his only aim that of seeing the celestial light. When he fixes his eyes on the tip of his nose he loses his sense of outside things, becomes enraptured with the invisible, learns the intangible, becomes detached from the world, dissolves, is aetherialized. That sublimation of the being by the tip of the nose is the most lofty phenomenon of the spirit, and the faculty for obtaining it doesn't belong to the fakir alone. It's universal. Every man has the need and the power to contemplate his own nose with an aim to see the celestial light, and such contemplation, whose effect is subordination to just one nose, constitutes the equilibrium of societies. If noses only contemplated each other, humankind wouldn't have lasted two centuries, it would have died out with the earliest tribes.

I can hear an objection on the part of the reader here. "How can it be like that," he asks, "if no one has ever seen men contemplating their own noses?"

Obtuse reader, that proves you've never got inside the brain of a milliner. A milliner passes by a hat shop, the shop of a rival who'd opened it two years before. It had two doors then, now it has four. It promises to have six or eight. The rival's customers are going in through the doors. The milliner compares that shop with his, which is older and has only two doors, and those hats with his, less sought after even though priced the same. He's naturally mortified, but he keeps on walking, concentrating, with his eyes lowered or straight ahead, pondering the reasons for the other man's prosperity and his own backwardness while he as a milliner is a much better milliner than the other milliner . . . At that moment his eyes are fixed on the tip of his nose.

The conclusion, therefore, is that there are two capital forces: love, which multiplies the species, and the nose, which subordinates it to the individual. Procreation, equilibrium.

L

Virgília Wed

"The one who'd got in from São Paulo was my cousin Virgília, married to Lobo Neves," Luís Dutra went on.

"Oh!"

"And today I learned something for the first time, you rogue . . ."

"What was that?"

"That you wanted to marry her."

"My father's idea. Who told you that?"

"She did herself. I talked about you a lot to her and then she told me everything."

The following day on the Rua do Ouvidor, in the doorway of Plancher the printer, I saw a splendid woman appear in the distance. It was she. I only recognized her when she was a few steps away, she was so different, nature and art had given her their final touch. We greeted each other. She went on her way, joined her husband in the carriage that was waiting for them a little farther on. I was astounded.

A week later I ran into her at a ball. I think we got to exchange two or three words. But at another ball given a month later at the house of a lady, whose salons were the jewel of the first reign and were no less that of the second, the meeting was broader and longer because we chatted and waltzed. The waltz is a delightful thing. We waltzed. I won't deny that as I pressed that flexible and magnificent body to my body I had a singular sensation, the sensation of a man who'd been robbed.

"It's very hot," she said when we finished. "Shall we go out onto the terrace?"

"No, you might catch cold. Let's go into the other room."

In the other room was Lobo Neves, who paid me many compliments for my political writings, adding that he couldn't say anything about the literary ones because he didn't understand them, but the political ones were excellent, well thought out and well written. I replied with an equal show of courtesy and we separated, pleased with each other.

About three weeks later I received an invitation from him for an intimate gathering. I went. Virgília greeted me with these gracious words: "You're going to waltz with me tonight." The truth was that I had the reputation of being an eminent waltzer. Don't be surprised over the fact that she preferred me. We waltzed once and once again. If a book brought on Francesca's downfall, here it was the waltz that brought on ours. I think I grasped her hand that night with great strength and she left it there, as if forgetful, and I embraced her, and with all eyes on us and on the others who were also embracing and twirling . . . Delirium.

L I

Mine

"She's mine!" I said to myself as soon as I passed her on to another gentleman. And I must confess that for the rest of the evening the idea was becoming embedded in my spirit, not with the force of a hammer, but with that of a drill, which is more insinuative.

"Mine!" I said when I got to the door of my house.

But there, as if fate or chance or whatever it was remembered to feed my passionate flight of fancy, a round, yellow thing was gleaming at me on the ground. I bent over. It was a gold coin, a half doubloon.

"Mine!" I repeated, and laughed.

That night I didn't think about the coin anymore, but on the following day, remembering the incident, I felt a certain revulsion in my conscience and a voice that asked me why the devil a coin that I hadn't inherited or earned but only found in the street should be mine. Obviously it wasn't mine, it belonged to somebody else, the one who'd lost it, rich or poor, and he might have been poor. Some worker who didn't have anything to feed his wife and children with. But even if he was rich my duty remained the same. It was proper to return the coin and the best method, the only method, was to do it through an advertisement or through the police. I sent a letter to the chief of police enclosing what I'd found and beseeching him by the means at his disposal to return it into the hands of its true owner.

I sent the letter off and ate a peaceful breakfast, I might even say a jubilant one. My conscience had waltzed so much the night before that it had lost its breath, but giving back the half doubloon was a window that opened onto the other side of morality. A wave of pure air came in and the lady breathed deeply. Ventilate your conscience! That's all I can tell you. Nevertheless, if for no other reason, my act was a nice one because it expressed the proper scruples, the feelings of a delicate soul. That was what my inner lady was telling me, in a way that was austere and tender at the same time. That was what she was telling me as I leaned on the sill of the open window.

"You did well, Cubas. You behaved perfectly. This air isn't only pure, it's balmy, it's the breath of the eternal gardens. Do you want to see what you did, Cubas?"

And the good lady took out a mirror and opened it before my eyes. I saw, I clearly saw the half doubloon of the night before, round, shiny, multiplying all by itself—becoming ten—then thirty—then five hundred—expressing in that way the benefits I would be given in life and in death by the simple act of restitution. And I was pouring out my whole being into the contemplation of that act, I was seeing myself in it again, I found myself good—great perhaps. A simple coin, eh? See what it means to have waltzed just a wee bit more.

So I, Brás Cubas, discovered a sublime law, the law of the equivalencies of windows, and I established the fact that the method of compensating for a closed window is to open another, so that morality can continuously aerate one's conscience. Maybe you don't understand what's entailed in that. Maybe you want something more concrete, a package, for example, a mysterious package. Well, here's the mysterious package.

L I I

The Mysterious Package

The matter is that a few days later on my way to Botafogo I tripped over a package lying on the beach. That's not quite exact. It was more of a kick than a trip. Seeing a bundle, not large but clean and neatly tied together with strong twine, something that looked like something, I thought about giving it a kick, just for the fun of it, and I kicked it, and the package resisted. I cast my eyes about. The beach was deserted. Some children were playing far off—beyond them a fisherman was drying his nets—no one could have seen my act. I bent over, picked up the package, and went on my way.

I went on my way but not without some hesitation. It might have been a trick being played by some boys. I got the idea of taking what I'd found back to the beach, but I felt it and rejected the idea. A little farther on I changed course and headed home.

"Let's have a look," I said as I entered my study.

And I hesitated for a moment, because of shame, I think. The suspicion of a trick struck me again. It was certain that there'd been no outside witness there. But I had an urchin inside myself who would whisper, wink, grunt, kick, jeer, cackle, do devilish things if he saw me open the package and find a dozen old handkerchiefs or two dozen rotting guavas inside. It was too late. My curiosity was sharpened, as the reader's must be. I unwrapped the bundle and I saw . . .,found . . . counted . . . recounted nothing less than five *contos*. Nothing less. Maybe ten *mil-réis* more. Five *contos* in good banknotes and coins, all clean and in neat order, a rare find. I wrapped them up again. At dinner it seemed to me that one of the black boys was speaking to the other with his eyes. Had they spied on me? I asked them discreetly and concluded that they hadn't. After dinner I went back to my study, examined the money, and laughed at my maternal worries regarding the five *contos*—I, who was well-off.

In order not to think about it any more I went to Lobo Neves' that night. He'd insisted that I not miss his wife's receptions. There I ran into the chief of police. I was introduced to him. He immediately remembered the letter and the half doubloon I'd sent him a few days before. He revealed the matter. Virgília seemed to be savoring my act and everyone of those present came up with some analogous anecdote to which I listened with the impatience of a hysterical woman.

The following night and during that whole week I gave as little thought as I could to the five *contos* and, I must confess, I left them ever so peaceful in my desk drawer. I liked talking about everything except money, and principally money that had been found. It wasn't a crime to find money, however, it was a happy thing, good luck, maybe even a stroke of Providence. It couldn't be anything else. Five *contos* aren't lost the way you lose a pouch of tobacco. Five *contos* are carried with thirty thousand feelings, you keep feeling them, you don't take your eyes off them, or your hands, or your thoughts, and for them to be lost foolishly like that on a beach it has to be . . . Finding them can't be a crime. Neither a crime, nor dishonor, nor anything that might sully a man's character. They were something discovered, a lucky strike, like the grand prize, like a winning bet on the horses, like the stakes in an honest gambling game, and I might even say that my good luck was deserved, because I didn't feel bad or unworthy of the rewards of Providence.

"These five *contos*," I said to myself three weeks later, "must be used for some good deed, maybe as the dowry of some poor girl, or something like that . . . I'll see . . ."

That same day I took them to the Banco de Brasil. There I was received with many gracious references to the matter of the half doubloon, the news of which was already spreading among people of my acquaintance. I replied with annoyance that the matter wasn't worth the great to-do. Then they praised my modesty—and since I got angry they answered that it was nothing more or less than something grand.

L I I I

• • • • •

Virgília was the one who no longer remembered the half doubloon. Her whole being was concentrated on me, on my eyes, on my life, on my thoughts—that was what she said and it was true.

There are some plants that are born and grow quickly. Others are late and stunted. Our love was like the former. It burst forth with such drive and so much sap that in a short while it was the broadest, leafiest, and most luxuriant creation in the forest. I can't tell you for certain the number of days that this growth took. I do remember that on a certain night the flower, or the kiss if you want to call it that, began to bud, a kiss that she gave me trembling—poor thing—trembling with fear, because it was by the gate in the yard. That single kiss united us—just as the moment was brief, so was the love ardent, the prologue to a life of delights, terrors, remorse, pleasures that ended in pain, afflictions that opened up into joy—a patient and systematic hypocrisy, the only check rein on an unchecked passion—a life of agitation, rage, despair, and jealousy, which one hour would pay for fully and more than enough, but another hour would come and swallow it all up along with everything else, leaving on the surface agitation and all the remains, and the remains of the remains, which are aversion and satiety. Such was the book with that prologue.

L I V

The Grandfather Clock

I left there savoring the kiss. I couldn't sleep. I lay down on my bed, of course, but it meant nothing. I heard the hours of night. Usually when I couldn't sleep, the chiming of the grandfather clock would upset me very much. The mournful tick-tock, slow and dry, seemed to say with every note that I was having one instant less of life. Then I would picture an old devil sitting between two sacks, that of life and that of death, taking out the coins of life and giving them to death, counting them like this:

"Another less . . ."
"Another less . . ."
"Another less . . ."
"Another less . . ."

The strangest thing is that if the clock stopped I would wind it up so it wouldn't stop ticking and I could count all of my lost instants. There are inventions that are transformed or come to an end; institutions themselves die. A clock is definitive and perpetual. The last man, as he says farewell to the cold and used-up sun, will have a watch in his pocket in order to know the exact time of his death.

On that night I didn't suffer that sad feeling of tedium but a different and delightful one. Fantasies swarmed inside of me, coming one on top of another like the devout women who crush forward in order to get a look at the singing angel in processions. I wasn't hearing the instants lost but the minutes gained. From a certain time forward I didn't hear anything at all because my thought, wily and frisky, leaped out the window and flapped its wings toward Virgília's house. There it found

Virgília's thought on a window sill. They greeted each other, remained chatting. We were tossing in bed, cold perhaps, in need of rest, and those two idlers there were repeating the old dialogue of Adam and Eve.

L V

The Old Dialogue of Adam and Eve

Brás Cubas

. . . .?

Virgília

. . . .

Brás Cubas

. . . .
. . . .

Virgília

. . . .!

Brás Cubas

. . . .

Virgília

. . . .
. . . .? . . . .
. . . .
. . . .

Brás Cubas

. . . .

Virgília

. . . .

Brás Cubas

. . . .
. . . .
. . . . !. .
. .!. . . . .
. . . .!

Virgília

. . . .?

Brás Cubas

. . . .!

Virgília

. . . .!

L V I

The Opportune Moment

But, dash it all! Who can explain the reason for this difference to me? At one time we kept company, discussed marriage, broke up, and separated, coldly, painlessly, because there'd been no passion. I only carried away a little spite and nothing else. The years pass, I see her again, we take three or four turns in a waltz, and here we are, madly in love with each other. Virgília's beauty, it's true, had reached a high degree of perfection, but we were substantially the same and I, for my part, hadn't become more handsome or more dashing. Who will explain the reason for that difference to me?

The reason couldn't have been anything else but the opportune moment, because if on that first occasion neither of us was too green for love, both of us were for *our* love, a fundamental distinction. No love is possible without the opportunity of the subjects. I found that explanation myself two years after the kiss one day when Virgília was complaining to me about a fop who kept flirting with her tenaciously.

"What a pest! How importune!" she said, putting on an angry face.

I shuddered, stared at her, saw that the indignation was sincere. Then it occurred to me that maybe I'd brought on that same frown at some time and I immediately understood the degree of my evolution. I'd gone from importune to opportune.

L V I I

Fate

Yes, sir, we were in love. Now that all the social laws forbade it, now was when we truly loved each other. We found ourselves yoked together like the two souls the poet encountered in Purgatory:

Di pari, come buoi, che vanno a giogo

and I'm wrong comparing us to oxen because we were a different species of animal, less sluggish, more roguish and lascivious. There we were, going along without knowing where to, on what secret roads, a problem that frightened me for a few weeks but whose outcome I turned over to fate. Poor Fate! Where can you be walking now, great supervisor of human affairs? Maybe you're growing a new skin, a different face, different ways, a different name, and it's even possible that . . . I forget where I was . . . Ah, yes, on secret roads. I said to myself that now it would be whatever God willed. It was our fate to fall in love. If it hadn't been, how could we explain the waltz and all the rest? Virgília was thinking the same thing. One day, after confessing to me that she had moments of remorse, since I'd told her that if she felt remorse it was because she didn't love me, Virgília clasped me in her magnificent arms, murmuring:

"I love you. It's the will of heaven."

And that wasn't just random words. Virgília was somewhat religious. She didn't go to mass on Sundays, it's true, and I even think she only went to church on feast days and when there was a vacant pulpit somewhere. But she prayed every night, fervently, or sleepily at least. She was afraid of thunder. On those occasions she'd cover her ears and mumble all the prayers in the catechism. In her bedroom she had a small carved jacaranda prie-dieu, three feet high and with images inside. But she never mentioned it to her friends. On the contrary, she would tag as fanatics those who were simply religious. For some time I suspected that there was a certain annoyance with belief in her and that her religion was a kind of flannel undergarment, hidden and cozy, but I was obviously mistaken.

L V I I I

Confidence

Lobo Neves gave me great fear at first. An illusion! He never tired of telling me how he loved his wife. He thought that Virgília was perfection itself, a combination of solid and refined qualities, loving, elegant, austere, a model woman. And the confidence didn't stop there. From the crack that it once was it grew to be a wide-open door. One day he confessed to me that he had a sad worm gnawing at his existence. He needed public glory. I bolstered his spirits, told him many nice things that he listened to with that religious unction of a desire that doesn't want to finish dying. Then I realized that his ambition was fatigued from beating its wings and being unable to take flight. Days later he told me about all his annoyance and weariness, the bitter pills he'd swallowed, spites, intrigues, perfidy, interests, vanity. There was obviously a crisis of melancholy there. I tried to fight against it.

"I know what I'm talking about," he replied sadly. "You can't imagine what I've been through. I went into politics because of a liking for it, the family, ambition, and a little bit because of vanity. You can see that I have in me all the motives that lead a man into public life. All I was missing was interest in a different way. I'd seen the theatre from the audience's side and, I swear, it was beautiful! Superb sets, life, movement and grace in the performance. I signed on. They gave me a role that ... but why am I boring you with all this? Let me keep my afflictions to myself. Believe me, I've spent hours, days ... There's no constancy of feelings, there's no gratitude, there's no nothing ... nothing ... nothing."

He fell silent, deeply downcast, his eyes in the air, not seeming to hear anything unless it was the echo of his own thoughts. After a few moments he stood up and held out his hand to me. "You must be laughing at me," he said, "but please forgive my letting things out. I had some business that was eating at my soul." And he laughed in a somber, sad way, then he asked me not to mention to anyone what had passed between us. I replied that absolutely nothing had happened. Two deputies and a district leader came in. Lobo Neves greeted them effusively, at first a little artificially, but then quite naturally. After half an hour no one would have said he wasn't the most fortunate of men. He chatted, joked, laughed, and everybody laughed.

L I X

An Encounter

P olitics must be an invigorating wine, I said to myself as I left Lobo Neves' house. And I kept walking on and on until, on the Rua dos Barbonos, I saw a carriage and in it one of the ministers, an old schoolmate of mine. We waved to each other affectionately, the carriage went on its way, and I kept walking on ... on ... on ...

"Why can't I be a minister?"

That idea, resplendent and grand—extravagantly clad, as Father Bernardes would have said—that idea started a swirl of somersaults and I let myself stand there watching it, finding it amusing. I wasn't thinking about Lobo Neves' sadness anymore, I felt the attraction of the abyss. I remembered that schoolmate, how we played around on the hills, our joys and our mischief, and I compared the boy with the man and asked myself why I couldn't be like him. I was turning into the Passeio Público then and everything seemed to be telling me the same thing—Why can't you be a minister, Cubas?—Cubas, why can't you be a minister of state? When I heard it a delightful feeling refreshed my whole organism. I went in, sat down on a bench, mulling that idea over. And how Virgília would enjoy it! A few moments later, coming toward me, I saw a face that didn't seem unknown to me. I recognized it from somewhere or other.

Imagine a man between thirty-eight and forty, tall, slim, and pale. His clothes, except for their style, looked as if they'd escaped from the Babylonian captivity. The hat was a contemporary of one of Gessler's. Imagine now a frock coat broader than the needs of his frame—or, literally, that person's bones. The fringe had disappeared some time ago, of the eight original buttons, three were left. The brown drill trousers had two strong knee patches, while the cuffs had been chewed by the heels of boots that bore no pity or polish. About his neck the ends of a tie of two faded colors floated, gripping a week-old collar. I think he was also wearing a dark silk vest, torn in places and unbuttoned.

"I'll bet you don't know me, my good Dr. Cubas," he said.

"I can't recall . . ."

"I'm Borba, Quincas Borba."

I drew back in astonishment . . . If only I'd been given the solemn speech of a Bossuet or a Vieira to describe such desolation! It was Quincas Borba, the amusing boy of times gone by and my schoolmate, so intelligent and so well-off. Quincas Borba! No, impossible. It couldn't be. I couldn't come to believe that this filthy figure, this beard tinted with white, this aging tatterdemalion, all that ruination was Quincas Borba. But it was. His eyes had something left over from other times and his smile hadn't lost a certain mocking air that was peculiar to him. In the meantime he withstood my astonishment. After a while I turned my eyes away. If the figure repelled me, the comparison grieved me.

"I don't have to tell you a thing, you can guess it all. A life of misery, tribulation, and struggle. Remember our parties where I played the part of the king? What a fiasco! I end up a beggar . . ."

And, lifting his right hand and his shoulders with an air of indifference, he seemed resigned to the blows of fortune and, I don't know, was
even happy perhaps. Happy perhaps. Impassive certainly. There was no
Christian resignation or philosophical acceptance in him. It seemed
that misery had calloused his soul to the point of taking away the feeling of the mud. He dragged his rags along just as he'd formerly done
with the royal purple, with a certain indolent grace.

"Look me up," I said. "I might be able to fix something up for you."

A magnificent smile opened his lips. "You're not the first to promise
me something and I don't know if you'll be the last not to do anything
for me. So what's the use? I'm not asking for anything, unless it's
money, money, yes, because I have to eat and eating-places don't give
credit, greengrocers either. A nothing, two *vinténs* worth of manioc
cake, the damned greengrocers won't even trust you for that . . . It's hell,
my . . . I was going to say friend . . . A hell! Devilish! Absolutely devilish! Look, I still haven't had any breakfast today."

"No?"

"No. I left home early. Do you know where I live? On the third landing of the São Francisco stairs, to the left of a person going up. You
don't have to knock on the door. A cool house, extremely cool. Well, I
left early and I still haven't eaten . . ."

I took out my wallet, picked a five *mil-réis* note—the least clean
one—and gave it to him. He took it with eyes that gleamed with greed.
He held the note up in the air and flourished it with enthusiasm.

"*In hoc signo vinces!*" he roared.

And then he kissed it with a great show of tenderness and such noisy
carrying on that it gave me a mixed feeling of nausea and pity. He was
sharp and he understood me. He became serious and asked my forgiveness for his joy, saying that it was the joy of a poor man who hadn't seen
a five *mil-réis* note in many a year.

"Well, it's in your hands to see a lot more of them," I said.

"Yes?" he hastened to say, lunging toward me.

"Working," I concluded.

He made a gesture of disdain. He fell silent for a few moments then
told me positively that he didn't want to work. I was disgusted with that
abjection, which was so comical and so sad, and I made ready to leave.

"Don't leave until I teach you my philosophy of misery," he said, taking a broad stance before me.

L X

The Embrace

I presumed that the poor devil was crazy and I was going to leave when he grabbed me by the wrist and stared for a few seconds at the diamond I was wearing on my finger. I could feel the quivers of greed in his hand, an itch for possession.

"Magnificent!" he said.

Then he began to walk all around me, examining me closely.

"You take good care of yourself," he said. "Jewelry, fine, elegant clothes, and . . . Just compare those shoes with mine. What a difference! There's no comparison! I tell you, you take good care of yourself. What about girls? How about them? Are you married?"

"No . . ."

"Me either."

"I live at . . ."

"I don't want to know where you live," Quincas Borba put in. "If we see each other again, give me another five *mil-réis* note. But allow me not to look you up at home. It's a kind of pride . . . Now, goodbye, I can see that you're impatient."

"Goodbye!"

"And thank you. Let me thank you a little more warmly."

And saying that he embraced me so swiftly that I couldn't avoid it. We finally separated, I with long strides, my shirt wrinkled from the embrace, annoyed and sad. The pleasant side of me no longer dominated, the other one did. I would have preferred to see him bearing this misery with dignity. Yet, I couldn't help comparing the man of today with the one of days gone by, growing sad as I faced the chasm that separates the hopes of one time from the reality of another . . .

"So, goodbye! Let's go have dinner," I said to myself.

I put my hand into my vest and I couldn't find my watch. The final disillusionment. Borba had stolen it during the embrace.

L X I

A Project

I dined in sadness. It wasn't the loss of the watch that tormented me, it was the image of the perpetration of the theft and the remembrances of childhood, and once again the comparison, the conclusion . . . Starting with the soup course the yellow, morbid flower from Chapter XXV began to open up in me and then I ate hurriedly in order to run to Virgília's. Virgília was the present. I wanted to take refuge in it so I could escape the burdens of the past, because the encounter with Quincas Borba had turned my eyes back to the past and I had really entered it, but it was a broken, abject, beggarly, and thievish past.

I left the house, but it was early. If I went now I'd find them still at the table. I thought about Quincas Borba again and then I got the desire to go back to the Passeio Público and see if I could find him. The idea of regenerating him rose up in me like a driving need. I went, but I couldn't find him now. I inquired of the guard, who told me that, indeed, "that fellow" came around there sometimes.

"At what time?"

"He doesn't have a set time."

It wouldn't be impossible for me to run into him on another occasion. I promised myself I'd be back. The need to regenerate him, get him back to working and having respect for his person was filling my heart. I was starting to get a comfortable feeling, one of uplift, of admiration for myself . . . At that point night began to fall. I went to meet Virgília.

L X I I

The Pillow

I went to meet Virgília. I quickly forgot Quincas Borba. Virgília was the pillow for my spirit. A soft, warm, aromatic pillow embroidered in cambric and lace. It was there that it was accustomed to rest away from all unpleasant feelings, those that were merely annoying or those that were even painful. And when things were put into proper balance, that was the only reason for Virgília's existence. There couldn't have been any other. Five minutes were enough to forget Quincas Borba completely, five minutes of mutual contemplation, with hands clasped together. Five minutes and a kiss. And off went the memory of Quincas Borba . . . Scrofula of life, rag out of the past, what do I care if you exist or not, if you bother the eyes of other people, since I have ten square inches of a divine pillow on which to close my eyes and sleep?

L X I I I

Let's Run Away!

Alas, not always to sleep. Three days later, going to Virgília's—it was four in the afternoon—I found her sad and downcast. She refused to tell me what it was, but since I insisted so much:

"I think that Damião suspects something. I've noticed some funny things about him lately . . . I don't know . . . He treats me well, there's no doubt about that. But his look doesn't seem the same. I'm not sleeping well. Just last night I woke up terrified. I was dreaming he was going to kill me. Maybe it's just an illusion, but I think he suspects . . ."

I calmed her down as best I could. I said that they might be political worries. Virgília agreed that they might be, but she was still very distraught and nervous. We were in the living room which, as it happened, faced the yard, where we'd exchanged our initial kiss. An open window let the breeze in, rustling the curtains slightly, and I sat staring at the curtains without seeing them. I was holding the binoculars of the imagination. In the distance I could make out a house of our own in which there wasn't any Lobo Neves or any marriage or any morality or any other bond that impeded the expansion of our will. That idea intoxicated me. With the elimination of world, morality, and husband in that way, all we had to do was go into that angelic dwelling.

"Virgília," I said, "I've got a proposition for you."

"What is it?"

"Do you love me?"

"Oh!" she sighed, putting her arms around my neck.

Virgília loved me furiously. That answer was her open wish. With her arms around my neck, silent, breathing heavily, she remained staring at me with her beautiful big eyes, which gave the singular impression of a moist light. I let myself remain watching them, looking lovingly at her mouth, as cool as dawn and as insatiable as death. Virgília's beauty had a tone of grandeur now, something it hadn't had before she was married. She was one of those figures carved in Pentelic marble, of noble workmanship, open and pure, tranquilly beautiful, like the statues but neither indifferent nor cold. On the contrary, she had the look warm natures have, and it could be said that in reality she summed up all love. She summed it up especially on that occasion, in which she was mutely expressing everything the human eye can say. But time was urgent. I clasped her hands, took them by the wrists, and, looking at her, asked if she had the courage.

"For what?"

"For running away. We'll go where it will be more comfortable for us, a house, big or small according to what you want, in the country or in the city, or in Europe, wherever you think, where nobody can bother us and there won't be any dangers for you, where we can live for each other . . . Yes? Let's run away. Sooner or later he's going to find out something and you'll be lost, because I'll kill him, I swear."

I stopped. Virgília had grown very pale. She dropped her arms and sat down on the settee. She remained that way for several minutes without saying anything to me, I don't know whether hesitating in her choice or terrified at the idea of discovery and death. I went over to her, insisted on the proposal, told her all of the advantages of a life alone together, without jealousies, terrors, or afflictions. Virgília listened to me in silence, then said:

"We might not escape. He'd catch up with me and kill me just the same."

I pointed out to her how it wouldn't be that way. The world was rather vast and I had the means to live wherever the air was pure and there was a lot of sunshine. He'd never get there. Only great passions are capable of great actions, and he didn't love her enough to be able to find her if we were far away. Virgília made a gesture of horror, almost indignation. She murmured that her husband loved her very much.

"Perhaps," I answered. "Perhaps he does . . ."

I went over to the window and began drumming my fingers on the sill. Virgília called to me. I stayed where I was, chewing on my jealousy, wanting to strangle her husband if I'd had him there at hand . . . At that precise moment Lobo Neves appeared in the yard. Don't tremble so, my pale lady reader. Relax, I'm not going to initial this page with a drop of blood. As soon as he appeared in the yard I gave him a friendly wave along with a gracious word. Virgília hurriedly left the room, which he entered three minutes later.

"Have you been here long?" he asked.

"No."

He'd come in serious, worried, his eyes open wide in a distracted way, a habit of his, but he immediately changed it into a true expression of joviality when he saw his son arrive, the little master, the future lawyer in Chapter VI. He took him in his arms, lifted him into the air, kissed him several times. I, who hated the child, drew away from both of them. Virgília came back into the room.

"Ah!" Lobo Neves said with a deep breath as he sat down on the sofa.

"Tired?" I asked.

"Very. I made a couple of hard coups, one in the chamber and the other in the street. And we've got a third one still to come," he added, looking at his wife.

"What is it?" Virgília asked.

"A . . . Make a guess!"

Virgília had sat down beside him, taken one of his hands, straightened his tie, and asked again what it was.

"A box at the opera no less."

"For Candiani?"

"For Candiani."

Virgília clapped her hands, got up, gave her son a kiss with an air of childish joy, which was quite out of tune with her appearance. Then she asked if the box was on the side or in the middle, consulted her husband in a low voice as to what she should wear, about what opera would be sung, and I don't know what other things.

"You're staying for dinner with us, doctor," Lobo Neves told me.

"That's precisely why he came," his wife confirmed. "He says that you have the best wine in Rio de Janeiro."

"He doesn't drink much even for that reason."

At dinner I belied his words. I drank more than I was accustomed to. Even so, less than was necessary for me to lose my reason. I was already upset and I became a little more so. It was the first great anger I'd felt for Virgília. I didn't look at her one single time during dinner. I talked about politics, the press, the ministry, I think I could have talked about theology had I known anything about it or remembered anything. Lobo Neves followed me with great calm and dignity, even with a certain superior benevolence. And all of that irritated me too and rendered the dinner all the more bitter and long. I took my leave as soon as we got up from the table.

"We'll see you later, right?" Lobo Neves asked.

"Maybe."

And I left.

L X I V

The Transaction

I wandered through the streets and retired at nine o'clock. Unable to sleep, I set about reading and writing. At eleven o'clock I was sorry I hadn't gone to the theater, consulted the clock, wanted to get dressed and go out. I calculated that I'd get there too late, however. Besides, it would be a proof of weakness. Obviously Virgília was beginning to be annoyed with me, I thought. And that idea made me desperate and cold successively, ready to forget her and to kill her. I could see her from there, reclining in her box with her magnificent arms bare—the arms that were mine, only mine—fascinating everyone's eyes with the superb dress she must have had on, her milky white breast, her hair in tight curls in the style of the time, and her diamonds, less brilliant than her eyes . . . I saw her like that and it pained me that others should see her. Then I began to undress her, put the jewels and silks aside, undo her hair with my voracious and lascivious hands, making her—I don't know whether more beautiful or more natural—making her mine, only mine, nothing but mine.

The next day I couldn't stand it. I went to Virgília's early, found her with eyes red from weeping.

"What happened?" I asked.

"You don't love me," was her answer. "You've never shown me the slightest sign of love. Yesterday you treated me as if you hated me. If I only knew what I'd done! But I don't know. Won't you tell me what it was?"

"What what was? I don't think there was anything."

"Wasn't anything? You treated me like a dog . . ."

With that word I took her hands, kissed them, and two tears appeared in her eyes.

"It's over, it's all right," I said.

I didn't have the heart to argue and, besides, argue about what? It wasn't her fault if her husband loved her. I told her that she hadn't done anything to me, that I was necessarily jealous of the other man, that I couldn't always bear him with a happy face. I added that maybe there was a lot of pretending on his part and the best way to shut the door on battles and disagreements was to accept my idea of the day before.

"I thought about it," Virgília repled. "A little house all our own, by itself, in the middle of a garden on some back street, isn't that it? I liked the idea, but why run away?"

She said that with the ingenuous and casual tone of someone who can think no evil, and the smile that slackened the corners of her mouth carried the same innocent expression. Then pushing me away, she retorted:

"You're the one who never loved me."

"I?"

"Yes, you're selfish! You'd rather see me suffer every day . . . You're an unspeakable egotist!"

Virgília began to weep, and so as not to attract anyone's attention she put her handkerchief into her mouth, suppressed her sobs in an outburst that disconcerted me. If anyone had heard her everything would have been lost. I leaned toward her, took her by the wrists, whispered the sweetest names of our intimacy to her. I pointed out the danger. The fear calmed her down.

"I can't," she said after a few moments, "I can't leave my son. If I took him along I'm sure he'd follow me to the ends of the earth. I can't. Kill me if you want, or let me die . . . Oh, Lord! Oh, Lord!"

"Calm down, someone might hear you."

"Let them hear, I don't care!"

She was still upset. I asked her to forget everything, to forgive me, that I was mad but that my insanity was because of her and would end because of her. Virgília wiped her eyes and held out her hand. We both smiled. A few minutes later we went back to the matter of the solitary little house on some back street . . .

L X V

Eyes and Ears

We were interrupted by the sound of a coach in the yard. A slave came in to announce the arrival of Baroness X. Virgília consulted me with her eyes.

"If you have a headache like that, madam," I said, "I should think it would be best not to receive her."

"Has she got down already?" Virgília asked the slave.

"She's already got down. She says she needs very much to talk to my lady!"

"Show her in!"

The baroness entered shortly. I don't know whether she expected to see me in the parlor, but she couldn't have shown any greater fluster.

"How good to see you!" she exclaimed. "Where have you been hiding, sir, that you never appear anywhere? Why, just yesterday I was surprised not to see you at the theater. Candiani was a delight. What a woman! Do you like Candiani? Naturally. Men are all alike. The baron was telling me last night in our box that a single Italian woman is worth five Brazilian women. Such impertinence! And the impertinence of an old man, which is worse. But why didn't you go to the theater last night?"

"A migraine."

"Hah! Some love affair, don't you think, Virgília? Well, my friend, you'd better hurry up because you must be forty . . . or close to it . . . Aren't you forty years old?"

"I can't say with certainty," I replied, "but if you'll excuse me, I'll go check my baptism certificate."

"Get along with you . . ." And holding out her hand to me, "Until what next time? We'll be at home on Saturday. The baron misses you . . ."

Out on the street I was sorry I'd left. The baroness was one of the people who was most suspicious of us. Fifty-five years old and looking forty, sleek, smiling, vestiges of beauty, elegant bearing, and refined manners. She didn't talk a lot or all the time. She possessed the great skill of listening to others, spying on them. At those times she would sit back in her chair, unsheathe her long, sharp vision, and take her ease. The others, not knowing what was going on, would talk, look, gesticulate, while she would simply look, sometimes staring, sometimes moving her eyes, carrying the ruse to the point of looking inside herself sometimes because she would let her eyelids droop. but since eyelashes are lattices, her glance would continue its work, rummaging in the souls and lives of others.

The second person was a relative of Virgília's, Viegas, a worthless old man of seventy winters, sucked dry and yellowish, who suffered from a chronic case of rheumatism, no less chronic asthma, and a heart lesion. He was a walking hospital ward. His eyes, however, gleamed with plenty of life and health. Virgília, during the first weeks, wasn't afraid of him at all. She told me that when Viegas seemed to be watching with his stare, he was simply counting money. He was, in fact, a great miser.

There was still Virgília's cousin, Luís Dutra, whom I disarmed now by dint of talking to him about his prose and poetry and introducing him to acquaintances. When the latter, linking the name to the person, showed themselves to be pleased with the introduction, there was no doubt but that Luís Dutra overflowed with happiness. And I made use of that happiness with the hope that he would never catch us. There were, finally, two or three ladies, several fops, and the servants, who naturally would avenge themselves for their servile status in that way, and all of them constituted a veritable forest of eyes and ears among which we had to slip along with the tactics and subtlety of serpents.

L X V I

Legs

Now, whenever I think about those people, my legs carry me off down the street so that without realizing it I found myself at the door of the Hotel Pharoux. I was in the habit of dining there. But, not having deliberately walked there, I deserved no credit for the act, but my legs, which had done so, did. Blessed legs! And there are those who treat you with disdain or indifference. Even I, until then, held you in low esteem, getting annoyed when you tired, when you couldn't go beyond a certain point and left me with a desire to flap my wings like a hen tied by the feet.

That time, however, it was a ray of light. Yes, legs, my friends, you left the task of thinking about Virgília to my head and you said to one another, "He's got to eat, it's dinnertime, let's take him to the Pharoux. Let's divide up his consciousness, one part can stay with the lady, we'll take over the other part so that he goes straight ahead, doesn't bump into people or carriages, tips his hat to acquaintances, and, finally, arrives safe and sound at the hotel." And you followed your plan to the letter, kind legs, which obliges me to immortalize you with this page.

L X V I I

The Little House

I dined and went home. There I found a box of cigars that Lobo Neves had sent me, wrapped in tissue paper and tied with a pink ribbon. I understood, I opened it, and took out this note:

My B . . .
They suspect us. All is lost. Forget me forever. We can't see each other again. Goodbye, forget the unhappy.

V . . . a

That letter was a blow. Nevertheless, immediately after nightfall I ran to Virgília's. I was on time, she regretted it. Through an open window she told me what had happened with the baroness. The baroness had told her quite frankly that there was a lot of talk at the theatre the night before regarding my absence from the Lobo Neves box. They'd commented on my relationship to the house. In short, we were the object of public suspicion. She finished by saying that she didn't know what to do.

"The best thing is to run away," I hinted.

"Never," she replied, shaking her head.

I saw that it was impossible to separate two things that were completely linked in her spirit: our love and public opinion. Virgília was capable of equal and great sacrifices to preserve both advantages, and flight left her with only one. I might have had a feeling similar to spite, but the commotion of those two days was already great and the spite quickly died. It's all set. Let's arrange the little house.

As a matter of fact, I found it a few days later, made to order in a corner of Gamboa. A jewel! New, freshly painted, with four windows in front and two on either side—all with brick-colored blinds—vines at the corners, a garden in front. Mystery and solitude. A jewel!

We arranged for a woman known to Virgília, in whose house she'd been a seamstress and servant, to go live there. Virgília held a real enchantment over her. She wouldn't tell her everything. She'd easily accept the rest.

For me this was a new situation in our love, an appearance of exclusive possession, of absolute dominion, something that would soothe my conscience and maintain decorum. I was already tired of the other man's curtains, chairs, carpet, couch, all the things that constantly brought our duplicity up before my eyes. Now I could avoid the frequent dinners, the teas every night, and, finally, the presence of their son, my accomplice and my enemy. The house rescued me completely. The ordinary world would end at its door. From there on there was the infinite, an eternal, superior, exceptional world, ours, only ours, without laws, without institutions, without any baroness, without eyes, without ears—one single world, one single couple, one single life, one single will, one single affection—the moral unity of all things through the exclusion of those that were contrary to me.

LXVIII

The Whipping

Such were my reflections as I walked along Valongo right after seeing and arranging for the house. They were interrupted by a gathering of people. It was because of a black man whipping another in the square. The other one didn't try to run away. He only moaned these words: "Please, I'm sorry, master. Master, I'm sorry!" but the first one paid no attention and each entreaty was answered with a new lashing.

"Take that, you devil!" he was saying. "There's sorry for you, you drunk!"

"Master!" the other one was moaning.

"Shut your mouth, you animal!" the whipper replied.

I stopped to look . . . Good Lord! And who did the one with the whip turn out to be? None other than my houseboy Prudêncio—the one my father had freed some years before. He came over to me, having ceased immediately, and asked for my blessing. I inquired if that black man was his slave.

"He is, yes, little master."

"What did he do?"

"He's a loafer and a big drunk. Only today I left him in the store while I went downtown and he went off to a bar to drink."

"It's all right, forgive him," I said.

"Of course, little master. Your word is my command. Get on home with you, you drunkard!"

I left the crowd of people who were looking at me with wonder and whispering conjectures. I went on my way, unraveling an infinite number of reflections that I think I've lost completely. They would have been material for a good and maybe happy chapter. I like happy chapters, they're my weakness. On the outside the Valongo episode was dreadful, but only on the outside. As soon as I stuck the knife of rationality deeper into it I found it to have a happy, delicate, and even profound marrow. It was the way Prudêncio had to rid himself of the beatings he'd received by transmitting them to someone else. As a child I used to ride on his back, put a bit into his mouth, and whip him mercilessly. He would moan and suffer. Now that he was free, however, he had the free use of himself, his arms, his legs, he could work, rest, sleep unfettered from his previous status. Now he could make up for everything. He bought a slave and was paying him back with high interest the amount he'd received from me. Just look at the subtlety of the rogue!

L X I X

A Grain of Folly

The case makes me remember a loony I knew. His name was Romualdo and he said he was Tamerlane. It was his great and only mania and he had a strange way of explaining it.

"I am the famous Tamerlane," he would say. "Formerly I was Romualdo, but I fell ill and I took so much tartar, so much tartar, so much tartar that I became a Tartar, and even king of the Tartars. Tartar has the property of producing Tartars."

Poor Romualdo! People laughed at his response, but it's likely that the reader isn't laughing, and rightfully so. I don't find it funny at all. When you first hear it, it has a touch of humor, but told like this, on paper, and with reference to a whipping received and passed on, I have to confess that it's much better to get back to the little house in Gamboa and put the Romualdos and Prudêncios aside.

L X X

Dona Plácida

L et's get back to the little house. You wouldn't be able to enter it today, curious reader. It grew old, blackened, rotting, and the owner tore it down to replace it with another three times bigger, but, I swear to you, lesser than the first one. The world may have been too small for Alexander, but the eaves of a garret are an infinity for swallows.

Take a look now at the neutrality of this globe that carries us through space like a lifeboat heading for shore: today a virtuous couple sleeps on the same plot of ground that once held a sinning couple. Tomorrow a churchman may sleep there, then a murderer, then a blacksmith, then a poet, and they will all bless that corner of earth that gave them a few illusions.

Virgília turned the house into a jewel. She arranged for household items that were just right and placed them about with the aesthetic intuition of an elegant woman. I brought in some books, and everything was under the care of Dona Plácida, the purported and in certain respects the real lady of the house.

It was very difficult for her to accept the house. She'd sniffed out the intention and her position pained her, but she finally gave in. I think she wept at the beginning, was sick with herself. What was certain at least was that she didn't lift her eyes to me during the first two months. She spoke to me with her look lowered, serious, frowning, sad sometimes. I wanted to win her over and didn't act offended, treating her with affection and respect. I made a great effort to win her good will, then her trust. When I obtained her trust, I made up a pathetic story about my love for Virgília, a situation before her marriage, her father's resistance, her husband's harshness, and I don't know how many other novelistic touches. Dona Plácida didn't reject a single page of the novel. She accepted them all. It was a necessity of her conscience. At the end of six months anyone who saw the three of us together would have said that Dona Plácida was my mother-in-law.

I wasn't ungrateful. I made her a special gift of five *contos*—the five *contos* found in Botafogoas—as a nest egg for her old age. Dona Plácida thanked me with tears in her eyes and from then on never ceased to pray for me every night before an image of the Virgin she had in her room. That was how her nausea ceased.

L X X I

The Defect of this Book

I'm beginning to regret this book. Not that it bores me, I have nothing to do and, really, putting together a few meager chapters for that other world is always a task that distracts me from eternity a little. But the book is tedious, it has the smell of the grave about it; it has a certain cadaveric contraction about it, a serious fault, insignificant to boot because the main defect of this book is you, reader. You're in a hurry to grow old and the book moves slowly. You love direct and continuous narration, a regular and fluid style, and this book and my style are like drunkards, they stagger left and right, they walk and stop, mumble, yell, cackle, shake their fists at the sky, stumble, and fall . . .

And they do fall! Miserable leaves of my cypress of death, you shall fall like any others, beautiful and brilliant as you are. And, if I had eyes, I would shed a nostalgic tear for you. This is the great advantage of death, which if it leaves no mouth with which to laugh, neither does it leave eyes with which to weep . . . You shall fall.

L X X I I

The Bibliomaniac

M aybe I'll leave out the previous chapter. Among other reasons because in the last lines there's a phrase that's close to being nonsense and I don't want to provide food for future critics.

Put the case that seventy years from now a skinny, sallow, graying chap who loves nothing but books leans over the previous page to see if he can discover the nonsense. He reads, rereads, reads again, disjoins the words, takes out a syllable, then another, and another still, and examines the remaining ones inside and out from all sides, up against the light, dusts them off, rubs them against his knee, washes them, and nothing doing. He can't find the absurdity.

He's a bibliomaniac. He doesn't know the author. This name of Brás Cubas doesn't appear in his biographical dictionaries. He found the volume by chance in the rundown shop of a second-hand book dealer. He bought it for two hundred *réis*. He inquired, investigated, searched about, and came to discover that I was a one-and-only copy . . . One and only! You people who not only love books but suffer from a mania for them know quite well the value of those words and you can imagine, therefore, my bibliomaniac's delight. He would reject the crown of the Indies, the Papacy, all the museums of Italy and Holland if he had to trade that one and only copy for them and not because it is that of my *Memoirs*. He would do the same with Laemmert's *Almanac* if it were a one-and-only copy.

The worst part is the absurdity. The man stays there, hunched over the page, a lens under his right eye, given over completely to the noble and wearing function of deciphering the absurdity. He's already promised himself to write a brief report in which he will relate the finding of the book and the discovery of the sublimity if there is to be one under that obscure phrase. In the end he discovers nothing and contents himself with ownership. He closes the book, looks at it, looks at it again, goes to the window and holds it up to the sun. A one-and-only copy. At that moment, passing under the window is a Caesar or a Cromwell on the path to power. He turns his back on him, closes the window, lies down in his hammock, and slowly thumbs through the book, lovingly, wallowing hard . . . A one-and-only copy!

L X X I I I

The Luncheon

T he absurdity made me lose another chapter. How much better it would have been to have said things smoothly, without all these jolts! I've already compared my style to a drunkard's gait. If the idea seems indecorous to you, let me say that it's what my meals with Virgília were like in the little house in Gamboa, where we would have our sumptuous feast sometimes, our luncheon. Wine, fruit, compotes. We would eat, it's true, but it was eating punctuated by loving little words, tender looks, childish acts, an infinity of those side comments of the heart in addition to the real, uninterrupted discourse of love. Sometimes a tiff would come to temper the excessive sweetness of the situation. She would leave me, take refuge in a corner of the settee or go inside to listen to Dona Plácida's pruderies. Five or ten minutes later we would pick up the thread of our conversation the way I pick up the thread of this narrative to let it unwind again. Let it be noted that far from being horrified at the method, it was our custom to invite it in the person of Dona Plácida, to sit down at the table with us, but Dona Plácida never accepted.

"You don't seem to like me anymore," Virgília told her one day.

"Merciful heavens!" the good lady exclaimed, lifting her arms up toward the ceiling. "Not like Iaiá? Who would I ever like in this world then?"

And taking her hands she would look into her eyes, look and look until her eyes watered from staring so hard. Virgília stroked her and I left her a small silver coin in the pocket of her dress.

L X X I V

Dona Plácida's Story

Never repent for being generous. The little silver coin brought me Dona Plácida's confidence and, consequently, this chapter. Days later, when I was alone in the house, we began a conversation and she told me her story in brief terms. She was the illegitimate child of a sexton at the cathedral and a woman who sold sweets on the street. She lost her father when she was ten. By then she was shredding cocoanut and doing all kinds of other chores of a sweets-maker fitting for her age. At fifteen or sixteen she married a tailor who died of tuberculosis a while later, leaving her with a daughter two years old and her mother, exhausted from a life of work. She had three mouths to feed. She made sweets, which was her trade, but she also sewed, day and night, assiduously, for three or four shops and she taught some girls in the neighborhood for ten *tostões* a month. The years passed that way, but not her beauty, because she'd never had any. Some courtships, proposals, and seductions came her way, which she resisted.

"If I could have found another husband," she told me, "I think I would have got married, but nobody wanted to marry me."

One of the suitors managed to get himself accepted, without being any more genteel than the others, however. Dona Plácida sent him packing and after sending him off wept a great deal. She continued doing sewing for the outside and keeping her pots boiling. Her mother was ill-tempered because of her age and her poverty. She railed at her daughter to take on one of the seasonal, temporary husbands who asked for her. And she would roar:

"Do you think you're better than me? I don't know where you get those stuck-up ideas of a rich person. My fine friend, life doesn't get straightened out just by chance. You can't eat the wind. What is this? Nice young fellows like Policarpo from the store, poor boy . . . are you waiting for some nobleman to come along?"

Dona Plácida swore to me that she wasn't waiting for any nobleman. It was her character. She wanted to be married. She knew quite well that her mother hadn't been and she knew some women who only had lovers. But it was her character and she wanted to be married. She didn't want her daughter to be anything else either. She worked hard, burning her fingers on the stove and her eyes sewing by the candleholder in order to eat and not lose everything. She grew thin, fell ill, lost her mother, buried her with the help of charity, and kept on working. Her daughter was fourteen, but she was very frail and didn't do anything except flirt with the sharpers who hung around the window grating. Dona Plácida worried a great deal, taking her with her when she had to deliver sewing jobs. The people in the shops stared and winked, convinced that she'd brought her along in order to catch a husband or something else. Some would make bad jokes, pay their respects. The mother began to get offers of money . . .

She paused for a moment and then went on:

"My daughter ran away. She went off with a fellow, I don't even want to know about it . . . She left me alone, but so sad, so sad that I wanted to die. I had nobody else in the world and I was getting old and sick. It was around that time that I got to know Iaiá's family, good people who gave me something to do and even gave me a home. I was there for several months, a year, over a year, a house servant, sewing. I left when Iaiá got married. Then I lived as God willed it. Look at my fingers, look at these hands . . ." And she showed her thick, wrinkled hands, the tips of her fingers pricked by needles . . . "You don't get this way by chance, sir. God knows how you get this way . . . Luckily Iaiá took care of me, and you too, doctor . . . I was afraid of ending up begging on the street . . ."

As she uttered the last phrase Dona Plácida shuddered. Then, as if recovered, she seemed to be worrying about the impropriety of that confession to the lover of a married woman and she began to laugh, retract, call herself silly, "full of beans," as her mother used to tell her. Finally, tired of my silence, she left the room. I stayed there staring at my shoetops.

L X X V

To Myself

G ive the possibility that one of my readers might have skipped the previous chapter, I must observe that it's necessary to read it in order to understand what I said to myself right after Dona Plácida left the room. What I said was this:

"Well, then, the sexton of the cathedral, assisting at mass one day, saw the lady, who was to be his partner in the creation of Dona Plácida, come in. He saw her on other days, for weeks on end, he liked her, he joshed with her, stepped on her foot as he went up to the altar on feast days. She liked him, they grew close, made love. From that conjunction of empty sensuality Dona Plácida came into bloom. It must be believed that Dona Plácida still couldn't talk when she was born, but if she could have, she might have said to the authors of her days, 'Here I am. Why did you call me?' And the sacristan and the sacristaness would naturally have answered her, 'We called you to burn your fingers on pots, your eyes in sewing, to eat poorly or not at all, to go from one place to another in drudgery, getting ill and recovering only to get ill and recover once again, sad now, then desperate, resigned tomorrow, but always with your hands on the pot and your eyes on the sewing until one day you end up in the mire or in the hospital. That's why we called you in a moment of sympathy.' "

L X X V I

Manure

S uddenly my conscience gave me a tug, accusing me of having Dona Plácida surrender her virtue, assigning her a shameful role after a long life of work and privation. Go-between was no better than concubine and I'd lowered her to that position by dint of gifts and money. That was what my conscience was saying to me. I spent a few minutes not knowing how to answer it. It added that I'd taken advantage of the fascination Virgília held over the ex-seamstress, of the latter's gratitude, ultimately, of her need. It made note of Dona Plácida's resistance, her tears during the early days, her grim expressions, her silences, her lowered eyes, and my skills at bearing up under all that until I could overcome it. And it tugged at me again in an irritated and nervous way.

I agreed that that was how it was, but I argued that Dona Plácida's old age was not protected from beggary. It was a compensation. If it hadn't been for our love affair, most likely Dona Plácida would have ended up like so many other human creatures, from which it can be deduced that vice many times is manure for virtue. And that doesn't prevent virtue from being a fragrant and healthy bloom. My conscience agreed and I went to open the door for Virgília.

L X X V I I

Appointment

Virgília entered, smiling and relaxed. Time had carried away her frights and vexations. How sweet it was to see her arrive during the early days, shameful and trembling! She traveled in a coach, her face veiled, wrapped in a kind of collared cape that disguised the curves of her figure. The first time she'd dropped onto the settee, breathing heavily, scarlet, with her eyes on the floor. And—word of honor!—never on any occasion had I found her so beautiful, perhaps because I had never felt myself more flattered.

Now, however, as I was saying, the frights and vexations were over. Our meetings were entering the chronometric stage. The intensity of love was the same, the difference was that the flame had lost the mad brightness of the early days and had become a simple sheaf of rays, peaceful and content, as with marriages.

"I'm very angry with you," she said as she sat down.

"Why?"

"Because you didn't go there yesterday as you'd told me you would. Damião asked several times if you weren't coming at least for tea. Why didn't you come?"

As a matter of fact, I had broken the promise I'd made and the fault was all Virgília's. A matter of jealousy. That splendid woman knew that it was and she liked to hear it said, whether aloud or in a whisper. Two days before at the baroness' she'd waltzed twice with the same dandy after listening to his courtly talk in a corner by the window. She was so merry! So open! So self-possessed! When she caught an interrogative and threatening wrinkle between my eyebrows, she showed no surprise, nor did she become suddenly serious, but she threw the dandy and his courtly talk overboard. Then she came over to me, took my arm, and led me into the other room, with fewer people, where she complained of being tired and said many other things with the childlike air she was accustomed to assume on certain occasions and I listened to her almost without replying.

Now, once more, it was difficult for me to reply, but I finally told her the reason for my absence . . . No, eternal stars, never have I seen such startled eyes. Her mouth half-open, her eyebrows arched, a visible, tangible stupefaction that was undeniable, such was Virgília's immediate reply. She nodded her head with a smile of pity and tenderness that confused me completely.

"Oh, you . . .!

And she went to take off her hat, cheerful, jovial, like a girl just back from school. Then she came over to me where I was seated, tapped me on the head with one finger, repeating, "This, this," and I couldn't help laughing, too, and everything ended up in fun. It was obvious I'd been mistaken.

L X X V I I I

The Presidency

On a certain day months later Lobo Neves arrived home saying that he might get the position of president of a province. I looked at Virgília, who'd grown pale. Seeing her grow pale, he asked:

"What, don't you like it, Virgília?"

Virgília shook her head.

"I'm not too pleased," was her reply.

Nothing more was said, but at night Lobo Neves brought up the project again a little more resolutely than during the afternoon. Two days later he declared to his wife that the presidency was all set. Virgília couldn't hide the dislike it caused her. Her husband replied to everything by saying political necessities.

"I can't refuse what they ask of me. And it even suits us, our future, our coat-of-arms, my love, because I promised that you'd be a marchioness and you're not even a baroness yet. Are you going to say I'm ambitious? I really am, but you mustn't put any weights on the wings of my ambition."

Virgília was disoriented. The next day I found her at the Gamboa house sad and waiting for me. She'd told everything to Dona Plácida, who was trying to console her as best she could. I was no less downcast.

"You've got to come with us," Virgília told me.

"Are you crazy? It would be madness."

"What then . . .?"

"Then we've got to change the plan."

"That's impossible."

"Has he already accepted?"

"It seems so."

I got up, tossed my hat onto a chair, and began pacing back and forth, not knowing what to do. I thought for a long time and couldn't come up with anything. Finally, I went over to Virgília, who was seated, and took her hand. Dona Plácida went over to the window.

"My whole existence is in this tiny hand," I said. "You're responsible for it. Do whatever you think best."

Virgília had an afflicted expression. I went over to lean against the sideboard across from her. A few moments of silence passed. We could only hear the barking of a dog and, I'm not sure, the sound of the water breaking on the beach. Seeing that she wasn't saying anything, I looked at her. Virgília had her eyes on the floor, motionless, dull, her hands resting on her knees with the fingers crossed in a sign of extreme despair. On another occasion, for a different reason, I would certainly have thrown myself at her feet and sheltered her with my reason and my tenderness. Now, however, it was necessary to have her make her own effort at sacrifice for the responsibility of our life together and, consequently, not shelter her, leave her to herself, and go away. That was what I did.

"I repeat, my happiness is in your hands," I said.

Virgília tried to hold me back, but I was already out the door. I managed to hear an outburst of tears and, I can tell you, I was on the point of going back to stanch them with a kiss, but I got control of myself and left.

L X X I X

Compromise

I would never finish were I to recount every detail of how I suffered during the first few hours. I vacillated between wanting and not wanting, between the compassion that was pulling me toward Virgília's house and a different feeling—selfishness, let us suppose—that was telling me: "Stay here. Leave her alone with the problem, leave her along because she'll resolve it in favor of love." I think those two forces were equal in intensity; they attacked and resisted at the same time, fervently, tenaciously, and neither was giving way at all. Sometimes I felt a tiny bite of remorse. It seemed to me that I was abusing the weakness of a guilty woman in love, without any sacrifice or risk on my part. And when I was about to surrender, love would come again and repeat the selfish advice to me and I would remain irresolute and restless, desirous of seeing her and wary that the sight of her would lead me to share the responsibility of the solution.

Finally a compromise between selfishness and compassion: I would go see her at her home, and only at her home, in the presence of her husband so as not to say anything to her, waiting for the effect of my intimation. In that way I'd be able to conciliate the two forces. Now, as I write this, I like to think that the compromise was a fraud, that compassion was still a form of selfishness and that the decision to go console Virgília was nothing more than a suggestion of my own suffering.

L X X X

As Secretary

The next night I did go to the Lobo Neves'. They were both home, Virgília quite sad, he quite jovial. I could swear that she was feeling a certain relief when our eyes met, full of curiosity and tenderness. Lobo Neves told me about the plans that would bring him the presidency, the local difficulties, the hopes, the solutions. He was so happy, so hopeful! Virgília, at the other end of the table, pretended to be reading a book but she would look at me over the page from time to time, questioning and anxious.

"The worst part," Lobo Neves told me, "is that I still haven't found a secretary."

"No?"

"No, but I've got an idea."

"Ah!"

"An idea . . . How'd you like to travel north?"

I don't know what I told him.

"You're rich," he went on, "you don't need the paltry salary, but if you'll do me the favor, you'll come along with me as secretary."

My spirit gave a leap backward, as if I'd seen a snake in front of me. I faced Lobo Neves, stared at him demandingly to see if some hidden thought had caught hold of him . . . Not a shadow of it. His look was direct and open, the calmness of his face was natural, not forced, a calmness sprinkled with joy. I took a deep breath and didn't have the courage to look at Virgília. I could feel her gaze over the page, also asking me the same. And I said yes, I'd go. In all truth, a president, a president's wife, a secretary was a way of resolving things in an administrative way.

L X X X I

Reconciliation

In spite of everything, as I left there I had the shadow of some doubts. I pondered about whether or not it would be an insane exposure of Virgília's reputation, if there wasn't some other reasonable way of combining government and Gamboa. I couldn't find any. The next day, as I got out of bed, my mind was made up and resolved to accept the nomination. At midday my servant came to tell me that a veiled lady was waiting for me in the parlor. I hurried out. It was my sister Sabina.

"It can't go on like this," she said. "Once and for all, let's make up. Our family's fallen apart, we mustn't go on acting like two enemies."

"But I couldn't ask for anything else, sister!" I shouted, holding out my arms to her.

I had her sit down beside me, asking her about her husband, her daughter, business, everything. Everything was fine. Their daughter was pretty as a picture. Her husband would come and show her to me if I'd let him.

"Come, now! I'll go see her for myself."

"Will you?"

"Word of honor."

"So much the better!" Sabina sighed. "It's time to put an end to all this."

I found her to be stouter and perhaps younger looking. She looked twenty and she was over thirty. Charming, affable, no awkwardness, no resentments. We looked at each other holding hands, talking about everything and nothing, like two lovers. It was my childhood coming to the surface, fresh, frisky, and golden. The years were falling away like the rows of bent playing cards I fooled with as a child and they let me see our house, our family, our parties. I bore the memory with some effort, but a neighborhood barber came to mind as he twanged on his classical fiddle and that voice—because up till then the memory had been mute—that voice out of the past, nasal and nostalgic, moved me to such a degree that . . .

Her eyes were dry. Sabina hadn't inherited the morbid yellow flower. What difference did it make? She was my sister, my blood, a part of my mother, and I told her that with tenderness, sincerity . . . Suddenly I heard knocking on the parlor door. I went to open it. It was a five-year-old little angel.

"Come in, Sara," Sabina said.

It was my niece. I picked her up, kissed her several times. The little one, frightened, pushed me off on my shoulder with her little hand, writhing to get down . . . At that moment a hat appeared in the door followed by a man, Cotrim, no less. I was so moved that I put the daughter down and threw myself into the arms of the father. That effusion may have disconcerted him a little because he seemed awkward to me. A simple prologue. Shortly after we were talking like two good old friends. No allusions to the past, lots of plans for the future, the promise to dine at each other's house. I didn't fail to mention that the exchange of dinners might have to have a slight interruption because I was thinking of traveling north. Sabina looked at Cotrim, Cotrim at Sabina. Both agreed that the idea made no sense. What the devil could I expect to find up north? Because wasn't it in the capital, right there in the capital, that I should continue to shine, showing up the young fellows of the time? Because, really, there wasn't a single one of them who could compare to me. He, Cotrim, had been following me from a distance and, in spite of a ridiculous quarrel, had always had an interest, pride, and vanity in my triumphs. He heard what was being said about me on the street and in salons. It was a concert of praise and admiration. And leave all that to go spend a few months in the provinces without any need to, without any serious reason? Unless it was political.

"Political, precisely," I said.

"Not even for that reason," he replied after a moment. And after another silence, "In any case, come dine with us tonight."

"Of course I will. But tomorrow or afterward you have to dine with me."

"I don't know, I don't know," Sabina objected. "At a bachelor's house . . . You have to get married, brother. I want a niece, too, do you hear?"

Cotrim stopped her with a gesture I didn't understand too well. It didn't matter. The reconciliation of a family is well worth an enigmatic gesture.

L X X X I I

A Matter of Botany

Let hypochondriacs say what they will: life is sweet. That was what I was thinking to myself watching Sabina, her husband, and her daughter troop down the stairs, sending lots of affectionate words up to where—on the landing—I was sending just as many others down to them. I kept on thinking that I really was lucky. A woman loved me, I had the trust of her husband, I was going to be secretary to them both, and I'd been reconciled with my family. What more could I ask for in twenty-four hours?

That same day, trying to prepare people's ideas, I began to bandy it about that I might be going north as provincial secretary in order to fulfill certain political designs of my own. I said so on the Rua do Ouvidor and repeated it the following day at the Pharoux and at the theater. Some people, tying my nomination to Lobo Neves', which was already rumored, smiled maliciously, others patted me on the back. At the theatre a lady told me that it was carrying a love of sculpture a bit far. She was referring to Virgília's beautiful figure.

But the most open allusion I received was at Sabina's three days later. It was made by a certain Garcez, an old surgeon, tiny, trivial, and a babbler who was capable of reaching the age of seventy, eighty, or ninety without ever having acquired the austere bearing that marks the gentility of the aged. A ridiculous old age is perhaps nature's saddest and final surprise.

"I know, this time you're going to read Cicero," he told me when he heard of the trip.

"Cicero?" Sabina exclaimed.

"What else? Your brother is a great Latinist. He can translate Virgil at sight. Note that it's Virgil and not Virgília . . . don't confuse them . . ."

And he laughed, a gross, vulgar, frivolous laugh. Sabina looked at me, fearful of some reply. But she smiled when she saw me smile and turned her face to hide it. The other people looked at me with expressions of curiosity, indulgence, and sympathy. It was quite obvious that they hadn't heard anything new. The matter of my love affair was more public than I could have imagined. Nevertheless, I smiled a quick, fugitive, swallowing smile—chattering like the Sintra magpies. Virgília was a beautiful mistake, and it's so easy to confess a beautiful mistake! At first I was accustomed to scowl when I heard some reference to our love affair, but—word of honor—inside I had a warm and flattered feeling. Once, however, I happened to smile and I continued doing so on other occasions. I don't know if there's anyone who can explain the phenomenon. I explain it this way: in the beginning the contentment, being inner, was, in a manner of speaking, that same smile but only a bud. With the passage of time the flower bloomed and appeared for the eyes of others. A simple matter of botany.

L X X X I I I

13

Cotrim drew me out of that pleasure, leading me to the window. "Do you mind if I tell you something?" he asked. "Don't take that trip. It's unwise, it's dangerous."

"Why?"

"You know very well why," he replied. "It's dangerous especially, quite dangerous. Here in the capital a matter like that gets lost in the mass of people and interests. But in the provinces it takes on a different shape. And since it's a question of political people, it really is unwise. The opposition newspapers, as soon as they sniff out the business, will proceed to print it in block letters, and out of that will come the jokes, the remarks, the nicknames . . ."

"But I don't understand . . ."

"You understand, you understand. Really, you wouldn't be much of a friend of ours if you denied what everybody knows. I've known about it for months. I repeat, don't take a trip like that. Bear up under her absence, which is better, and avoid any great scandal and greater displeasure . . ."

He said that and went inside. I remained there looking at the street light on the corner—an old oil lamp—sad, obscure, and curved, like a question mark. What was I to do? It was Hamlet's case, either to suffer fortune's slings and arrows or fight against them and subdue them. In other words, to sail or not to sail. That was the question. The street light wasn't telling me anything. Cotrim's words were echoing in the ears of my memory in quite a different way from those of Garcez. Maybe Cotrim was right. But would I be able to separate from Virgília?

Sabina came over and asked me what I was thinking about. Nothing, I answered, that I was sleepy and was going home. Sabina was silent for a moment. "I know what you need. It's a girlfriend. Let me arrange a girlfriend for you." I left there oppressed, disoriented. Everything ready for sailing—heart and soul—and that gatekeeper of social rules appears and asks me for my card of admission. I said to hell with social rules and along with them the constitution, the legislative body, the ministry, everything.

The next day I open a political newspaper and read that by a decree dated the 13th Lobo Neves and I had been named president and secretary of the Province of ***. I immediately wrote to Virgília and two hours later went to Gamboa. Poor Dona Plácida! She was getting more and more upset. She asked me if we were going to forget our old lady, if our absence would be for long and if the province was far away. I consoled her, but I needed consolation myself. Cotrim's objections were bothering me. Virgília arrived a short time later, lively as a swallow, but when she saw that I was downcast she got serious.

"What's wrong?"

"I'm not sure," I said. "I don't know if I should accept."

Virgília dropped onto the settee laughing. "Why not?" she asked.

"It's not proper. It's too obvious . . ."

"But we're not going anymore."

"What do you mean?"

She told me that her husband had turned down the nomination and for reasons that he only told her, charging her to the greatest secrecy. He couldn't admit it to anyone else. "It's childish," he observed, "ridiculous, but in the end for me it's a powerful reason." He told me that the decree was dated the 13th and that that number carried a mournful memory for him. His father had died on the 13th, thirteen days after a dinner where thirteen people had been present. The house in which his mother died was Number 13. Etc. It was a fateful figure. He couldn't admit such a thing to the minister. He would tell him that he had personal reasons for not accepting. I was left as the reader must be—a little startled at that sacrifice to a number, but since he was an ambitious man the sacrifice must have been sincere . . .

L X X X I V

The Conflict

F ateful number, can you remember how many times I blessed you? That, too, must have been the way the red-haired virgins of Thebes blessed the mare with a russet mane that took their place in Pelopidas' sacrifice—a charming mare who died there covered with flowers without anyone's ever having given her a word of fond remembrance. Well, I give you one, pitiful mare, not only because of the death you suffered but because among the spared maidens it's not impossible that a grandmother of the Cubases figured . . . Fateful number, you were our salvation. Her husband didn't confess the reason for his refusal to me. He told me, too, that it was because of personal business and the serious, convinced face with which I listened to him did honor to human hypocrisy. He was the only one who had trouble covering up the sadness eating at him. He spoke little, was self-absorbed, stayed home reading. On other occasions he would receive and then he would converse and laugh a lot, with noise and affection. Two things were oppressing him—ambition, which had had its wings clipped by a scruple and immediately following doubt and perhaps regret, but a regret that would return if the hypothesis were repeated, because the superstitious basis still existed. He had his doubts about the superstition without arriving at its rejection. That persistence of a feeling that was repugnant to the individual himself was a phenomenon worthy of some attention. But I preferred that she couldn't bear seeing a toad turned on its back.

"What is there about that?" I asked her.

"It's evil," was her answer.

Only that, the single answer that was worth as much as the book with seven seals for her. It's evil. They'd told her that when she was a child with no other explanation and she was content with the certainty of harm. The same thing happened when there was talk of pointing at a star. That she knew perfectly well could cause a wart.

A wart or anything else, what was that to someone who'd lost the presidency of a province? A gratuitous or cheap superstition can be tolerated. What cannot be is one that carries away part of your life. That was the case with Lobo Neves along with doubt and the terror of having been ridiculous. And the added fact that the minister hadn't believed in any personal reasons. He attributed Lobo Neves' refusal to political maneuvers, a complicated illusion because of certain aspects. He treated him shabbily, conveyed his lack of trust to colleagues. Incidents arose. Finally, with time, the resigned president went over to the opposition.

L X X X V

The Summit

A person who has escaped a danger loves life with new intensity. I began to love Virgília even more ardently after being on the brink of losing her and the same things happened with her. In that way the presidency had only given new life to our original affection. It was the drug with which we made our love more delightful and also more esteemed. During the first days following that episode we entertained ourselves by imagining the pain of separation had there been a separation, how sad we both would have been, how far the sea would have stretched out between us like an elastic cloth. And just as children snuggle up to their mother's breast to escape a simple scowl, we fled the imagined danger by squeezing each other with hugs.

"My wonderful Virgília!"

"My love!"

"You're mine, aren't you?"

"Yours, yours . . ."

And thus we picked up the thread of our adventure the same as the Sultaness Scheherezade had done with the thread of her stories. That was, to my mind, the high point of our love, the summit of the mountain from where, for a time, we could make out the valleys to the east and west and the tranquil blue sky above us. Having rested for that time, we began to descend the slope, holding hands or apart, but descending, descending . . .

L X X X V I

The Mystery

As I perceived her to be somewhat different on the way down, I don't know whether downcast or something else, I asked her what was wrong. She was silent, with an expression of annoyance, upset, fatigue. I persisted and she told me that . . . A thin fluid ran through my whole body, a strong, quick, singular sensation that I'll never be able to put down on paper. I grasped her hands, pulling her softly to me, and kissed her on the brow with the solemnity of Abraham. She shuddered, took my head between her hands, stared into my eyes, then stroked me with a maternal gesture . . . There's a mystery there. Let's give the reader time to decipher that mystery.

L X X X V I I

Geology

A disaster occurred around that time: the death of Viegas. Viegas had passed through by chance, his seventy years oppressed by asthma, disjointed by rheumatism, and a damaged heart to boot. He was one of the delicate observers of our adventure. Virgília nourished great hopes that this old relative, avaricious as a tomb, would protect her son's future by means of some legacy. And if her husband had similar thoughts he covered them or choked them off. Everything must be told: there was a certain fundamental dignity in Lobo Neves, a layer of rock that resisted dealings with people. The others, the outer layers, loose earth and sand, had been brought to him by life in its perpetual overflow. If the reader remembers Chapter XXIII he will observe that this is the second time I've compared life to an overflow, but he must also notice that this time I add an adjective: perpetual. And God knows the strength of an adjective, above all in young, hot countries.

What's new to this book is Lobo Neves' moral geology, and probably that of the gentleman reading me. Yes, these layers of character that life alters, preserves, or dissolves according to their resistance, these layers deserve a chapter that I'm not going to write so as not to make the narration too long. I'm only going to say that the most honest man I ever met in my life was a certain Jacó Medeiros or Jacó Valadares, I can't remember his name too well. Maybe it was Jacó Rodrigues, in any case, Jacó. He was probity personified. He could have been rich by going counter to the tiniest scruple and he refused. He let no less than four hundred *contos* slip through his fingers. His probity was so exemplary that it got to be punctilious and wearisome. One day as we were alone together at his place in the midst of a pleasant chat they came to tell him that Doctor B., a boring fellow, was looking for him. Jacó told them to say he wasn't at home.

"It won't work," a voice roared in the hallway, "because I'm already inside."

And, indeed, it was Doctor B. who appeared at the parlor door. Jacó got up to receive him, stating that he'd thought it was someone else, not he, adding that he was very pleased with his visit, which subjected us to an hour and a half of deadly boredom and no more because Jacó took out his watch. Doctor B then asked him if he was going out.

"With my wife," Jacó answered.

Doctor B. left and we gave a sign of relief. Once we got through with our sighing, I told Jacó that he'd just lied four times in less than two hours. The first time by contradicting himself, the second by showing happiness at the presence of the intruder, the third by saying that he was going out, the fourth by adding that it was with his wife. Jacó reflected for a moment, then confessed the accuracy of my observation, but he defended himself by saying that absolute veracity was incompatible with an advanced social state and that the peace of cities could only be obtained at the cost of reciprocal deceits . . . Ah! Now I remember. His name was Jacó Tavares.

L X X X V I I I

The Sick Man

Needless to say, I refuted such a pernicious doctrine with the most elementary arguments, but he was so annoyed with my observation that he resisted to the end, displaying a certain fictitious heat, perhaps in order to confuse his conscience.

Virgília's case was a bit more serious. She was less scrupulous than her husband. She openly showed the hope she had for the legacy, showering her relative with all manner of courtesies, attentions, and allurements that could bring on a codicil at the very least. Properly speaking, she flattered him, but I have observed that women's flattery is not the same as that of men. The latter tends toward servility, the former is mingled with affection. The gracefully curved figure, the honeyed word, their very physical weakness give women's flattery a local hue, a legitimate look. The age of the one being flattered doesn't matter. A woman will always have a certain air of mother or sister for his—or even that of a nurse, another feminine position in which the most skillful of men will always lack a *quid*, a fluid, something.

That was what I was thinking when Virgília broke out into a warm greeting for her old relative. She went to meet him at the door, talking and laughing, took his hat and cane, gave him her arm and led him to a chair, or to *the* chair, because in the house it was "Viegas' chair," a special piece of work, cozy, made for ill or aged people. She would go close the nearest window if there was a breeze or open it if it was hot, but carefully seeing to it that he wouldn't get a draft.

"So? You're a little stronger today . . ."

"Ha! I had a rotten night. I can't shake off this hellish asthma."

And the man was puffing, gradually recovering from the fatigue of arriving and climbing the steps, not from the walk because he always came in a carriage. Beside him, a little to the front, Virgília would sit on a stool, her hands on the sick man's knees. In the meantime the young master would come into the room without his usual leaping about, more discreet, meek, serious. Viegas was very fond of him.

"Come here, young master," he would say to him and with great effort would put his hand into his wide pocket, take out a pillbox, put one in his mouth and give another to the boy. Asthma pills. The boy said they tasted very good.

This would be repeated with variations. Since Viegas liked to play checkers, Virgília would follow his desire, enduring it for a long spell as he moved the pieces with his weak, slow hand. At other times they would go out to stroll in the yard, with her offering him her arm, which he wouldn't always accept, saying that he was solid and capable of walking a league. They would walk, sit down, walk again, talk about different things, sometimes about some family matter, sometimes about drawing-room gossip, sometimes, finally, about a house he was thinking of building for his own residence, a house of modern design because his was an ancient one, going back to the time of King John VI, like some that can still be seen today (I think) in the São Cristóvão district with their thick columns in front. He thought that the big house where he was living could be replaced and he'd already ordered a sketch from a well-known mason. Ah!, then indeed, Virgília would see what an old man of good taste was like.

He spoke, as can be imagined, slowly and with difficulty, with pauses for gasping, which were uncomfortable for him and for others. From time to time he would have a coughing attack. Bent over, groaning, he would lift his handkerchief to his mouth and inspect it. When the attack had passed he would go back to the plans for the house, which would have this and that room, a terrace, a coach house, a thing of beauty.

L X X X I X

In Extremis

"Tomorrow I'm going to spend the day at Viegas'," she told me one time. "Poor thing! He hasn't got anybody . . ."

Viegas had been put to bed once and for all. His married daughter had fallen ill precisely at that time and couldn't keep him company. Virgília would go there from time to time. I took advantage of the occasion to spend the whole day next to her. It was two in the afternoon when I got there. Viegas was coughing so hard that it made my chest burn. Between attacks he was haggling over the price of a house with a skinny fellow. The fellow was offering him thirty *contos*, Viegas demanded forty. The buyer kept insisting, like someone afraid of missing a train, but Viegas wouldn't give in. First he refused the thirty *contos*, then two more, then three more, and finally fell into a severe attack that shut off his speech for fifteen minutes. The buyer was most solicitous to him, rearranging his pillows, offering him thirty-six *contos*.

"Never!" the sick man groaned. He asked for a bundle of papers on his desk. Not having the strength to take off the rubber band that held the papers, he asked me to do it. I did. They were the accounts for the construction of the house: bills from the mason, the carpenter, the painter. Bills for the wallpaper in the parlor, the dining room, the bedrooms, the studies. Bills for the hardware, the cost of the lot. He was opening them one by one with a trembling hand and he asked me to read them and I read them.

"See? One thousand two hundred, paper at one thousand two hundred a room. French hinges . . . Look, it's a giveaway," he concluded after the last bill was read.

"Well, all right . . . but . . ."

"Forty *contos*. I won't give it to you for anything less. The interest alone . . . add up the interest . . ."

He coughed out those words in gushes, syllable by syllable as if they were the crumbs of a crumbling pair of lungs. In their deep sockets his eyes rolled and flashed, reminding me of a night light. Under the sheet the bony outline of his body was sketched out, coming to points in two places, his knees and his feet. His yellowed, slack, wrinkled skin barely covered the skull of an expressionless face. A white cotton cap covered the cranium that had been shaved by time.

"So?" the skinny fellow then said.

I signaled him not to go on and he was silent for a few moments. The sick man stared at the ceiling, silent, gasping hard. Virgília turned pale, got up, went to the window. She sensed death and was afraid. I made an attempt to talk about other things. The skinny fellow told an anecdote but got onto the house again, raising his bid.

"Thirty-eight *contos*," he said.

"Huh? . . ." the sick man grunted.

The skinny fellow went over to the bed, took his hand and it felt cold. I went to the sick man, asked him if he felt like something, if he wanted a glass of wine.

"No . . . no . . . for . . . fort . . . for . . . for . . ."

He had a coughing attack and it was his last. Shortly thereafter he expired, to the great consternation of the skinny fellow, who confessed to me afterward that he was ready to offer forty *contos*. But it was too late.

X C

The Ancient Dialogue Between Adam and Cain

Nothing. No remembrance in the will, not even an asthma pill so that when it was all over he wouldn't seem ungrateful or forgetful. Nothing. Virgília swallowed that bit of failure in anger and she told me with a certain caution, not because of the matter itself but because she'd mentioned it to her son, whom she knew I didn't like very much or very little. I suggested that she shouldn't give any more thought to such a thing. It was best to forget the deceased, an imbecile, a damned skinflint, and think about happy things. Our child, for example . . .

There, I've revealed the deciphering of the mystery, that sweet mystery of a few weeks before when Virgília seemed a bit different from what she normally was. A child. A being made from my own being! That was my only thought from that moment on. The eyes of the world, the suspicions of her husband, the death of Viegas, nothing interested me at that time, neither political conflicts, nor revolutions, nor earthquakes, nor anything. I only thought about that anonymous embryo of obscure paternity and a secret voice told me: "It's your child." My child! And I would repeat those two words with a certain indefinable voluptuous feeling and I don't know how many feelings of pride. I felt myself a man.

The best thing was that we would both converse, the embryo and I, talking about present and future things. The rascal loved me, he was a funny little rogue, giving me little pats on the face with his chubby little hands or then sketching out the shape of a lawyer's robe, because he was going to be a lawyer and he would make a speech in the chamber of deputies. And his father would listen to him from a box, his eyes gleaming with tears. From lawyer he would go back to school again, tiny, slate and books under his arm, or then he would drop into his cradle and stand up again as a man. I sought in vain to fix the spirit in one age, one appearance. That embryo had my eyes, all of my forms and gestures. He suckled, he wrote, he waltzed, he was interminable in the limits of a quarter hour—baby and deputy, schoolboy and dandy. Sometimes, beside Virgília, I would forget about her and everything. Virgília would shake me, scold me for my silence. She said that I didn't love her anymore at all. The truth is I was having a dialogue with the embryo. It was the ancient dialogue between Adam and Cain, a conversation without words, between life and life, mystery and mystery.

X C I

An Extraordinary Letter

A round that time I was in receipt of an extraordinary letter accompanied by an object that was no less extraordinary. Here is what the letter said:

My dear Brás Cubas,
   Sometime back on the Passeio Público I borrowed a watch from you. It gives me great satisfaction to return it to you with this letter. The difference is that it's not the same watch but another, I won't say better, but equal to the first. *Que voulez-vous, monseigneur,* as Figaro said, *c'est la misère.* Many things have happened since our encounter. I shall proceed to recount them in detail if you won't slam the door on me. Know, then, that I'm not wearing those caduceus boots nor have I put on a famous frock coat whose flaps have been lost in the night of the ages. I've given up my step on the São Francisco stairs. Finally, I eat lunch.
   Having said this, I ask your permission to come by one of these days to place a piece of work before you, the fruit of long study, a new philosophical system that not only explains and describes the origin and consummation of things, but takes a great step beyond Zeno and Seneca, whose stoicism was really child's play alongside my moral recipe. This system of mine is singularly astonishing. It rectifies the human spirit, suppresses pain, assures happiness, and will fill our country with great glory. I call it Humanitism, from *Humanitas,* the guiding principle of things. My first inclination showed great presumption. It was to call it Borbism, from Borba, a vain title as well as being crude and bothersome. And it was certainly less expressive. You will see, my dear Brás Cubas, you will see that it truly is a monument. And if there is anything that can make me forget the bitterness of life it is the pleasure of finally having grasped truth and happiness. There they are in my hand, those two slippery things. After so many centuries of struggle, research, discovery, systems, and failures, there they are in the hands of man. Goodbye for now, my dear Brás Cubas. Remembrances from

Your old friend
Joaquim Borba dos Santos.

I read this letter without understanding it. It was accompanied by a pouch containing a handsome watch with my initials engraved on it along with these words: *A Remembrance of Old Quincas.* I went back to the letter, read it slowly, attentively. The return of the watch precluded any idea of a jape. The lucidity, the serenity, the conviction—a touch boastful, of course—seemed to eliminate any suspicion of lunacy. Naturally, Quincas Borba had come into an inheritance from some relative of his in Minas Gerais and the abundance had given him back his early dignity. I won't say entirely so. There are things that can't be recouped completely, but, still, regeneration wasn't impossible. I put the letter and the watch away and I awaited the philosophy.

X C I I

An Extraordinary Man

L et me put an end to extraordinary things now. I'd just put away the letter and watch when a thin, middling man came to see me with a note from Cotrim inviting me to dinner. The bearer was married to a sister of Cotrim's and had just arrived from the north a few days before. His name was Damasceno and he'd been involved in the revolution of 1831. He himself told me that within the space of five minutes. He'd left Rio de Janeiro because of a disagreement with the Regent, who was an ass, a little less of an ass than the minister who served under him. Furthermore, revolution was knocking at the door again. At that point, even though his political ideas were somewhat muddled, I managed to get an organized and formulated idea of the government of his preference: it was moderate despotism—not with sweet talk, as they say elsewhere, but with the plumed helmets of the National Guard, except that I couldn't tell whether he wanted a despotism of one, three, thirty, or three hundred people. He had opinions on many different things, among others the development of the African slave trade and the expulsion of the English. He liked the theater very much. As soon as he arrived he went to the São Pedro Theater where he saw a superb drama, *Maria Joana,* and a very interesting comedy, *Kettly, or the Return to*

Switzerland. He'd also enjoyed Deperini very much in *Sappho* or *Anna Boleyn*, he couldn't remember which. But Candiani! Yes, sir, she was top-drawer. Now he wanted to hear *Ernani*, which his daughter sang at home to the piano: *Ernani, Ernani, involami* . . . And he said that standing up and half-singing; those things only reached the north as an echo. His daughter was dying to hear all the operas. His daughter had a lovely voice. And taste, very good taste. Oh, he'd been so anxious to return to Rio de Janeiro. He'd already gone up and down the city, filled with nostalgia . . . He swore that in some places he felt like crying. But he'd never sail again. He'd got very seasick on board, like all the other passengers except for an Englishman . . . The English could go to hell! Things would never be right until they all sailed away. What can England do to us? If he could find some stout-hearted men he could expel those Limeys in one night . . . Thank God he was a patriot—and he pounded his chest—which wasn't surprising because it was in the family. He was descended from a very patriotic old captain-major. Yes, he wasn't a nobody. If the occasion arose and he had to show what kind of wood his boat was made of . . . But it was getting late and I told him that I wouldn't miss dinner and for him to expect me there for a longer chat. I took him to the parlor door. He stopped, saying that he felt very close to me. When he'd gotten married I was in Europe. He knew my father, an upright man he'd joined in a dance at a famous ball at the Praia Grande . . . Things! Things! He'd talk about it later, it was getting late, he had to carry the answer to Cotrim. He left. I closed the door behind him.

XCIII

The Dinner

W hat a torture the dinner was! Fortunately, Sabina seated me next to Damasceno's daughter, a Dona Eulália, or, more familiarly, Nhã-loló, a charming girl, a little bashful at first, but only at the beginning. She lacked elegance, but she made up for it with her eyes, which were superb and had the only defect of being fixed on me except when they went down to her plate. But Nhã-loló ate so little that she scarcely looked at her meal. Later in the night she sang. Her voice was, as her father had said, "quite lovely." Nevertheless, I slipped away. Sabina came to the door with me and asked me what I thought of Damasceno's daughter.

"Nice enough."

"Quite nice, don't you think?" she put in. "She needs a little refining, but what a good heart! She's a pearl. She'd make a good bride for you."

"I don't like pearls."

"Grumpy! When are you going to settle down? When you fall off the tree, when you're ripe, I know. Well, my fine fellow, whether you want to or not, you're going to marry Nhã-loló."

And as she said that she tapped my face with her fingers, light as a dove and at the same time firm and resolute. Good Lord! Could that have been the reason for the reconciliation? I was a bit disconsolate with the idea, but a mysterious voice was calling me to the Lobo Neves house. I said goodbye to Sabina and her threats.

X C I V

The Secret Cause

"How's my darling little mother?" At that word Virgília pouted as always. She was by a window, all alone, looking at the moon, and she greeted me merrily, but when I mentioned our child she pouted. She didn't like that mention, she was bothered by my anticipated paternal caresses. I, for whom she was now a sacred person, a divine ampulla, left her alone. I imagined at first that the embryo, that unknown figure entering into our adventure, had brought back her sense of sin. I was wrong. Virgília had never seemed more expansive, less reserved, less concerned about other people and her husband. There was no remorse. I also imagined that the conception might have been nothing but an invention, a way of tying me to her, a recourse that wouldn't last long and perhaps was beginning to bother her. The hypothesis wasn't absurd. My sweet Virgília lied sometimes, and so gracefully!

That night I discovered the real reason. It was fear of childbirth and the annoyance of pregnancy. She'd suffered a great deal with the birth of her first child. During that hour made up of minutes of life and minutes of death, she'd experienced the chills of the gallows in her imagination. As for the annoyance, it was complicated all the more by the forced deprivation of certain habits of her elegant life. That must have been it, most certainly. I gave her to understand that, scolding her a little by my rights as a father. Virgília stared at me. She immediately turned her eyes away and smiled in an incredulous way.

X C V

The Flowers of Yesteryear

Where are they, the flowers of yesteryear? One afternoon, after a few weeks of gestation, the whole structure of my paternal dreams crumbled. The embryo went away at the point when you couldn't tell Laplace from a turtle. I got the news from the mouth of Lobo Neves, who left me in the parlor and accompanied the doctor to the bedroom of the frustrated mother. I leaned against the window, looking out into the yard where the orange trees were green, with no flowers. Where had they gone, the flowers of yesteryear?

X C V I

The Anonymous Letter

I felt a touch on my shoulder. It was Lobo Neves. We faced each other for a few minutes, mute, inconsolable. I asked about Virgília, then we stayed chatting for half an hour. At the end of that time they brought him a letter. He read it, turned very pale, and folded it with a trembling hand. I think I noticed a movement in him as if he wanted to pounce on me, but I can't remember too well. What I do remember clearly is that over the following days he greeted me coldly and taciturnly. A few days later in Gamboa, Virgília finally told me everything.

Her husband had shown her the letter as soon as she recovered. It was anonymous and it informed on us. It didn't say everything. It spoke, for example, of our outside meetings. It limited itself to cautioning him about our intimacy and added that the suspicions were a matter of public knowledge. Virgília read the letter and said with indignation that it was a vile libel.

"Libel?" Lobo Neves asked.

"Vile."

Her husband took a deep breath, but as he went back to the letter it seemed that every word in it was making a negative sign with its finger, every letter was crying out against his wife's indignation. That man, otherwise intrepid, was now the most fragile of creatures. Perhaps his imagination was showing him that famous eye of public opinion staring sarcastically at him from a distance with its rascally look. Maybe an invisible voice was repeating into his ear the hints that he'd previously heard or mentioned. He demanded that his wife confess everything to him, because he would forgive her everything. Virgília saw that she was safe. She pretended to be irritated over his insistence, swore that she'd only heard words of jest and courtesy from me. The letter must have been from some luckless suitor. And she named a few—one who'd flirted with her openly for three weeks, another who'd written her a letter, and still others, and others. She gave him their names, the circumstances, studying her husband's eyes and ended up saying that in order not to give the libel any room she'd treat me in such a way that I wouldn't be coming back.

I listened to all this a little perturbed, not by the addition of the dissimulation it would be necessary to employ from then on until I kept
completely away from the Lobo Neves house, but by Virgília's moral
calm, her lack of upset, fear, memories, and even remorse. Virgília noticed my concern, lifted up my head, because I was staring at the floor
then, and told me with a certain bitterness:

"You don't deserve the sacrifices I'm making for you."

I didn't say anything to her. It was useless to have her ponder how a
little despair and terror would give our situation the caustic taste of the
early days. But if I told her that it could have been possible that, slowly
and artificially, she would reach that touch of despair and terror. I didn't
say anything to her. She was tapping the floor nervously with the tip of
her shoe. I went over and kissed her on the forehead. Virgília drew back
as if it had been the kiss of a dead man.

X C V I I

Between Mouth and Forehead

I can sense that the reader has shuddered—or should have shuddered. Naturally, the last words suggested three or four reflections to
him. Take a good look at the picture. In a little house in Gamboa two
people who've been in love for a long time, one leaning over the other,
giving her a kiss on the forehead and the other drawing back as if she
felt the contact of the mouth of a corpse. There you have in the short
space between mouth and forehead, before the kiss and after it, there
you have enough room for a lot of things—the contraction of a resentment—the wrinkle of mistrust—or, finally, the pale and drowsy nose
of satiety . . .

X C V I I I

Suppressed

We separated in a happy mood. I dined reconciled with the situation. The anonymous letter was bringing back the salt of mystery and the pepper of danger to our adventure, and in the end it was good that Virgília hadn't lost her self-control in that crisis. That night I went to the São Pedro Theater. They were putting on a great play in which Estela was bringing out tears. I went in, ran my eyes over the boxes. In one of them I saw Damasceno and his family. The daughter was dressed with a new elegance and a certain stylishness, something difficult to explain because the father only earned enough to go into debt. Maybe that was the reason.

I went to visit them during intermission. Damasceno greeted me with lots of words, his wife with lots of smiles. As for Nhã-loló, she didn't take her eyes off me. She seemed prettier to me than at the time of the dinner. I found in her a certain ethereal softness wedded to the polish of earthly forms—a vague expression and worthy of a chapter in which everything must be vague. Really, I don't know how to tell you, I didn't feel too bad beside the girl who was done up smartly in a fine dress, a dress that gave me the itching of a Tartuffe. As I contemplated how it chastely and completely covered her knee, I made a subtle discovery, to wit, that nature foresaw human clothing, a condition necessary for the development of our species. Habitual nudity, given the multiplicity of the works and cares of the individual, would tend to dull the senses and retard sex, while clothing, deceiving nature, sharpens and attracts desires, activates them, reproduces them, and, consequently, drives civilization. A blessed custom that gave us Othello and transatlantic packets.

I had an urge to suppress this chapter. This is a slippery slope. But, after all, I'm writing my memoirs and not yours, my peaceable reader. Alongside the charming maiden I seemed to be taken with a double and indefinable feeling. She was the complete expression of Pascal's duality, *l'ange et la bête*, with the difference that the Jansenist wouldn't admit the simultaneity of the two natures, while there they were quite together—*l'ange*, who was saying certain heavenly things—and *la bête*, who . . . No, I am most certainly going to suppress this chapter.

X C I X

In the Orchestra

In the orchestra seats I found Lobo Neves chatting with some friends. We spoke superficially, coldly, both constrained. But during the next intermission, with the curtain about to go up, we ran into each other in one of the corridors where there was nobody about. He came over to me with great affability and laughter, pulled me into one of the theatre's bay windows, and we talked for a long time, mostly he, who seemed the most tranquil of men. I got to ask him about his wife. He answered that she was fine, but then he turned the conversation to general matters, expansive, almost jolly. Whoever wants to can make a guess as to the cause of the difference. I fled from Damasceno, who was spying on me from the door of his box.

I didn't hear any of the second act, neither the words of the actors nor the applause of the audience. Leaning back in my chair I was picking the shreds of my conversation with Lobo Neves out of my memory, re-creating his manners, and I concluded that the new situation was much better. All we needed was Gamboa. Visiting the other house would only sharpen suspicions. We could rigorously go without speaking every day. It was even better, it put the longing during our breaks back into our love. Besides, I was going on forty and I wasn't anything, not even a district elector. It was urgent that I do something, if only for the love of Virgília, who would be proud to see my name shine . . . I think that there was loud applause at that moment, but I can't swear to it. I was thinking about something else.

Multitude, whose love I coveted until death, that was how I got my revenge on you sometimes. I let humankind bustle around my body without hearing them, just as the Prometheus of Aeschylus did with his torturers. Oh, did you try to chain me to the rock of your frivolity, your indifference, or your agitation? Fragile chains, my friends. I would break them with the action of a Gulliver. It's quite ordinary to go off to ponder in the wilderness. The voluptuous, extraordinary thing is for a man to insulate himself in a sea of gestures and words, of nerves and passions, and declare himself withdrawn, inaccessible, absent. The most they can say when he becomes himself again—that is, when he becomes one of the others—is that he's come down from the world of the moon. But the world of the moon, that luminous and prudent garret of the brain, what else is it if not the disdainful affirmation of our spiritual freedom? By God, that's a good way to end a chapter.

C

The Probable Case

If this world weren't a region of inattentive spirits it wouldn't be necessary to remind the reader that I'm only attesting to certain laws when, in truth, I possess them. With others I restrict myself to the admission of their probability. An example of the second case is the basis of the present chapter, whose reading I recommend to all people who love the study of social phenomena. It would seem, and it's not improbable, that there exists between the events of public life and those of private life a certain reciprocal, regular, and perhaps periodic action—or, to use an image, something similar to the tides on the beach in Flamengo and others equally surging. Indeed, when the wave attacks the beach it floods it for several feet inland. But those same waters return to the sea with variable force and go on to form part of the wave about to come and which must return the same as the first. That's the image. Let's have a look at its application.

I said elsewhere that Lobo Neves, nominated for president of a province, had turned down the nomination because of the date of the decree, which was the 13th. A serious act whose consequence was the break between the minister and Virgília's husband. In that way the private event of the evil omen of a number produced the phenomenon of political discord. It remains to be seen how, sometimes afterward, a political event determined a cessation of motion in private life. Since it's not suitable to the method of this book to describe that other phenomenon immediately, I shall limit myself for now to say that Lobo Neves, four months after our meeting in the theatre, made up with the minister, a fact that the reader must not lose sight of if he wishes to penetrate the subtlety of my thought.

C I

The Dalmatian Revolution

It was Virgília who gave me the news of her husband's political about-face one certain October morning between eleven o'clock and noon. She spoke to me about meetings, conversations, a speech . . .

"So this time you're going to become a baroness," I interrupted.

She turned down the corners of her mouth and shook her head from side to side. But that gesture of indifference was contradicted by something less definable, less clear, an expression of pleasure and expectation. I don't know why, but I imagined that the imperial letter of nomination was capable of drawing her into virtue, I won't say because of virtue in herself, but out of gratitude for her husband. Because she was sincerely in love with nobility. One of the greatest displeasures to come up in our life was the appearance of a dandy from a legation—let us call it the legation of Dalmatia—Count B. V., who chased after her for three months. That man, a genuine nobleman by blood, had turned Virgília's head a little, for she, among other things, had a diplomatic vocation. I can't get to what might have become of me if a revolution hadn't broken out in Dalmatia that overthrew the government and cleaned out its embassies. The revolution was bloody, painful, formidable. With every ship arriving from Europe the newspapers described the horrors, calculated the bloodshed, counted the heads. Everybody was seething with indignation and pity . . . Not I. Inside I blessed the tragedy that had removed a pebble from my shoe. And, then, Dalmatia was so far away!

C I I

At Rest

B ut this same man who was overjoyed by the departure of the other, a while later practiced . . . No, I won't talk about it on this page. Let that chapter wait for when my annoyance is at rest. A crass, low act, with no possible explanation . . . I repeat, I'm not going to recount the matter on this page.

C I I I

Distraction

N o, sir, it's not done. Excuse me, but it's just not done. Dona Plácida was right. No gentleman arrives an hour late to the place where his lady is waiting for him. I came in panting, Virgília had left. Dona Plácida told me that she'd waited a long time, that she'd got annoyed, that she'd wept, that she'd sworn contempt for me, and other things that our housekeeper said with sobs in her voice, asking me not to abandon Iaiá, that it was being very unfair to a girl who'd sacrificed everything for me. I explained to her then that it was a mistake . . . And it wasn't. I think that it was only distraction. A word, a conversation, an anecdote, anything. Only distraction.

Poor Dona Plácida! She really was upset. She was walking back and forth shaking her head, breathing heavily, peeping through the blind. Poor Dona Plácida! With what skill had she tucked in, caressed, and pampered the wiles of our love! What a fertile imagination for making the hours more pleasurable and brief! Flowers, sweets—the delicate sweets of other times—and lots of laughter, lots of caressing, laughter and caressing that grew with time, as though she wanted to preserve our adventure or give it back its first bloom. Our confidante and house-keeper forgot nothing, not even lies, because she would mention signs and longings she hadn't witnessed. Nothing, not even calumny, because once she even accused me of a new love. "You know I couldn't love any other woman," was my reply when Virgília spoke to me about something similar. And those simple words, with no protest or reproof, did away with Dona Plácida's calumny and left her sad.

"All right," I said after a quarter of an hour. "Virgília's got to recognize that I wasn't at all to blame . . . Would you take a note to her right now?"

"She must be very sad, the poor thing! Look, I don't want anyone to die, but if you, sir, but if you ever got to where you could marry Iaiá, then, yes, you'd see what an angel she is!"

I remember that I turned my face away and looked at the floor. I recommend that gesture to people who don't have a response ready or even those who are reluctant to face the pupils of other eyes. In such cases some prefer to recite a stanza from the *Lusiads*, others adopt the recourse of whistling *Norma*. I'll stick with the gesture mentioned. It's simpler and it calls for less effort.

Three days later everything had been explained. I imagine that Virgília was a little startled when I asked forgiveness for the tears she'd shed on that occasion. I can't remember if inside I attributed them to Dona Plácida. Indeed, it could have been that Dona Plácida had wept when she saw her disappointment and through a phenomenon of vision the tears she had in her own eyes seemed to be falling from Virgília's. Whatever it was, everything had been explained, but not forgiven, much less forgotten. Virgília had some harsh things to say to me, threatened me with separation, and ended up praising her husband. There, yes, you had a worthy man, quite superior to me, charming, a model of courtesy and affection. That's what she said while I, sitting with my hands on my knees, looked at the floor, where a fly was dragging an ant that was biting its leg. Poor fly! Poor ant!

"But, haven't you got anything to say?" Virgília asked, standing over me.

"What is there for me to say? I've explained everything. You persist in getting angry. What is there for me to say? Do you know what I think? I think you're tired, that you're bored, that you want to stop . . ."

"Exactly!"

She put on her hat, her hand trembling, enraged . . . "Goodbye, Dona Plácida," she shouted to the back. Then she went to the door. She was going to leave. I grabbed her by the waist. "It's all right, it's all right," I said to her. Virgília still struggled to leave. I held her back, asked her to stay, to forget about it. She came away from the door and sat down on the settee. I sat down beside her, told her a lot of loving things, some humble, some funny. I'm not sure whether our lips got as close as a cambric thread or even closer. That's a matter of dispute. I do remember that in the agitation one of Virgília's earrings had fallen off and I leaned over to pick it up and that the fly of a little while back had climbed onto the earring still carrying the ant on its leg. Then I, with the inborn delicacy of a man of our century, took that pair of mortified creatures into the palm of my hand. I calculated the distance between my hand and the planet Saturn and asked myself what interest there could be in such a wretched episode. If you conclude from it that I was a barbarian, you're wrong, because I asked Virgília for a hairpin in order to separate the two insects. But the fly guessed my intention, opened its wings, and flew off. Poor fly! Poor ant. And God saw that it was good, as Scripture says.

C I V

It Was He!

I gave the hairpin back to Virgília and she returned it to her hair and made ready to leave. It was late, it had already struck three. Everything was forgotten and forgiven. Dona Plácida, who'd been watching for the right moment for leaving, suddenly shut the window and exclaimed:

"Holy Mother of God! Here comes Iaiá's husband!"

The moment of terror was short but complete. Virgília turned the color of the lace on her dress. She ran to the door of the bedroom. Dona Plácida, who'd closed the blind, was also trying to close the inside door. I got ready to wait for Lobo Neves. That short instant passed. Virgília returned to her senses, pushed me into the bedroom, told Dona Plácida to go back to the window. The confidante obeyed.

It was he. Dona Plácida opened the door to him with all sorts of exclamations of surprise. "You here, sir? Honoring the house of your old woman? Please come in. Guess who's here . . . You don't have to guess, that's the only reason you came . . . Come out, Iaiá."

Virgília, who was in a corner, ran to her husband. I was spying on them through the keyhole. Lobo Neves came in slowly, pale, quiet, with no furor, and cast a glance about the room.

"What's this?" Virgília exclaimed. "What are you doing here?"

"I was passing and I saw Dona Plácida in the window so I came to say hello to her."

"Thank you very much," Dona Plácida hastened to say. "And they say old women don't amount to anything . . . Just look! Iaiá looks jealous." And, stroking her, "This angel is the one who's never forgotten old Plácida. Poor thing! She's got her mother's exact face. Sit down, sir . . ."

"I can't stay."

"Are you going home?" Virgília asked. "We can leave together."

"I am."

"Let me have my hat, Dona Plácida."

"Here it is."

Dona Plácida went to get a mirror, opened it in front of her. Virgília put on her hat, tied the ribbons, fixed her hair, talking to her husband, who wasn't saying anything in reply. Our good old lady was prattling too much. It was a way of covering up the shaking of her body. Virgília, having overcome the first moment, had regained control of herself.

"All set," she said. "Goodbye, Dona Plácida. Don't forget to come by, do you hear?" The other one promised she would and opened the door for them.

C V

The Equivalency of Windows

D ona Plácida closed the door and dropped onto a chair. I immediately left the bedroom and took two steps on my way out to the
street to tear Virgília away from her husband. That was what I said and
it was good that I said it because Dona Plácida held me back by the
arms. After a time I got to imagine that I'd only said it so she would
hold me back. But simple reflection is enough to show that after ten
minutes in the bedroom it could only have been a most genuine and
sincere gesture. And that was because of the famous law of the equiva-
lency of windows that I had the satisfaction of discovering and formu-
lating in Chapter LI. It was necessary to air out one's conscience. The
bedroom was a closed window. I opened another with the gesture of
leaving, and I breathed.

C V I

A Dangerous Game

I breathed and sat down. Dona Plácida was clamoring with exclamations and wailing. I listened without saying anything. I was pondering to myself whether it might have been better to have shut Virgília up
in the bedroom and to have stayed in the parlor. But I immediately realized that it would have been worse. It would have confirmed suspicions,
reached the point of an explosion and a bloody scene . . . It had been so
much better that way. But what about afterwards? What was going to
happen to Virgília? Would her husband kill her, beat her, lock her up,
throw her out? Those questions ran slowly through my brain, the way

little specks and dark commas run across the field of vision of sick or tired eyes. They came and went, with their dry and tragic look, and I couldn't grasp one of them and say: It's you, you and no other.

Suddenly I saw a black shape. It was Dona Plácida, who'd gone inside, put on her cloak, and was offering to go to the Lobo Neves house for me. I cautioned her that it was risky, because he would be suspicious of such a quick visit.

"Don't worry," she interrupted. "I'll know how to do it. If he's at home I won't go in."

She left. I remained there pondering what had happened and the possible consequences. In the end it seemed to me that it was playing a dangerous game and I asked myself if it wasn't time to get up and take a little walk. I felt taken by a longing for marriage, by a desire to straighten my life out. Why not? My heart still had things to explore. I didn't feel incapable of a chaste, austere, pure love. In reality, adventures are the torrential and giddy part of life, the exception, that is. I was weary of them. I may even have felt the prick of some remorse. As soon as I thought about that I let myself go to follow my imagination. I immediately saw myself married, alongside an adorable woman, looking at a baby sleeping in the arms of a nursemaid, all of us in the back of a shady green yard, and peeping at us through the trees was a strip of blue sky, an extremely blue sky . . .

C V I I

A Note

"**N**othing happened, but he suspects something. He's very serious and not talking. He just went out. He smiled only once, at Nhonhô, after staring at him for a long time, frowning. He didn't treat me either badly or well. I don't know what's going to happen. God willing, this will pass. Be very cautious for now, very cautious."

C V I I I

Perhaps Not Understood

There's the drama, there's the tip of Shakespeare's tragic ear. That little scrap of paper, scribbled on in part, crumpled by hands, was a document for analysis, which I'm not going to do in this chapter, or in the next, or perhaps in all the rest of the book. Could I rob the reader of the pleasure of noting for himself the coldness, the perspicacity, and the spirit of those few lines jotted down in haste and, behind then, the storm of a different brain, the concealed rage, the despair that brings on constraint and meditation, because it must be resolved in the mud, in blood, or in tears?

As for me, if I tell you that I read the note three or four times that day, believe it, because it's the truth. If I tell you, further, that I reread it the next day, before and after breakfast, you can believe it; it's the naked truth. But if I tell you the upset I had, you might doubt that assertion a bit and not accept it without proof. Neither then nor even now have I been able to make out what I felt. It was fear and it wasn't fear. It was pity and it wasn't pity. It was vanity and it wasn't vanity. In the end, it was love without love, that is, without delirium, and all that made for a rather complex and vague combination, something that you probably don't understand, as I didn't understand it. Let's just suppose that I didn't say anything.

C I X

The Philosopher

Since it's known that I reread the letter before and after breakfast, it's known, therefore, that I had breakfast, and all that remains to be said is that the breakfast was one of the most frugal of my life: an egg, a slice of bread, a cup of tea. I haven't forgotten that small circumstance. In the midst of so many important things that were obliterated, that breakfast escaped. The main reason might have been my disaster, but it wasn't. The main reason was a reflection made to me by Quincas Borba, who visited me that day. He told me that frugality wasn't necessary in order to understand Humanitism, much less to practice it. That philosophy enjoyed easy accommodation with the pleasures of life, including table, theatre, and love, and that, quite the contrary, frugality could be an indication of a certain tendency toward asceticism, which was the perfect expression of human idiocy.

"Look at Saint John," he went on, "he lived off grasshoppers in the wilderness instead of growing peacefully fat in the city while making Pharisaism in the synagogue lose weight."

God spare me the narration of Quincas Borba's story, which I listened to in its entirety on that sad occasion, a long, complicated yet interesting story. And since I won't be telling the story, I'll also dispense with describing his person, quite different from the one that had appeared to me on the Passeio Público. I shall be silent. I will only say that if a man's main characteristic isn't in his features but in his clothing, he wasn't Quincas Borba: he was a judge without a robe, a general without a uniform, a businessman without a budget. I noted the perfection of his frock coat, the whiteness of his shirt, the shine of his shoes. His very voice, hoarse before, seemed to have been restored to its original sonority. As for his mannerisms, without having lost the previous vivacity, they no longer had the disorder and were subject to a certain method. But I don't wish to describe him. If I were to speak, for example, about his gold stickpin and the quality of the leather of his shoes, it would initiate a description that I am omitting in the name of brevity. Be satisfied to know that his shoes were of patent leather. Know, furthermore, that he'd inherited a few braces of *contos* from an old uncle in Barbacena.

My spirits (allow me a child's comparison here!), my spirits on that occasion were a kind of shuttlecock. Quincas Borba's narration hit it, it went up, and when it was about to drop, Virgília's note hit it again, and it was hurled into the air once more. It would descend and the episode on the Passeio Público would receive it with another stroke, equally as firm and effective. I don't think I was born for complex situations. That pushing and shoving of opposite things was getting me off balance. I had an urge to wrap up Quincas Borba, Lobo Neves, and Virgília's note in the same philosophy and send them to Aristotle as a gift. Nevertheless, our philosopher's narrative was instructive. I especially admired the talent for observation with which he described the gestation and growth of vice, the inner struggles, the slow capitulations, the covering of slime.

"Look," he observed. "The first night I spent on the São Francisco stairs, I slept right through as though it had been the softest down. Why? Because I went gradually from a bed with a mattress to a wooden cot, from my own bedroom to the police station, from the police station to the street . . ."

Finally, he wanted to explain the philosophy to me. I asked him not to. "I'm terribly preoccupied today and I wouldn't pay attention. Come back another time. I'm always home." Quincas Borba smiled in a sly way. Maybe he knew about my affair, but he didn't say anything more. He only spoke these last words to me at the door:

"Come to Humanitism. It's the great bosom for the spirit, the eternal sea into which I dove to bring out the truth. The Greeks made it come out of a well! What a base conception! A well! But that's precisely why they never hit upon it. Greeks, Sub-Greeks, Anti-Greeks, the whole long series of mankind has leaned over that well to watch truth come out, but it isn't there. They wore out ropes and buckets. Some of the more audacious ones went down to the bottom and brought up a toad. I went directly to the sea. Come to Humanitism."

C X

31

A week later Lobo Neves was named president of a province. I clung to the hope of a refusal, that the decree would again come out dated the 13th. The date was the 31st, however, and that simple transposition of ciphers eliminated any diabolical substance in them. How deep are the springs of life!

C X I

The Wall

As it isn't my custom to cover up or hide anything, on this page I shall tell about the wall. They were ready to embark. In the meantime at Dona Plácida's house I caught sight of a small piece of paper on the table. It was a note from Virgília. She said she would expect me at night in the yard, without fail. And she ended: "The wall's low on the alley side."

I made a gesture of displeasure. The letter seemed uncommonly audacious to me, poorly thought out, even ridiculous. It wasn't just inviting scandal, it was inviting ridicule along with it. I pictured myself climbing over the wall, even though it was low on the alley side. And just as I was about to get over it I saw myself in the clutches of a policeman who took me to the station house. The wall is low! And what if it was low? Virgília didn't know what she was doing, naturally. It was possible that she was already sorry. I looked at the piece of paper, wrinkled but inflexible. I had an itch to tear it up into thirty thousand pieces and throw them to the wind as the last remnants of my adventure. But I retreated in time. Self-respect, the vexation of the running away, the idea of fear . . . There was nothing to do but go.

"Tell her I'm coming."

"Where?" Dona Plácida asked.

"Where she said she expects me."

"She didn't say anything to me."

"On this piece of paper."

Dona Plácida focused her eyes. "But I found that paper in your drawer this morning and I thought that . . ."

I had a strange sensation. I reread the piece of paper, looked at it, looked at it again. It was, indeed, an old note of Virgília's received during the beginning of our love affair, a certain meeting in the yard, which had, indeed, led to my leaping over the wall, a low and discreet wall. I put the paper away . . . I had a strange sensation.

C X I I

Public Opinion

B ut it was written that the day was to be one of dubious moves. A few hours later I ran into Lobo Neves on the Rua do Ouvidor. We talked about the presidency and politics. He took advantage of the first acquaintance who passed and left me after all manner of pleasant words. I remember that he was withdrawn, but it was a withdrawal he was struggling to hide. It seemed to me then (and may the critics forgive me if this judgment of mine is too bold), it seemed to me that he was afraid—not afraid of me, or of himself, or of the law, or of his conscience. He was afraid of public opinion. I imagined that that anonymous and invisible tribunal in which every member accuses and judges was the limit set for Lobo Neves' will. Maybe he didn't love his wife anymore and therefore it was possible that his heart was indifferent in its indulgence of her latest acts. I think (and again I beg the critics' good will), I think he was probably prepared to break with his wife, as the reader has probably broken with many personal relationships, but public opinion, that opinion which would drag his life along all the streets, would open a minute investigation into the matter, would put together, one by one, all circumstances, antecedents, inductions, proofs, would talk about them in idle backyard conversations, that terrible public opinion, so curious about bedrooms, stood in the way of a family breakup. At the same time, it made vengeance, which would be an admission, impossible. He couldn't appear resentful toward me without also seeking a conjugal breakup. Therefore he had to pretend the same ignorance as before and, by deduction, similar feelings.

I think it was quite hard for him. In those days especially, I saw how hard it must have been for him. But time (and this is another point in which I hope for the indulgence of men who think!), time hardens sensibility and obliterates the memory of things. It was to be supposed that the years would dull the thorns, that a removal from events would smooth the sore spots, that a shadow of retrospective doubt would cover the nakedness of reality. In short, that public opinion would occupy itself a bit with other adventures. The son, as he grew up, would try to satisfy the father's ambitions. He would be heir to all his affection. This

and constant activity and public prestige and old age, then illness, decline, death, a dirge, an obituary, and the book of life was closed without
a single blood-stained page.

C X I I I

Glue

The conclusion, if the previous chapter has one, is that public opinion is a good glue for domestic institutions. It's not entirely impossible that I'll develop that thought before finishing the book, but it's
also not impossible that I'll leave it the way it is. One way or another,
public opinion is a good glue, both in domestic order and in politics.
Some bilious metaphysicians have arrived at the extreme of presenting
it as the simple product of foolish or mediocre people. But it's obvious
that even when a conceit as extreme as that doesn't bring out an answer
by itself, it's sufficient to consider the salutary effects of public opinion
and conclude that it's the superfine work of the flower of mankind, to
wit, the greatest number.

C X I V

End of a Dialogue

"Yes, it's tomorrow. Are you going to come on board?"

"Are you mad? That's impossible."

"Goodbye, then!"

"Goodbye!"

"Don't forget Dona Plácida. Go see her from time to time. Poor thing! She came to say goodbye to us yesterday. She cried a lot, said I'd never see her again . . . She's a good person, isn't she?"

"Of course."

"If we have to write, she'll get the letters. Goodbye for now then, un-til . . ."

"Two years maybe?"

"Oh, no! He says it's only until they hold elections."

"Is that so? So long, then. Watch out, they're looking at us."

"Who?"

"Over there on the sofa. We'd better break up."

"It's awfully hard for me."

"But we have to. Goodbye, Virgília!"

"See you later. Goodbye!"

C X V

Lunch

I didn't see her leave, but at the designated hour I felt something that wasn't pain or pleasure, a mixed sort of thing, relief and longing all mixed in together in equal doses. The reader shouldn't be irritated by this confession. I know quite well that in order to titillate the nerves of fantasy I should have suffered great despair, shed a few tears, and not eaten lunch. It would have been like a novel, but it wouldn't have been biography. The naked truth is that I did eat lunch, as on every other day, succoring my heart with the memories of my adventure and my stomach with the delicacies of M. Prudhon . . .

. . . Old people from my time, perhaps you remember that master chef at the Hotel Pharoux, a fellow who, according to what the owner of the place said, had served in the famous Véry and Véfour in Paris and later on in the palaces of the Count Molé and the Duke de la Rochefoucauld. He was famous. He arrived in Rio de Janeiro along with the polka . . . The polka, M. Prudhon, the Tivoli, the foreigners' ball, the Casino, there you have some of the best memories of those times, but above all, the master's delicacies were delicious.

They were, and on that morning it was as if the devil of a fellow had sensed our catastrophe. Never had ingenuity and art been so favorable to him. What a delight of spices! What a delicacy of meats! What refinement in the shapes! You ate with your mouth, with your eyes, and with your nose. I can't remember the bill on that day. I know that it was expensive. Oh, the sorrow of it! I had to give magnificent burial to my love affair. It was going off there, out to sea, off into space and time, and I was staying behind at a corner table with my forty-some-odd years, so lazy and so hazy. It was left for me never to see them again, because she might come back and she did come back , but who asked for an outpouring of morning from the evening sunset?

C X V I

The Philosophy of Old Pages

The end of the last chapter left me so sad that I was capable of not writing this one, of taking a little rest, purging my spirit of the melancholy that encumbers it and then continuing on. But no, I don't want to waste any time.

Virgília's departure left me with a sample of what it's like to be widowed. During the first few days I stayed home, catching flies like Domitian, if Suetonius is telling the truth, but catching them in a particular way, with my eyes. I would catch them one by one, lying in the hammock in the rear of a large room with an open book in my hands. It was everything: nostalgia, ambitions, a bit of tedium, and a lot of aimless daydreaming. My uncle the canon died during that interval along with two cousins. I didn't feel shocked. I took them to the cemetery as one takes money to the bank. What am I saying? As one takes letters to the post office. I sealed the letters, put them in the box, and left it to the postman to see that they were delivered into the right hands. It was also around that time that my niece Venância, Cotrim's daughter, was born. Some were dying, others were being born. I continued with the flies.

At other times I would get agitated. I would open drawers, shuffle through old letters from friends, relatives, sweethearts (even those from Marcela), and open all of them, read them one by one, and revive the past ... Uninstructed reader, if you don't keep the letters from your youth, you won't get to know the philosophy of old pages someday, you won't enjoy the pleasure of seeing yourself from a distance, in the shadows, with a three-cornered hat, seven-league boots, and a long Assyrian beard, dancing to the sound of Anachreonic pipes. Keep the letters of your youth!

Or, if the three-cornered hat doesn't suit you, I'll use the expression of an old sailor, a friend of the Cotrims. I'll say that if you keep the letters of your youth, you'll find a chance to "sing a bit of nostalgia." It seems that our sailors give that name to songs of the land sung on the high seas. As a poetic expression it's something that can make you even sadder.

C X V I I

Humanitism

Two forces, however, along with a third, compelled me to return to my usual agitated life. Sabina and Quincas Borba. My sister was pushing the conjugal candidacy of Nhã-loló in a truly impetuous way.

When I became aware, I practically had the girl in my arms. As for Quincas Borba, he finally laid out Humanitism for me. It was a philosophical system destined to be the ruination of all others.

"Humanitas," he said, "the principle of things, is nothing but man himself divided up into all men. Humanitas has three phases: the *static*, previous to all creation; the *expansive*, the beginning things; the *dispersive*, the appearance of man; and it will have one more, the *contractive*, the absorption of man and things. The *expansion*, starting the universe, suggested to Humanitas the desire to enjoy it, and from there the *dispersion*, which is nothing but the personified multiplication of the original substance."

Since that explanation didn't seem sufficiently clear to me, Quincas Borba developed it in a profound way, pointing out the main lines of the system. He explained to me that on the one side Humanitism was related to Brahmanism, to wit, in the distribution of men throughout the different parts of the body of Humanitas, but what had only a narrow theological and political meaning in the Indian religion, in Humanitism was the great law of personal worth. Thus, descending from the chest or the kidneys of Humanitas, that is, being *strong*, wasn't the same as descending from the hair or the tip of the nose. Therefore the necessity to cultivate and temper muscles. Hercules was only an anticipatory symbol of Humanitism. At that point Quincas Borba pondered whether or not paganism might have reached the truth if it hadn't been debased by the amorous part of its myths. Nothing like that will occur with Humanitism. In this new church there will be no easy adventures, or falls, or sadness, or puerile joys. Love, for example, is a priestly function, reproduction a ritual. Since life is the greatest reward in the universe and there's no beggar who doesn't prefer misery to death (which is a delightful infusion of Humanitas), it follows that the transmission of life, far from being an occasion of lovemaking, is the supreme moment of the spiritual mass. From all of which there is truly only one misfortune: that of not being born.

"Imagine, for example, that I had not been born," Quincas Borba went on. "It's positive that I wouldn't be having the pleasure of chatting with you now, of eating this potato, of going to the theatre, or, to put it all into one word, living. Note that I'm not making a man a simple vehicle of Humanitas. He is vehicle, passenger, and coachman all at the same time. He is Humanitas itself in a reduced form. It follows from that that there is a need for him to worship himself. Do you want a proof of the superiority of my system? Think about envy. There is no moralist, Greek or Turkish, Christian or Muslim, who doesn't thunder against the feeling of envy. Agreement is universal, from the fields of Idumea to the heights of Tijuca. So, then, let go of old prejudices, forget about shabby rhetoric, and study envy, that ever so subtle and so noble feeling. With every man a reduction of Humanitas, it's clear that no man is fundamentally opposed to another man, whatever contrary appearances may be. Thus, for example, the headsman who executes the condemned man can excite the vain clamor of poets. But, substantially, it is Humanitas correcting in Humanitas an infraction of the law of Humanitas. I will say the same of an individual who disembowels another. It's a manifestation of the force of Humanitas. There is nothing to prevent (and there are examples) his being disemboweled just the same. If you've understood well, you will easily understand that envy is nothing but an admiration that fights, and since fighting is the main function of humankind, all bellicose feelings are the ones that best serve its happiness. It follows, then, that envy is a virtue."

Why deny it? I was flabbergasted. The clarity of the exposition, the logic of the principles, the rigor of the deductions, all of that seemed great to the highest degree, and it became necessary for me to break off the conversation for a few minutes while I digested the new philosophy. Quincas Borba couldn't conceal the satisfaction of his triumph. He had a chicken wing on his plate and he was gnawing on it with philosophical serenity. I voiced a few objections still, but they were so feeble that he didn't waste much time in knocking them down.

"In order to understand my system well," he concluded, "it's necessary never to forget the universal principle, distributed and summed up in every man. Look. War, which looks like a calamity, is a convenient operation, which we could call the snapping of Humanitas' fingers; hunger (and he sucked philosophically on his chicken wing), hunger is proof that Humanitas is subject to its own entrails. But I don't need any other documentation of the sublimity of my system than this chicken right here. It nourished itself on corn, which was planted by an African, let us suppose imported from Angola. That African was born, grew up, was sold. A ship brought him here, a ship built of wood cut in the forest by ten or twelve men, propelled by sails that eight or ten men sewed together, not to mention the rigging and other parts of the nautical apparatus. In that way, this chicken, which I have lunched on just now, is the result of a multitude of efforts and struggles carried out with the sole aim of satisfying my appetite."

Between cheese and coffee Quincas Borba demonstrated to me how his system meant the destruction of pain. Pain, according to Humanitism, is pure illusion. When a child is threatened with a stick, even before being struck, he closes his eyes and trembles. That *predisposition* is what constitutes the basis of the human illusion, inherited and transmitted. It's not enough, of course, to adopt the system in order to do away with pain immediately, but it is indispensable. The rest is the natural evolution of things. Once man gets it completely into his head that he is Humanitas itself, there's nothing else to do but raise his thought up to the original substance in order to prevent any painful sensation. The evolution is so profound, however, that it can only take place over a few thousand years.

For a few days after that Quincas Borba read me his *magnum opus*. It consisted of four handwritten volumes, a hundred pages each, in a cramped hand and with Latin quotations. The last volume was a political treatise based on Humanitas. It was, perhaps, the most tedious part of the system, since it was conceived with a formidable rigor of logic. With society reorganized by his method, not even then would war, insurrection, a simple beating, an anonymous stabbing, hunger, or illness be eliminated. But since those supposed plagues were really errors of understanding, because they were nothing but external movements of the internal substance destined not to have any influence over man except as a simple break in universal monotony, it was clear that their existence would not be a barrier against human happiness. But even when such plagues (a basically false concept) corresponded in the future to the narrow conception of former times, not even then would the system be destroyed, and for two reasons: first, because Humanitas being the creative and absolute substance, every individual would find the greatest delight in the world in sacrificing himself to the principle from which he descends; second, because even then it wouldn't diminish man's spiritual power over the earth, invented solely for his recreation, like the stars, breezes, dates, and rhubarb. Pangloss, he said to me as he closed the book, wasn't as dotty as Voltaire painted him.

C X V I I I

The Third Force

The third force that called me into the bustle was the pleasure of making a show and, above all, an incapacity to live by myself. The multitude attracted me, applause was my love. If the idea of the poultice had come to me at that time, who knows. I might not have died so soon and would have been famous. But the poultice didn't come. What did come was a desire to be active in something, with something, and for something.

C X I X

Parenthesis

I want to leave in parenthesis here half a dozen maxims from the many I wrote down around that time. They're yawns of annoyance. They can serve as epigraphs to speeches that have no subject:

———————————————————

Bear your neighbor's bellyache with patience.

———————————————————

We kill time; time buries us.

———————————————————

A philosophical coachman used to say that the pleasure of a coach would be less if we all traveled in coaches.

———————————————————

Believe in yourself, but don't always doubt others.

It's beyond understanding why a Botocudo Indian pierces his lip to adorn it with a piece of wood. This is the reflection of a jeweler.

Don't be irritated if you're poorly paid for a service. It's better to fall down from out of the clouds than from a third-story window.

C X X

Compelle Intrare

No, sir, right now, like it or not, you've got to get married, Sabina told me. What a pretty future! An old bachelor with no children. No children! The idea of having children gave me a start. The mysterious fluid was running through me again. Yes, it was fitting for me to be a father. The life of a celibate may have certain advantages of its own, but they would be tenuous and purchased at the price of loneliness. No children! No, impossible! I was ready to accept everything, even the relationship with Damasceno. No children! Since I'd already placed great trust in Quincas Borba by then, I went to see him and laid out my inner movement toward paternity to him. The philosopher listened to me with great excitement. He declared to me that Humanitism was at work in my breast. He encouraged me to get married. He pondered the fact that there were some more guests knocking at the door, etc. *Compelle intrare*, as Jesus said. And he wouldn't leave me without proving that the allegory in the Gospels was nothing but a foretoken of Humanitism, mistakenly interpreted by priests.

C X X I

Downhill

A t the end of three months everything was going along marvelously. The fluid, Sabina, the girl's eyes, the father's desires were among the many impulses driving me toward marriage. The memory of Virgília would appear at the door from time to time and with it a black demon who would hold a mirror up to my face in which I would see Virgília, far away, drowning in tears. But a different demon would come, pink, with another mirror in which the figure of Nhã-loló was reflected, tender, luminous, angelic.

I won't speak of the years. I didn't feel them. I'll even add that I put them aside one certain Sunday when I went to mass at the chapel on Livramento Hill. Since Damasceno lived in Cajueiros, I would accompany him to mass many times. The hill was still bare of houses except for the old mansion on top where the chapel was. So, one Sunday as I was descending with Nhã-loló on my arm, some kind of phenomenon, I don't know what, took place, taking off two years here, four there, then five farther on, so that when I got to the bottom I was only twenty years old, just as lively as I had been at that age.

Now, if you want to know under what circumstances the phenomenon took place, all you have to do is read this chapter to the end. We were coming from mass, she, her father, and I. Halfway down the hill we came upon a group of men. Damasceno, who was walking beside us, noticed what it was and went ahead, all excited. We followed along. And this is what we saw: men of all ages, sizes, and colors, some in shirtsleeves, others wearing jackets, others in tattered frock coats, in different positions, some squatting, others with their hands on their knees, these sitting on stones, those leaning against the wall, and all watching the center, with their souls leaning out of the windows of their eyes.

"What is it?" Nhã-loló asked me.

I signaled her to be quiet, carefully opened a path, and they all made room for me with none of them really seeing me. The center held their eyes. It was a cockfight. I saw the two contenders, two roosters with sharp spurs, fiery eyes, and filed beaks. Both were shaking their bloody combs, The breasts of both were without feathers and ruddy colored, weariness was coming over them. But they kept on fighting, eyes staring at eyes, beak down, beak up, a peck from this one, a peck from that, quivering and enraged. Everything else was lost for Damasceno. The spectacle had eliminated the whole universe for him. I told him in vain that it was time to go down. He didn't answer, he didn't hear, he was concentrating on the duel. Cockfights were one of his passions.

It was on that occasion that Nhã-loló tugged me softly on the arm, saying we should be on our way. I accepted her advice and went on with her. I've already said that the hill was uninhabited at the time. I also said that we were coming from mass, and since I didn't say it was raining, it was clear that the weather was good, a delightful sun. And strong. So strong that I immediately opened the parasol, held it by the center of the handle, and tilted in a way that was an aid to a page out of Quincas Borba's philosophy: Humanitas kissed Humanitas . . . That was how the years fell away from me on the way downhill.

We stopped at the base for a few minutes waiting for Damasceno. He arrived after a while, surrounded by bettors and commenting with them about the fight. One of them, the holder of the bets, was distributing a bundle of old ten *tostão* notes, which the winners took with redoubled joy. As for the roosters, they came along under the arms of their respective owners. One of them had his comb so badly pecked away and bloody that I recognized him immediately as the loser, but I was mistaken—the loser was the other one, who had no comb at all. They both had their beaks open and had trouble breathing, exhausted. The bettors, on the other hand, were merry in spite of the strong commotion of the fight. They recounted the lives of the contenders, recalled the deeds of both. I went along in vexation. Nhã-loló was especially vexed.

C X X I I

A Very Delicate Intention

What had upset Nhã-loló was her father. The ease with which he'd joined the bettors brought out old habits and social affinities and Nhã-loló had become afraid that a father-in-law like that would seem unworthy to me. The difference she was making in herself was notable. She would study herself and study me. Elegant and polished life attracted her, principally because she thought it the surest way to blend our personalities. Nhã-loló would observe, imitate, and guess. At the same time she undertook an effort to conceal her family's inferiority. On that day, however, her father's display was so great that it made her quite sad. I then sought to get her mind off the matter, telling her a string of jokes and jests, all in good taste. A vain effort that didn't make her any happier. Her depression was so deep, she was so obviously downcast, that I came to see in Nhã-loló the positive intention of separating her cause from her father's cause in my mind. I thought that a most elevated feeling. It was one more affinity we had in common.

"There's no other way," I said to myself. "I'm going to pluck that flower out of that bog."

C X X I I I

The Real Cotrim

In spite of my forty-some-odd years, since I loved harmony in the family, I understood that I shouldn't bring up the matter of marriage without first speaking to Cotrim. He listened to me and answered seriously that he had no opinions when it came to his relatives. They might imagine some special interest if he happened to praise the rare qualities of Nhã-loló. That's why he kept quiet. Furthermore, he was sure that his niece had a real passion for me, but if she consulted him his advice would be negative. It wasn't brought about by any hate, he appreciated my good qualities—they couldn't be more praiseworthy, it was true, and as for Nhã-loló, he could never deny that she was an excellent bride, but from there to advise marriage there was a wide gap.

"I wash my hands of it completely," he concluded.

"But the other day you thought I should get married as soon as possible . . ."

"That was something else. I think it's indispensable that you get married, especially with your political ambitions. You must know that celibacy is a drawback in politics. As to the bride, though, I can't approve, I don't want to, I shouldn't, it's against my honor. I think Sabina went too far, giving you certain hints, according to what she's said. But, in any case, she's not a blood relative of Nhã-loló like me. Look . . ., but no . . ., I won't say . . ."

"Say it."

"No, I won't say anything."

Perhaps Cotrim's scruples will seem excessive to one who didn't know that he possessed an extremely honorable character. I myself was unjust with him during the years following my father's will. I recognize now that he was a model. They accused him of avarice and I think they were right, but avarice is only the exaggeration of a virtue, and virtues should serve as evaluations. Oversupply is better than deficit. Since he was very cold in his manners, he had enemies who even accused him of being a barbarian. The only fact alleged in that particular was his frequent sending of slaves to the dungeon, from where they would emerge dripping blood. But, alongside the fact that he only sent recalcitrants and runaways, it so happens that, having been long involved in the smuggling of slaves, he'd become accustomed to a certain way of dealing that was a bit harsher than the business required, and one can't honestly attribute to the original nature of a man what is simply the effect of his social relations. The proof that Cotrim had pious feelings could be found in his love for his children and the grief he suffered when Sara died a few months after that. Irrefutable proof, I think, and not the only one. He was the treasurer of a confraternity and brother in several brotherhoods and even a redeemed brother in one of them, which doesn't jibe too well with his reputation for avarice. The truth is that the beneficence didn't fall on barren ground: the brotherhood (of which he was a judge) ordered a portrait of him in oils to be painted. He wasn't perfect, needless to say. He had, for example, the bad habit of letting the press know about his various charities—a reprehensible and not praiseworthy custom I must agree. But he defended himself by saying that good works were contagious when public. An argument that's not without some weight. I do believe (and here I give him the highest praise) that he only practiced those occasional charities with an aim to arousing the philanthropy of others, and if such was his intent, I must confess that publicity is a sine qua non. In short, he may have been owing in a few courtesies, but he didn't owe anyone a penny.

C X X I V

As an Interlude

What is there between life and death? A short bridge. Nevertheless, if I hadn't put this chapter together the reader would have suffered a strong shock, quite harmful to the effect of the book. Jumping from a portrait to an epitaph can be a real and common act. The reader, however, is only taking refuge in the book to escape life. I'm not saying the thought is mine. I'm saying that there's a grain of truth in it and the form, at least, is picturesque. And, I repeat, it's not mine.

C X X V

Epitaph

HERE LIES

DONA EULÁLIA DAMASCENA DE BRITO

DEAD

AT THE AGE OF NINETEEN

PRAY FOR HER!

C X X V I

Disconsolate

The epitaph says everything. It's worth more than my telling you about Nhã-loló's illness, her death, the despair of the family, the burial. Just know that she died. I will add that it was on the occasion of the first inroad of yellow fever. I won't say anything more except that I accompanied her to her final resting place and said goodbye sadly, but without tears. I concluded that perhaps I didn't really love her.

See now how excesses can lead to unawareness. I was pained a little by the blindness of the epidemic that was killing right and left and also carried off a young lady who was to be my wife. I couldn't get to understand the necessity of the epidemic, much less of that death. I think that I felt it to be even more absurd than all the other deaths. Quincas Borba, however, explained to me that epidemics were useful for the species, even though disastrous for a certain portion of individuals. He made me take notice that as horrible as the spectacle might be, there was a very weighty advantage: the survival of the greater number. He got to ask me in the midst of the general mourning if I didn't feel some secret joy in having escaped the clutches of the plague. But that question was so absurd that it went without an answer.

Since I haven't recounted the death, neither shall I speak about the seventh-day mass. Damasceno's sadness was profound. The poor man looked like a ruin. I was with him two weeks later. He was still inconsolable and he said that the great pain God had inflicted upon him was increased all the more by that inflicted on him by men. He didn't tell me anything else. Three weeks later he got back onto the subject and then he confessed to me that in the midst of the irreparable disaster he would have liked to have had the consolation of the presence of his friends. Only twelve people, and three-quarters of them Cotrim's friends, had accompanied the corpse of his beloved daughter to her grave. And he'd sent out eighty notices. I argued that with the losses being so widespread he could easily forgive that apparent lack of concern. Damasceno shook his head in an incredulous and sad way.

"Ah!" he moaned, "they deserted me."

Cotrim, who was present, said:

"The ones who came were the ones who had a true interest in you and in us. The eighty would have come as a formality, they would have talked about the government's inertia, druggists' panaceas, the price of houses, or something like that . . ."

Damasceno listened in silence, shook his head again, and sighed:

"But they would have come!"

C X X V I I

Formality

It is a great thing to have received a particle of wisdom from heaven, the gift of finding the relationship of things, the faculty of comparing them, and the talent for drawing a conclusion! I had the psychic distinction. I'm thankful for it, even now at the bottom of my grave.

In fact, the ordinary man, if he'd heard Damasceno's last words, wouldn't remember them when some time later he was to look at a print showing six Turkish ladies. But I remembered. They were six ladies from Constantinople—modern—in street clothes, faces covered not by a thick cloth that really covered them, but by a thin veil that pretended to reveal only the eyes and in reality exposed the whole face. And I was amused by that cunningness of Muslim coquetry, which in that way hides the face and follows usage, but doesn't cover it, displaying its beauty. There's apparently nothing to connect the Turkish ladies and Damasceno, but if you're a profound and penetrating spirit (and I doubt very much that you will deny me that), you'll understand that in both cases there arises the tip of a rigid yet gentle companion of social man . . .

Yes, pleasant Formality, you are the staff of life, the balm of hearts, the mediator among men, the link between heaven and earth. You wipe away the tears of a father, you capture the indulgence of a Prophet. If grief falls asleep and conscience is accommodated, to whom, except you, is that huge benefit owed? The esteem that extends to the hat on one's head doesn't say anything to the soul, but the indifference that courts it leaves it with a delightful impression. The reason is that, contrary to an old absurd formula, it isn't the letter that kills; the letter gives life, the spirit is the object of controversy, of doubt, of interpretation, and consequently of life and death. You live, pleasant Formality, for the peace of Damasceno and the glory of Mohammed.

C X X V I I I

In the Chamber

A nd take good notice that I saw the Turkish print two years after Damasceno's words and I saw it in the Chamber of Deputies, in the midst of a great hubbub while a deputy was discussing an opinion of the budget commission, for I was also a deputy. For those who've read this book there's no need to discuss my satisfaction further, and for the others it's equally useless. I was a deputy and I saw the Turkish print as I leaned back in my seat between a colleague who was telling a story and another who was sketching the profile of the speaker in pencil on the back of an envelope. The speaker was Lobo Neves. The wave of life had brought us to the same beach like two bottles from shipwrecked sailors, he holding in his resentment, I holding in my remorse perhaps. And I use that suspensive, doubtful, or conditional form meaning to say that there was nothing to be held there unless it was my ambition to be a cabinet minister.

C X X I X

No Remorse

I had no remorse. If I had the proper chemical apparatus, I would include a page of chemistry in this book because I would break down remorse into its most simple elements with an aim to knowing in a positive and conclusive way the reason for Achilles' dragging the corpse of his adversary around the walls of Troy and Lady Macbeth's walking about the room with her spot of blood. But I don't have any chemical apparatus, just as I didn't have any remorse. What I had was the desire to be a minister of state. Therefore, if I am to finish this chapter, I must say that I didn't want to be either Achilles or Lady Macbeth, and that if I had to be either one, better Achilles, better dragging the corpse in triumph than carrying the spot. Priam's pleas are finally heard and a nice military and literary reputation is gained. I wasn't listening to Priam's pleas but to Lobo Neves' speech, and I had no remorse.

C X X X

To Be Inserted in Chapter CXXIX

The first time I was able to speak to Virgília after the presidency was at a ball in 1855. She was wearing a superb gown of blue grosgrain and was displaying the same pair of shoulders as in previous times. It wasn't the freshness of her early years, quite the contrary, but she was still beautiful, with an autumnal beauty enhanced by the night. I remember that we talked a lot without referring to anything out of the past. Everything was understood. A remote, vague comment or a look, perhaps, and nothing else. A short while later she left. I went to watch her go down the steps and I don't know by what means of cerebral ventriloquism (I beg the forgiveness of philologists for this barbarous expression) I murmured to myself the profoundly retrospective word:

"Magnificent!"

This chapter should be inserted between the first and second sentences of Chapter CXXIX.

C X X X I

Concerning a Calumny

Just after I had said that to myself through the ventriloquo-cerebral process—or what was simple opinion and not remorse—I felt someone put his hand on my shoulder. I turned. It was an old friend, a naval officer, jovial, impudent in his manners. He smiled maliciously and said to me:

"You old devil! Memories of the past, eh?"

"Hurray for the past!"

"You've got your old job back, naturally."

"Easy, you rogue!" I told him, wagging my finger at him.

I must confess that the dialogue was an indiscretion—principally my last response. And I confess it with so much greater pleasure because women are the ones who have the fame of being indiscreet and I don't wish to end the book without setting that notion of the human spirit straight. In matters of amorous adventures I have found men who smiled or had trouble denying it, in a cold way, with monosyllables, and so forth, while their female equivalents wouldn't admit it and would swear by the Holy Gospels that it was all calumny. The reason for this difference is that women (excepting the hypothesis in Chapter CI and other hypotheses) surrender out of love, whether it be either Stendhal's love-passion, or the purely physical love of certain Roman ladies, for example, or Polynesian, Laplander, Kaffir, and possibly those of other civilized races. But men—I speak of men belonging to an elegant and cultured society—men couple their vanity to the other sentiment. In addition to that (and I'm still referring to forbidden cases) women, when they love another man, think they're betraying a duty and therefore must conceal it with the greatest skill, must refine the perfidy, while men, enjoying their being the cause of the infraction and the victory over the other man as well, are legitimately proud and immediately pass on to that other less harsh and less secret sentiment—that fine fatuousness that is the luminous sweat of merit.

But whether my explanation is true or not, it's sufficient for me to leave written on this page for the use of the ages that the indiscretion of women is a trick invented by men. In love, at least, they're as silent as the tomb. They've been ruined many times by being clumsy, restless, unable to stand up in the face of looks and gestures, and that's why a great lady and delicate spirit, the Queen of Navarre, somewhere employed a metaphor to say that all amorous adventures will of necessity be discovered sooner or later: "There is no puppy so well trained that we do not hear its bark in the end."

C X X X I I

Which Isn't Serious

B y quoting the Queen of Navarre's remark, it occurs to me that among our people when a person sees another irritated, it's customary to ask him: "Say, who killed your puppies?" as if to say, "Who exposed your love affair, your secret adventure, etc." But this chapter isn't serious.

C X X X I I I

Helvetius's Principle

W e were at the point where the naval officer got the confession of my affair with Virgília out of me and here I will improve on Helvetius' principle—or if not, I'll explain it. It was in my interest to keep quiet. To confirm the suspicions of an old thing was to arouse some forgotten hate, give rise to a scandal, at most to acquire the reputation of an indiscreet person. It was in my interest and if I understand Helvetius' principle in a superficial way, that's what I should have done. But I've already given the reasons for masculine indiscretion: before that interest in *security* there was another, that of *pride*, which is more intimate, more immediate. The first was reflexive, with the supposition of a previous syllogism. The second was spontaneous, instinctive, it came from the subject's insides. Finally, the first had a remote effect, the second a close one. Conclusion: Helvetius' principle is true in my case. The difference is that it wasn't a case of apparent interests but the hidden ones.

C X X X I V

Fifty Years Old

I still haven't told you—but I'll say it now—that when Virgília was going down the steps and the naval officer touched me on the shoulder, I was fifty years old. It was, therefore, my life that was going downstairs—or the best part of it at least, a part full of pleasures, agitations, frights—disguised with dissimulation and duplicity—but, all in all, the best if we must speak in the usual terms. If, however, we employ other, more sublime ones, the best part was what remained, as I shall have the honor of telling you in the few pages left in this book.

Fifty! It wasn't necessary to confess it. You're already getting the feeling that my style isn't as nimble as it was during the early days. On that occasion, when the conversation with the naval officer came to an end and he put on his cape and left, I must confess that I was left a bit sad. I went back to the main room. I felt like dancing a polka, being intoxicated by the lights, the flowers, the chandeliers, the pretty eyes, and the quiet and sprightly bubble of individual conversations. And I'm not sorry. I was rejuvenated. But a half hour later, when I left the ball at four in the morning, what did I find inside the coach? My fifty years. There they were, insistent, not numb from the cold, not rheumatic—but dozing off from fatigue, a little longing for bed and rest. Then—and just look to what point the imagination of a sleepy man can reach—then I seemed to hear from a bat who was climbing up the roof of the vehicle: Mr. Brás Cubas, the rejuvenation was in the room, the chandeliers, the lights, the silk—in short, in other people.

C X X X V

Oblivion

A nd now I have the feeling that if some lady has followed along these pages she closes the book and doesn't read the rest. For her, the interest in my love, which was love, has died out. Fifty years old! It isn't invalidism yet, but it's no longer sprightliness. With ten more years I'll understand what an Englishman once said, I'll understand that "it's a matter of not finding anyone who remembers my parents and the way in which I must face my own OBLIVION."

Put that name in small caps. OBLIVION! It's only proper that all honor be paid to a personage so despised and so worthy, a last-minute guest at the party, but a sure one. The lady who dazzled at the dawn of the present reign knows it and, even more painfully, the one who displayed her charms in bloom during the Paraná ministry, because the latter is closer to triumph and she is already beginning to feel that others have taken her carriage. So if she's true to herself she won't persist in a dead or expiring memory. She won't seek in the looks of today the same greeting as in yesterday's looks, when it was others who took part in the march of life with a merry heart and a swift foot. *Tempora mutantur.* She understands that this whirlwind is like that, it carries off the leaves of the forest and the rags of the road without exception or mercy. And if she has a touch of philosophy she won't envy but will feel sorry for the ones who have taken her carriage because they, too, will be helped down by the footman OBLIVION. A spectacle whose purpose is to amuse the planet Saturn, which is quite bored with it.

C X X X V I

Uselessness

B ut, I'm either mistaken or I've just written a useless chapter.

C X X X V I I

The Shako

N ot really. It sums up the reflections I made to Quincas Borba the following day, adding that I felt downhearted and a thousand other sad things. But that philosopher, with the elevated good sense he had at his disposal, shouted at me that I was sliding down the fatal slope of melancholy.

"My dear Brás Cubas, don't let yourself be overcome by those vapors. Good Lord! You've got to be a man! Be strong! Fight! Conquer! Dominate! Fifty is the age of science and government. Courage, Brás Cubas. Don't turn fool on me. What have you got to do with that succession from ruin to ruin, from flower to flower? Try to savor life. And be aware that the worst philosophy is that of the weeper who lies down on the riverbank to mourn the incessant flow of the waters. Their duty is never to stop. Make an adjustment to the law and try to take advantage of it."

The value of the authority of a great philosopher is found in the smallest things. Quincas Borba's words had the special virtue of shaking me out of the moral and mental torpor I was caught up in. Let's get to it. Let's get into the government, it's time. Up till then I hadn't participated in the great debates. I was courting a minister's portfolio by means of flattery, teas, commissions, and votes. And the portfolio never came. It was urgent that I make a speech.

I began slowly. Three days later during the discussion of the budget for the ministry of justice, I took advantage of an opening to ask the minister modestly if it wouldn't be useful to reduce the size of the National Guard's shakos. The object of the question wasn't far-reaching, but even so I demonstrated how it wasn't unworthy of the cogitations of a statesman and I cited Philopaemen, who ordered the replacement of his troops' shields, which were small, by other larger ones, and also their spears, which were too light, a fact that history didn't find out of line with the gravity of its pages. The size of our shakos called for a profound cut, not only to make them more stylish, but also to make them more hygienic. On parade in the sun the excessive heat they produce could be fatal. Since it was a well-known fact that it was a precept of Hippocrates that a person should keep his head cool, it seemed cruel to oblige a citizen, from the simple consideration of being in uniform, to risk his health and his life and, consequently, the future of his family. The chamber and the government should keep in mind that the National Guard is the rampart of freedom and independence, and that a citizen called up for service freely given, frequent, and arduous, had the right to have the onus of it lessened by a decree calling for a light and easy-fitting uniform. I added that the shako, because of its weight, lowered a citizen's head, and the nation needed citizens whose brow could be raised, proud and serene, in the face of power. And I concluded with this idea: the weeping willow, which bends its branches toward the earth, is a graveyard tree. The palm tree, erect and firm, is a tree of the wilderness, public squares, and gardens.

The impressions made by the speech were varied. As regards the form, the quick eloquence, the literary and philosophical part, the opinion was unanimous. Everyone told me it was perfect and that no one had ever been able to extract so many ideas from a shako. But the political part was considered deplorable by many. Some thought my speech was a parliamentary disaster. Lastly, they told me that others now considered me in the opposition, among them oppositionists in the chamber who went so far as to hint that it was a convenient moment for a vote of no confidence. I energetically rejected such an interpretation, which was not only erroneous but libelous in view of my prominent support of the cabinet. I added that the need to reduce the size of the shako was not so great that it couldn't wait a few years and, in any case, I was ready to compromise in the extent of the cut, being content with three-quarters of an inch or less. In the end, even though my idea wasn't adopted, it sufficed for me to have it introduced in parliament.

Quincas Borba, however, made no restrictions. I'm not a political man, he told me at dinner, I don't know whether you did the right thing or not. I do know that you made an excellent speech. And then he noted the most outstanding parts, the strong arguments with that modesty of praise that's so fitting in a great philosopher. Then he took the subject into account and attacked the shako with such strength, such great lucidity that he ended up by effectively convincing me of its danger.

C X X X V I I I

To a Critic

My dear critic,

A few pages back when I said I was fifty, I added: "You're already getting the feeling that my style isn't as nimble as it was during the early days." Maybe you find that phrase incomprehensible, knowing my present state, but I call your attention to the subtlety of that thought. I don't mean I'm older now than when I began the book. Death doesn't age one. I do mean that in each phase of the narration of my life I experience the corresponding sensation. Good Lord! Do I have to explain everything?

C X X X I X

How I Didn't Get to Be a Minister of State

. . . .
. . . .
. . . .

C X L

Which Explains the Previous One

There are things that are better said in silence. Such is the material of the previous chapter. Unsuccessful ambitious people will understand it. If the passion for power is the strongest of all, as some say, imagine the despair, the pain, the depression on the day I lost my seat in the Chamber of Deputies. All my hopes left me, my political career was over. And take note that Quincas Borba, through philosophical inductions he made, found that my ambition wasn't a true passion for power, but a whim, a desire to have some fun. In his opinion that feeling, no less profound than the other one, is much more vexing because it matches the love women have for lace and coiffures. A Cromwell or a Bonaparte, he added, for the very reason that they were burning with the passion for power, got there by sheer strength, either by the stairs on the right or the ones on the left. My feelings weren't like that. Not having that same strength in themselves, they didn't have certainty in the results and that was why there was greater affliction, greater disappointment, greater sadness. My feelings, according to Humanitism . . .

"Go to the devil with your Humanitism," I interrupted him. "I'm sick and tired of philosophies that don't get me anything."

The harshness of the interruption in the case of a philosopher of his standing was the equivalent of an insult. But he forgave the irritation with which I spoke to him. They brought us coffee. It was one o'clock in the afternoon, we were in my study, a lovely room that looked out on the backyard, good books, *objets d'art*, a Voltaire among them, a bronze Voltaire who on that occasion seemed to be accentuating the sarcastic little smile with which he was looking at me, the scoundrel, excellent chairs. Outside the sun, a big sun, which Quincas Borba, I don't remember whether as a jest or as poetry, called one of nature's ministers. A cool breeze was blowing, the sky was blue. In each window—there were three—hung a cage with birds, who were trilling their rustic operas. Everything had the appearance of a conspiracy of things against man: and even though I was in *my* room, looking at *my* yard, sitting in *my* chair, listening to *my* birds, next to *my* books, lighted by *my* sun, it wasn't enough to cure me of the longing for that other chair that wasn't mine.

C X L I

Dogs

"So what do you plan to do now?" Quincas Borba asked me, going over to put his empty coffee cup on one of the window sills.

"I don't know. I'm going to hide out in Tijuca, get away from people. I'm disgraced, disgusted. So many dreams, my dear Borba, so many dreams, and I'm nothing."

"Nothing?" Quincas Borba interrupted me with a look of indignation.

In order to take my mind off it he suggested we go out. We went in the direction of Engenho Velho, on foot, philosophizing about things. I'll never forget how beneficial that walk was. The words of that great man were the stimulating brandy of wisdom. He told me that I couldn't run away from the fight. If the oratorical rostrum was closed to me, I should start a newspaper. He came to use less elevated speech, showing that philosophical language can, now and then, fortify itself with the slang of the people. Start a newspaper, he told me, and "bring down that whole stinking mess."

"A great idea! I'm going to start a newspaper. I'm going to shatter them into a thousand pieces. I'm going to . . ."

"Fight. You can shatter them or not, the essential thing is for you to fight. Life is a fight. A life without fight is a dead sea in the center of the universal organism."

A short while later we came upon a dogfight. Sometimes that would be of no consequence in the eyes of an ordinary man. Quincas Borba made me stop and watch the dogs. There were two of them. I notice that there was a bone under their feet, the motive for their war, and I couldn't help having my attention called to the fact that there was no meat on the bone. Just a naked bone. The dogs were biting each other, growling, with fury in their eyes . . . Quincas Borba put his cane under his arm and seemed ecstatic.

"Isn't that beautiful?" he said from time to time.

I wanted to get away from there but I couldn't. He was rooted to the ground and he only started walking again when the fight was completely over and one of the dogs, bitten and defeated, took his hunger off someplace else. I noticed that Quincas had been truly happy, even though he held his happiness in as befits a great philosopher. He made me observe the beauty of the spectacle, recalled the object of contention, concluded that the dogs were hungry. But deprivation of food was nothing for the general effects of philosophy. Nor did he forget to remember that in some parts of the world the spectacle is on a grander scale: human beings are the ones who fight with dogs over bones and other less appetizing tidbits. A fight that becomes quite complicated because entering into action is man's intelligence along with the whole accumulation of sagacity that the centuries have given him, etc.

C X L I I

The Secret Request

So many things in a minuet!, as the saying goes. So many things in a dogfight! But I was no servile or weak-hearted disciple who was not about to make one or another adequate objection. As we walked along I told him that I had some doubts. I wasn't too sure of the advantage of fighting with dogs over a meal. He answered with exceptional softness:

"It's more logical to fight over it with other men, because the status of the contenders is the same and the stronger one gets the bone. But why shouldn't it be a grand spectacle to fight over it with dogs? Locusts are eaten voluntarily, as in the case of the One Who Goes Before or, even worse, that of Ezequiel, therefore, what's awful is edible. It remains to be seen whether or not it's more worthy for a man to fight over it by virtue of a natural necessity or to prefer it in obedience to religious, that is, mutable, exaltation, while hunger is eternal, like life and like death."

We were at the door of my house. I was given a letter, which they said was from a lady. We went in and Quincas Borba, with the discretion proper to a philosopher, went over to read the spines of the books on a shelf while I read the letter, which was from Virgília:

My good friend,

Dona Plácida is very ill. I'm asking you the favor of doing something for her. She's living on the Beco das Escadinhas. Could you see if you can get her admitted to Misericórdia Hospital for the indigent?

Your sincere friend,

It wasn't Virgília's delicate and correct hand, but heavy and uneven. The V of the signature was nothing but a scribble with no alphabetical intent, so that from the looks of the letter it was very hard to attribute its authorship to her. I turned the piece of paper over and over. Poor Dona Plácida! But I'd left her with the five *contos* from the beach at Gamboa, and I couldn't understand why . . .

"You'll understand," Quincas Borba said, taking a book off the shelf.

"What?" I asked, startled.

"You'll understand that I was telling nothing but the truth. Pascal is one of my spiritual grandfathers, and even though my philosophy is worth more than his, I can't deny that he was a great man. Now, what does he say on this page?" And with his hat still on his head, his cane under his arm, he pointed out the place with his finger. "What does he say? He says that man has 'a great advantage over the rest of the universe; he knows that he is going to die, while the universe is completely ignorant of the fact.' Do you see? The man who fights over a bone with a dog, has the great advantage over him of knowing that he's hungry. And that's what makes it a grand fight, as I was saying. 'He knows that he is going to die' is a profound statement, but I think my statement is more profound: He knows that he's hungry. Because the fact of death limits, in a manner of speaking, human understanding. The consciousness of extinction lasts only for a brief instant and ends forever, while hunger has the advantage of coming back, of prolonging the conscious state. It seems to me (at the risk of some immodesty) that Pascal's formula is inferior to mine, without ceasing to be a great thought, however, or Pascal a great man."

C X L I I I

I'm Not Going

W hile he was putting the book back on the shelf I reread the note. At dinner, seeing that I wasn't talking very much, chewing without really swallowing, staring into a corner of the room, or at the edge of the table, or at a plate, or at an invisible fly, he said: "Something's not right with you. I'll bet it was that letter." It was. I felt really bothered, annoyed with Virgília's request. I'd given Dona Plácida five *contos*. I doubt very much that anyone had been more generous than I, or even equally as generous. Five *contos*! And what had she done with them? She'd thrown them away, naturally, squandered them on big parties, and now she's ready for Misericórdia and I'm the one to get her in! You can die anywhere. Furthermore, I didn't know or didn't recall any Beco das Escadinhas. But judging from its name as an alley I imagined it to be some dark and narrow corner of the city. I would have to go there, attract neighbors' attention, knock on the door and all that. What a nuisance! I'm not going.

C X L I V

Relative Usefulness

B ut night, which is a good counselor, reflected that courtesy demanded I obey the wishes of my former lady.

"Bills that fall due have got to be paid," I said on arising.

After breakfast I went to Dona Plácida's place. I found a bundle of bones wrapped in rags lying on an old and revolting cot. I gave her some money. The next day I had her taken to Misericórdia, where she died a week later. I'm lying. She was found dead in the morning. She'd sneaked out of life just the way she'd come into it. I asked myself again, as in Chapter LXXV, if that was why the sexton of the cathedral and the candymaker had brought Dona Plácida into the world at a specific moment of affection. But I realized immediately that if it hadn't been for Dona Plácida my affair with Virgília might have been interrupted or broken off suddenly in its full effervescence. Such, therefore, was the usefulness of Dona Plácida's life. A relative usefulness, I admit, but what the devil is absolute in this world?

CXLV

A Simple Repetition

As for the five *contos*, it's not worth mentioning that a neighborhood stonemason pretended to be in love with Dona Plácida, succeeded in arousing her feeling or her vanity, and married her. At the end of a few months he invented some business deal, cashed in their savings, and fled with the money. It's not worth it. It's a case like Quincas Borba's dogs: a simple repetition of a chapter.

C X L V I

The Prospectus

It was urgent that I found the newspaper. I drew up the prospectus, which was a political application of Humanitism. Except that since Quincas Borba hadn't published his book yet (which he went on perfecting year by year), we agreed not to make any reference to it. Quincas Borba only asked for a signed and confidential declaration that certain principles applied to politics had been drawn from his still-unpublished book.

It was a choice prospectus. It promised a cure for society, an end to abuses, a defense of the sound principles of liberty and conservation. It appealed to commerce and to labor. It quoted Guizot and Ledru-Rollin and ended with this threat, which Quincas Borba found petty and local: "The new doctrine that we profess will inevitably bring down the present government." I must confess that given the political climate of the moment, the prospectus looked like a masterpiece to me. The threat at the end, which Quincas Borba found petty, was shown to him to be saturated with the purest Humanitism, and later on he himself allowed that it was. Since Humanitism excluded nothing, the Napoleonic Wars and a fight between goats, according to our doctrine, possessed the same sublimity, with the difference being that Napoleon's soldiers knew that they were going to die, something that apparently wasn't true with the goats. So I was only applying our philosophical formula to the circumstances: Humanitas wanted to replace Humanitas for the consolation of Humanitas.

"You are my beloved disciple, my caliph!" Quincas Borba roared with a touch of tenderness I hadn't heard in him till then. "I can say like the great Mohammed: Even if the sun and the moon come against me, I will not turn back from my ideas. Believe me, my dear Brás Cubas, this is the eternal truth, before the world and after the ages."

C X L V I I

Madness

I immediately sent a discreet notice to the press saying that within a few weeks an opposition paper edited by Dr. Brás Cubas would begin publication. Quincas Borba, to whom I read the notice, picked up a pen and with true humanistic brotherhood added this phrase after my name: "one of the most glorious members of the previous Chamber of Deputies."

The next day Cotrim stopped by my place. He was a bit upset, but he hid it, affecting calm and even happiness. He'd seen the news of the paper and felt that as a friend and relative he should dissuade me from an idea like that. It was a mistake, a serious mistake. He pointed out how I would be putting myself in a difficult situation and, in a certain way, locking the doors of parliament to me. The government not only seemed excellent to him, which couldn't be my opinion of course, but it would also certainly endure for a long time. So what could I gain by turning it unfavorable to me? He knew that some of the ministers liked me. It wasn't impossible that a vacancy, and . . . I interrupted him at that point to tell him that I had meditated a great deal about the step I was going to take and I wouldn't retreat an inch. I got to the point of suggesting that he read the prospectus, but he refused vehemently, saying that he didn't want to share the tiniest part of my madness.

"It's absolute madness," he repeated. "Think it over for a few days and you'll see that it's madness."

Sabina said the same thing at the theatre that night. She left her daughter in the box with Cotrim and took me out into the corridor.

"Brother Brás, what are you doing?" she asked me with affliction. "What kind of an idea is that, provoking the government for no reason when you could . . ."

I explained to her that it wasn't for me to go about begging for a seat in parliament, that my idea was to bring down the government because I didn't think it was equal to the situation—and a certain philosophical formula. I promised always to use courteous although energetic language. Violence wasn't a spice for my palate. Sabina tapped the tips of her fingers with her fan, lowered her head, and picked up the matter again, alternating between pleas and threats. I told her no, no, no. Disappointed, she threw into my face the idea that I preferred the advice of strange and envious people to hers and her husband's. "So, then, just keep on with what seems best to you," she concluded. "We've done our duty." She turned her back on me and returned to her box.

C X L V I I I

The Unsolvable Problem

I published the newspaper. Twenty-four hours later a declaration by Cotrim appeared in other papers saying in substance that given the fact that he was not a member of either of the parties into which the nation was divided, he found it expedient to make it quite clear that he had no influence on or any direct or indirect part in the journal of his brother-in-law Dr. Brás Cubas, whose ideas and political directions he disapproved of. The present government (like any other composed of equally competent members) seemed to him to be working for the public good.

It was hard for me to believe my eyes. I rubbed them once or twice and reread the inopportune, unusual, and enigmatic declaration. If he had nothing to do with the parties, what was an incident as minor as the publication of a newspaper to him? Not all citizens who find a government good or bad make declarations like that to the press, nor are they obliged to do so. Really, Cotrim's intrusion into that affair was a mystery, no less than his personal attack. Our relations until then had been smooth and pleasant. I couldn't remember any dissension, any shadow, anything, after the reconciliation. On the contrary, the memory was one of genuine good will. As, for example, when I was a deputy I was able to obtain some supply contracts for the naval arsenal for him, contracts that he continued fulfilling with the greatest punctuality and concerning which he spoke to me a few weeks earlier, saying that at the end of three more years they might bring him two hundred *contos*. Well, then, shouldn't the memory of such a large favor be enough to stop him from going public and tarnishing his brother-in-law's reputation? The reasons behind his declaration must have been very powerful in order to make him commit an act of impertinence and an act of ingratitude at the same time. I must confess, it was an unsolvable problem.

CXLIX

The Theory of Benefits

    So unsolvable that Quincas Borba couldn't handle it in spite of having studied it for a long time and quite willingly. "So goodbye, then!" he concluded. "Not every philosophical problem is worth five minutes' attention."

As for the censure of ingratitude, Quincas Borba rejected it out of hand, not as unprobable, but as absurd, because it didn't obey the conclusions of a good humanistic philosophy.

"You can't deny one fact," he said, "which is that the pleasure of the benefactor is always greater than that of the benefactee. What is a benefit? It's an act that brings a certain deprivation of the one benefited to an end. Once the essential effect has been produced, once the deprivation has ceased, that is, the organism returns to its previous state, a state of indifference. Just suppose that the waist of your trousers is too tight. In order to relieve the uncomfortable situation you unbutton the waist, you breathe, you enjoy an instant of pleasure, the organism returns to indifference and you forget about the fingers that performed the operation. If there's nothing that lasts, it's natural that memory should disappear, because it's not an aerial plant, it needs earth. The hope for other favors, of course, always holds the benefactee in a remembrance of the first one, but that fact, also one of the most sublime that philosophy can find in its path, is explained by the memory of deprivation or, using a different formula, by deprivation's continuing on in memory, which echoes the past pain and advises alertness for an opportune remedy. I'm not saying that even without this circumstance it doesn't sometimes happen that the memory of the favor will persist, accompanied by a certain more or less intense affection. But they're true aberrations with no value whatever in the eyes of a philosopher."

"But," I replied, "if there's no reason for the memory of the favor to last in the favored, there must be even less in relation to the favorer. I'd like you to explain that point for me."

"What's obvious by its nature can't be explained," Quincas Borba replied, "but I'll say one thing more. The persistence of the benefit in the memory of the one performing it is explained by the very nature of the benefit and its effects. In the first place, there's the feeling of a good deed and, deductively, the awareness that we're capable of good acts. In the second place, a conviction of superiority over another being is received, a superiority in status and means, and this is one of the most legitimately pleasant things for the human organism according to the best opinions. Erasmus, who wrote some good things in his *In Praise of Folly*, called attention to the complacency with which two donkeys rub against each other. I'm far from rejecting that observation by Erasmus, but I shall say what he didn't say, to wit, that if one of the donkeys rubbed better than the other, he would have some special indication of satisfaction in his eyes. Why is it that a pretty woman looks into a mirror so much if not because she finds herself pretty and, therefore, it gives her a certain superiority over a multitude of women less pretty or absolutely ugly? Conscience is just the same. It looks at itself quite often when it finds itself pretty. Nor is remorse anything else but the twitch of a conscience that sees itself repugnant. Don't forget that since everything is a simple irradiation of Humanitas, a benefit and its effects are perfectly admirable phenomena.

C L

Rotation and Translation

E very enterprise, attachment, or age contains a complete cycle of human life. The first number of my paper filled my soul with a vast awakening, crowned me with garlands, restored the quickness of youth to me. Six months later the hour of old age struck, and two weeks later that of death, which was in secret, like Dona Plácida's. On the day the paper was found dead in the morning, I sighed deeply, like a man who'd come back from a long journey. So if I were to say that human life feeds other more or less ephemeral lives, the way a body feeds its parasites, I don't think I would be saying something completely absurd. But in order not to risk a less neat and adequate image like that, I prefer an astronomical one: man executes, to the turn of the wheel of the great mystery, a double movement of rotation and translation. Its days are unequal, like those of Jupiter, and they comprise its more or less long year.

At the moment I was finishing my movement of rotation, Lobo Neves was concluding his movement of translation. He died with his foot on the ministerial step. It had been rumored for several weeks that he was going to be a minister. And since the rumor filled me with a great deal of irritation and envy, it's not impossible that the news of his death left me with a touch of tranquility, relief, and one or two minutes of pleasure. Pleasure may be an exaggeration, but it was true. I swear to the ages that it was absolutely true.

I attended the funeral. At the mortuary I found Virgília by the casket, sobbing. When she lifted her head I saw that she was really weeping. Before leaving the funeral she embraced the coffin with affliction. They came to pull her off and take her away. I tell you, the tears were genuine. I went to the cemetery and, to say it outright, I didn't feel much like speaking. A stone was stuck in my throat or in my conscience. At the cemetery, most of all when I dropped the spadeful of lime onto the coffin at the bottom of the grave, the dull thud of the lime gave me a shudder, a fleeting one, it's true, but unpleasant. And afterwards the afternoon had the weight and color of lead. The cemetery, the black clothing . . .

C L I

The Philosophy of Epitaphs

I left, keeping away from the groups of people and pretending to read the epitaphs. Besides, I like epitaphs. Among civilized people they're an expression of that pious and secret selfishness that induces us to pull out of death a shred at least of the shade that has passed on. That may be the origin of the inconsolable sadness of those who know their dead are in potter's field. They feel the anonymous rotting reaching themselves.

C L I I

Vespasian's Coin

They'd all gone. Only my carriage was waiting for its owner. I lighted a cigar. I left the cemetery behind. I couldn't shake the burial ceremony from my eyes or Virgília's sobs from my ears. The sobs, most of all, had the vague and mysterious sound of a problem. Virgília had betrayed her husband, sincerely, and now she was weeping for him, sincerely. There you have a difficult combination whose trajectory I was unable to follow completely. At home, however, getting out of the carriage, I suspected that the combination was possible and even easy. Gentle Nature! The tax of grief is like Vespasian's coin: it doesn't smell of its origins and can be collected just as well from evil as from good. Morality might condemn my accomplice. That's of no account, implacable friend, once you have punctually received the tears. Gentle, thrice gentle Nature!

C L I I I

The Alienist

I was beginning to get dotty and I preferred sleeping. I slept, I dreamed I was a nabob and I woke up with the idea of being a nabob. I sometimes liked to imagine those contrasts of region, status, and belief. A few days earlier I'd thought about the hypothesis of a social, religious, and political revolution that would transform the Archbishop of Cantuária into a simple tax collector in Petrópolis, and I made long calculations to find out if the tax collector would eliminate the archbishop or if the archbishop would reject the tax collector or what portion of an archbishop could remain in a tax collector or what amount of a tax collector could combine with an archbishop, and so forth. Insoluble questions, apparently, but in reality perfectly soluble if one considers that there can be two archbishops in one archbishop—the one from the bull and the other one. It's all set, I'm going to be a nabob.

It was nothing but drollery. I mentioned it to Quincas Borba, however, who looked at me with a certain caution and sorrow, being so good as to inform me that I was crazy. I laughed at first, but the noble conviction of the philosopher instilled a certain fear in me. The only objection to Quincas Borba's word was that I didn't feel crazy, but since crazy people generally have no other concept of themselves, such an objection was worthless. And see now if there isn't some basis to the popular belief that philosophers are men who are far removed from petty things. The next day Quincas Borba sent an alienist to see me. I knew him, I was aghast. He, however, behaved with the greatest delicacy and poise, taking his leave so merrily that it encouraged me to ask him if he really thought I was crazy.

"No," he said. "There are few men so much in command of their faculties as you."

"So Quincas Borba was mistaken?"

"Completely." And then, "On the contrary, if you're his friend . . . I ask you to distract him . . . because . . ."

"Good heavens! Do you think . . .? A man of such spirit, a philosopher!"

"That makes no difference. Madness can enter any house."

You can imagine my affliction. The alienist, seeing the effect of his words, realized that I was a friend of Quincas Borba and tried to lessen the gravity of the warning. He observed that it might not be anything and added even that a grain of folly, far from doing harm, gives a certain spice to life. Since I rejected that opinion with horror, the alienist smiled and told me something extraordinary, so extraordinary that the least it deserves is a chapter of its own.

C L I V

The Ships of The Piraeus

"You no doubt recall," the alienist told me, "that famous Athenian maniac who imagined that all ships entering the Piraeus were his property. He was nothing but a poor wretch who probably didn't even have a tub to sleep in as Diogenes had, but the imaginary ownership of the vessels was worth all the drachmas in Hellas. Well, we all have an Athenian madman in us. And anyone who swears that he didn't possess at least two or three schooners mentally, has to know that he swears falsely."

"Including you?" I asked.

"Including me."

"Including me?"

"Including you. And your servant as well, if that man shaking rugs out the window is your servant."

As a matter of fact it was one of my servants who was beating rugs while we spoke in the garden alongside. The alienist then noted that he'd opened all the windows wide and kept them that way, had raised the curtains, had revealed the richly furnished room as much as possible so it could be seen from outside, and he concluded, "That servant of yours has the Athenian's mania. He thinks that the ships are his. One hour of illusion that gives him the greatest happiness on Earth."

C L V

A Cordial Reflection

I f the alienist is right, I said to myself, there isn't much to pity in
Quincas Borba. It's a question of degree. Still, it's only proper to
keep an eye on him and prevent manias of other origins from entering
his brain.

C L V I

The Pride of Servanthood

Q uincas Borba differed with the alienist regarding my servant. "It's
possible as an image," he said, "to attribute the Athenian's mania
to your servant, but images are not ideas or observations taken from nature. What your servant has is a feeling that's noble and perfectly in line
with the laws of Humanitism: it's the pride of servanthood. His intention is to show that he isn't *just anybody's* servant." Then he called my attention to the coachmen in great houses, more haughty than their
masters, to hotel servants, whose solicitude depends upon the social
variations of the guest, etc. And he concluded that all of it was an expression of that delicate and noble sentiment—full proof that so many
times man, even when shining shoes, is sublime.

C L V I I

A Brilliant Phase

"You're the sublime one," I shouted, throwing my arms around his neck. Indeed, it was impossible to believe that such a profound man could have reached dementia. That was what I told him after my embrace, revealing the alienist's suspicions to him. I can't describe the impression that the revelation made on him. I remember that he trembled and turned pale.

It was around that time that I became reconciled once again with Cotrim, without getting to know the cause of our falling-out. An opportune reconciliation, because solitude was weighing on me and life for me was the worst kind of weariness, which is weariness without working. A short time later I was invited by him to join a Third Order, which I didn't do without first consulting Quincas Borba.

"Go ahead if you want," he told me, "but temporarily. I'm trying to attach a dogmatic and liturgical part to my philosophy. Humanitism must also be a religion, the one of the future, the only true one. Christianity is good for women and beggars, and the other religions aren't worth much more. They're all equal with the same vulgarity or weakness. The Christian paradise is a worthy emulation of the Muslim one. And as for Buddha's Nirvana, it's nothing more than a concept for paralytics. You'll see what the humanistic religion is. The final absorption, the *contractive* phase, is the reconstitution of substance, not is annihilation, etc. Go where you are called, but don't forget that you're my caliph."

And now have a peek at my modesty. I joined the Third Order of * * * and filled a few positions in it. That was the most brilliant phase of my life. Nevertheless, I shall be silent, I shan't say anything, I won't talk about my service, what I did for the poor and the infirm, or the recompense I received, nothing, I shall say absolutely nothing.

Perhaps the social economy could profit somewhat if I were to show how each and every outside reward is worth little alongside the subjective and immediate reward. But that would be breaking the silence I've sworn to maintain at this point. Besides, the phenomena of conscience are difficult to analyze. On the other hand, if I told one thing I would have to tell every one that's connected to it and I'd end up writing a chapter on psychology. I shall only state that it was the most brilliant phase of my life. The pictures in it were sad. They had the monotony of misfortune, which is as boring as that of pleasure, perhaps worse. But the joy given to the souls of the sick and the poor is a recompense of some value. And don't tell me that it's negative because the only one receiving it is the one taken care of. No. I received it in a reflexive way, and even then it was great, so great that it gave me an excellent idea of myself.

C L V I I I

Two Encounters

After a few years, three or four, I'd had enough of the service and I left it, not without a substantial donation, which gave me the right to have my portrait hung in the sacristy. I won't finish this chapter, however, without mentioning that in the hospital of the Order I witnessed the death of—guess who . . .?—the beautiful Marcela. And I watched her die on the same day that, while visiting a slum to distribute alms, I found . . . you're incapable of guessing now . . . I found the flower of the shrubbery, Eugênia, the daughter of Dona Eusébia and Vilaça, as lame as I'd left her and sadder still.

When she recognized me she turned pale and lowered her eyes. But it was only a matter of an instant. She immediately raised her head and looked straight at me with dignity. I understood that she wouldn't accept alms from my pocket and I held out my hand to her as I would have to the wife of a capitalist. She greeted me and shut herself up in her tiny room. I never saw her again. I learned nothing about her life or whether her mother was dead or what disaster had brought her to such poverty. I know that she was lame and sad. It was with that profound impression that I reached the hospital where Marcela had been admitted the day before and where I saw her expire a half hour later, ugly, thin, decrepit . . .

C L I X

Semidementia

I understood that I was old and needed some strength. But Quincas Borba had left for Minas Gerais six months earlier and he'd taken the best of philosophies with him. He returned four months later and came into my house one certain morning almost in the state in which I'd seen him in the Passeio Público. The difference was that his gaze was different. He was demented. He told me that in order to perfect Humanitism he'd burned the whole manuscript and was going to start all over again. The dogmatic part was finished, although not written down. It was the true religion of the future.

"Do you swear by Humanitas?" he asked me.

"You know I do."

My voice could barely come out of my chest and, besides, I hadn't discovered the whole cruel truth. Quincas Borba was not only mad, but he knew that he was mad, and that remnant of awareness, like a dim lamp in the midst of the shadows, greatly complicated the horror of the situation. He knew it and wasn't bothered by the illness. On the contrary, he told me, it was one more proof of Humanitas, which in that way was playing with itself. He recited long chapters of the book to me, and antiphonies, and spiritual litanies. He even got to go through a sacred dance he'd invented for the rites of Humanitism. The lugubrious grace with which he lifted up and shook his legs was singularly fantastic. At other times he would sulk in a corner with his eyes staring into space, eyes in which, at long intervals, a persistent ray of reason would gleam, as sad as a tear . . .

He died a short time later, in my house, swearing and repeating always that pain was an illusion and that Pangloss, the calumnied Pangloss, was not as dotty as Voltaire supposed.

C L X

On Negatives

Between Quincas Borba's death and mine the events narrated in the first part of the book took place. The principal one was the invention of the *Brás Cubas Poultice*, which died with me because of the illness I'd contracted. Divine poultice, you would have given me first place among men above science and wealth because you were the genuine and direct inspiration of heaven. Fate determined the contrary. And so, all of you must remain eternally hypochondriac.

This last chapter is all about negatives. I didn't attain the fame of the poultice, I wasn't a minister, I wasn't a caliph, I didn't get to know marriage. The truth is that alongside these lacks the good fortune of not having to earn my bread by the sweat of my brow did befall me. Furthermore, I didn't suffer the death of Dona Plácida or the semidementia of Quincas Borba. Putting one and another thing together, any person will probably imagine that there was neither a lack nor a surfeit and, consequently, that I went off squared with life. And he imagines wrong. Because on arriving at this other side of the mystery I found myself with a small balance, which is the final negative in this chapter of negatives—I had no children, I haven't transmitted the legacy of our misery to any creature.

Afterword

COSMOPOLITAN STRATEGIES IN
THE POSTHUMOUS MEMOIRS OF BRÁS CUBAS

A Strange Book

The Posthumous Memoirs of Brás Cubas thwarts the reader's expectations in more than just its disenchanted narrator's sarcastic tone. Within the corpus of nineteenth-century Brazilian letters it is something of an anomaly: for instance, it challenges the accepted modes of representation, best exemplified by Zola. And like the work of Sterne, it takes stylistic liberties, both typographically (LV, CXXXX) and through its oblique plot and frequent digressions. Over time, however, the interest in this curious amalgam has only grown more keen.

Brazilian history from the days of João VI's arrival in 1808 to the end of the Second Empire in 1889—the fall of Napoleon, the Regency, the winning of independence, slavery, and political life—makes discreet incursions into this text permeated by European literary and historical references and quotes. Thus we approach the fictional realm dominated by Brás Cubas, a wealthy, indolent bachelor who enjoys his good fortune in the agrarian slave-based economy of nineteenth-century Brazil. He hobnobs with the epoch's elite in a cultural milieu given to the pleasures of reading and traveling.

The stage is set for a novel of a very special character, one in which a peculiar dialogue with European literature is continually taking place. The reader is as likely to bump up against Buffon as Shakespeare or

Voltaire. Our deceased narrator leads the reader on a fascinating journey through a diverse realm where fiction is overlaid by fiction.

Many of Machado de Assis' French contemporaries set their unique stamp on the momentous developments of their century, pondering in their major works the seminal historical events they observed as partisans in the play of shifting ideologies. There was Chateaubriand with his *Mémoires d'outre-tombe*, Napoleon dictating *Mémorial de Sainte-Hélène* to Las Cases. Stendhal, Musset, Vigny, and Alexander Dumas, as well, left records of their impressions of the great evens in which they took part.

But our narrator, unlike his French confreres, is not interested in projecting himself onto the broad canvas of history but in recording the significant moments of a far from exemplary life, often exposing the least savory aspects of an existence he doesn't seek to embellish.

> No, sensitive soul, I'm not a cynic, I was a man. My brain was a stage on which plays of all kinds were presented, sacred dramas, austere, scrupulous, elegant comedies, wild farces, short skis, buffoonery, pandemonium, sensitive soul, a hodgepodge of things and people in which you could see everything, from the rose of Smyrna to the rue in your own backyard. (Ch. XXXIV)

An Urban Narrator

By leaving the glamorous movers and shakers of history aside, the reader can narrowly focus his gaze on characters of apparently insignificant stature. Thus we can appreciate the gossiping Dona Plácida, Eugênia, the disfigured girl of humble origins, and Prudêncio, the former slave who in turn becomes the master of another.

Nevertheless we shouldn't place undue emphasis on the narrator's predisposition toward detailed description. Despite precise references to public parks or charitable organizations, these details don't add up to the usual chronicle and are not meant to be read as picturesque or exotic elaborations on the city of Rio de Janeiro.

> I won't deny that when I caught sight of my native city I had a new sensation. It was not the effect of my political homeland, it was that of the place of my childhood, the street, the tower, the fountain on the corner, the woman in a shawl, the black street sweeper, the things and scenes of boyhood engraved in my memory. (Ch. XXIII)

The thoroughly urban landscape allows us to immerse ourselves in a few decades of a city's life which only gradually became modern, retaining nuances of the Portuguese colonial and baroque styles of architecture, but, thanks to the French Mission contracted by João VI in 1816, mixing in some neoclassicism. Rio de Janeiro struggled incessantly both against the tropical climate and plagues (the yellow fever in Ch. CXXVI) and hosted a considerable number of foreign residents—the typographer Plancher, and the hotelier Pharoux. It was the capital of a country clamoring for independence (Ch. XIV) yet constrained by its basically agrarian, slave-based, export economy.

Rio de Janeiro, the political and cultural center of nineteenth-century Brazil, offered a variety of entertainments that set it apart from the rest of the country: theatres, newspapers, bookstores, confectionary shops, jewelry stores, high fashion. The elegant Ouvidor street, where the fashionable met, with its showpiece. The capital city sought its models in England and, more than anywhere else, in France.

> . . . Old people from my time, perhaps you remember that master chef at the Hotel Pharoux, a fellow who, according to what the owner of the place said, had served in the famous Véry and Véfour in Paris and later on in the palaces of the Count Molé and the Duke de la Rochefoucauld. He was famous. (Ch. CXV)

Cosmopolitan Rio de Janeiro did not need just a chronicler, but rather a keen observer attuned to a panorama of changing relationships between people and the new foreign influences. Its variegated face demanded an ever-evolving psychological complexity. Before turning to Brás Cubas' cosmopolitan strategies, however, it is worth considering his shrewdness as a narrator, his peculiar and particular point of view, and his skepticism toward all ideals and certainties, especially those favored in the nineteenth century.

The Shrewdness of Brás Cubas

> Cats may be less sly and magnolias are certainly less restless than I was in my childhood. (Ch. XI)

The narrative displays a certain anxiety here and there, a fitful questioning of itself beyond the scope of its modus operandi. The narrator himself realizes that he is implicated. Restricted by formal commitments to tradition, he nevertheless thrusts his own amusing critique of those traditions and literary conventions into the text itself.

What is there between life and death? A short bridge. Nevertheless, if I hadn't put this chapter together the reader would have suffered a strong shock, quite harmful to the effect of the book. Jumping from a portrait to an epitaph can be a real and common act. The reader, however, is only taking refuge in the book to escape life. I'm not saying the thought is mine. I'm saying that there's a grain of truth in it and the form, at least, is picturesque. And, I repeat, it's not mine. (Ch. CXXIV)

The reader would be wise not to yield completely to the narrative vagaries—after all he actively participates in them—and must always keep in mind the narrator's special circumstances. Brás Cubas, the posthumous narrator, is more audacious about telling the truth than are the living, an advantage he used to reveal not only secrets but follies, treachery, rivalries, and deceptions, all quite jarring in terms of the era's expectations of the memoir.

Neither should we expect that the story be told in a linear fashion or be altogether faithful to common experience. Brás Cubas meanders through his narrative collage, a shrewd narrator intent on throwing the reader off the scent, offering explanations in one chapter only to qualify them in the next in a continual process of affirmation and equivocation. This technique tends to go against the grain of verities established in the eighteenth century concerning narrative development. And by constantly throwing the reader off the track with equivocation, humorous digressions, the questioning of fictional convention, and assertions and denials, the narrator weaves a symbolic web that does not hide its allegiance to a particular class perspective.

Some insight into class helps us understand the significance of citing Stendhal:

That Stendhal should have confessed to have written one of his books for a hundred readers is something that brings on wonder and concern. Something that will not cause wonder and probably no concern is whether this other book will have Stendhal's hundred readers, or fifty, or twenty, or even ten. (To the Reader)

Here Brás Cubas is referring to the preface of the second edition of *De L'Amour* in which Stendhal discusses the concept of the "happy few." The winds of 1789 swept away the old system of arts patronage. What remained was an avid reading and theatre-going public, eager, above all, to be entertained. The book had become a piece of merchandise, something merely to sell and to consume. Now the question was how to seduce the typical reader armed with "common sense" and a bulging pocket book. This hypothetical figure terrorized and obsessed the man of letters represented by Stendhal, and takes on unique dimensions in the musings of Brás Cubas who doesn't hesitate to prove his superior discernment by using a Stendhalian formulation.

Points of View

Brás Cubas writes from the point of view of one doubly exempt from the mundane. For one thing our narrator is a rich, idle Brazilian for whom tedious labor and the bitter flavor of poverty and financial preoccupation are not important considerations. The narrator's relationship with Quincas Borba is exemplary in this regard. As a classmate (in a double sense), Borba becomes an object of worship among his peers for always affecting a regal air. Later the beggary to which he is reduced makes our narrator sick. But even after Borba robs him (snatching his watch), Borba regains his extraordinary stature when he is restored to his accustomed place by an inheritance. The narrator's attitude toward Dona Plácida's birth resembles his stance toward Eugênia's dignity. Brás Cubas belongs to a social stratum to which individual expression must always be subordinated.

The narrator's point of view is also shaped by death. It is within this realm that the author is born, now definitively free from the responsibilities of the living. Death offers him the indolence of eternity. Everything is past, already lived, frozen for the narrator's use in a kind of crude bas-relief that displays a particular social milieu with its characteristic constraints and obligations.

> The gaze of public opinion, that sharp and judgmental gaze, loses its virtue the moment we tread the territory of death. I'm not saying that it doesn't reach here and examine and judge us, but we don't care about the examination or the judgment. My dear living gentlemen and ladies, there's nothing as incommensurable as the disdain of the deceased. (Ch. XXIV)

The text, however, does not function as an apologia for the Brazilian upper classes of the nineteenth century. The reader does not end up identifying with the narrator or defending his point of view, thus subverting the era's understanding of the memoir. There is surely a subtly ironic thwarting of the reader's expectations as well in the treatment of the social misfits of the book: Brás Cubas, Cotrim, and Quincas Borba.

The Meaning of Delirium

In the delirium chapter the lack of a coherent ethical structure sets the stage for a discourse on the futility of all human action, a discourse that perfectly coincides with the vision of the dominant classes in Brazil in the nineteenth century. But it goes further than a narrow discussion of class and proffers a discourse with a metaphysical twist—set forth slyly by the narrator as a delirium which compromises his credibility and leaves the reader wondering how much to believe.

> I must confess now, however, that I felt some sort of prick of curiosity to find out where the origin of the centuries was, if it was as mysterious as the origin of the Nile, and most of all, whether the consummation of those same centuries was really worth anything: the reflections of a sick mind. (Ch. VII)

This "sick mind" will produce an image whose name is not Jehovah or God, rather Nature or Pandora, a mix of Mother (because it engenders) and Nemesis (because it causes suffering and metes out death). There are no underlying moral principles implied in the action of this being which engenders life; nor are there moral guidelines for those beings thrust out into the vortex of history without the possibility of redemption or final knowledge.

> You great lascivious man, the voluptuosity of nothingness awaits you. (Ch. VII)

Protected by the knowledge conveyed to him by Nature/Pandora and by death, Brás Cubas realizes that his century, along with the history of humanity with its ideologies, institutions, and images, is an illusion. Such reasoning makes the final words of the book comprehensible: because he is without offspring the narrator at least can state that he wills the legacy of miserable human history to nobody.

Why narrate, then? The narrative justifies itself as a summing up of personal experience despite the superimposed dimension of class. In each individual, whether rich or poor, the gifts offered by nature resonate: knowledge, life, the will to live, and that scourge of the species— hope—surely one of the foundations of any belief.

The perspective under discussion is a radical one, deceptive and systematically elusive. But within narrated material everything is justified: the ideals of loyalty to country, God, ethnicity, progress, and the other givens of the nineteenth-century worldview, along with all the mistaken

and contradictory viewpoints that make the following surprising comparison possible:

> Moses, who also wrote about his death, didn't place it at the opening but at
> the close: a radical difference between this book and the Pentateuch. (Ch. I)

Illuminated by Nature's aura, divested of its original mythic significance,
the figure of Moses is transformed into just another element buffeted
about within the vortex of time. The Bible becomes a text like any
other, subordinate to the narrator's whim.

Through this metamorphosis Brás Cubas becomes St. Thomas
Aquinas' *Summa Theologica* itself. Ironically the two discourses, one on
the verities of faith and the other on the verities of philosophy, blend,
with the *Summa* representing just one more monument to the written
word, a stage in the inexorable journey toward annihilation and the loss
of one's precious identity (name, rank, social milieu). The *Summa* is an
achievement only outdone by Nature, which seeks not to individuate,
but to erase distinctions, and to whom the goings on of a Chinese barber and the writings of a church father are equivalent.

Nevertheless, one has to live to enjoy the brief time which Nature con-
cedes to us. And preferably one should live in Rio de Janeiro in the middle of the nineteenth century looking for ways to satisfy one's condition as
a lazy man of means lacking in neither cultivated social discourse nor the
consolation of literature. So let us return to Brás Cubas' cosmopolitanism.

Oceanic Culture

Broadly speaking a dependence on foreign culture nourishes the social
imagination of Rio's reigning elite, to which Brás Cubas is inextricably
linked. The mix of European and tropical culture is evident in the conversation of a recent arrival at the capital:

> He liked the theatre very much. As soon as he arrived he went to the São
> Pedro Theatre where he saw a superb drama, *Maria Joana*, and a very in-
> teresting comedy, *Kettly, or the Return to Switzerland*. He'd also enjoyed
> Deperini very much in *Sappho* or *Anna Boleyn*, he couldn't remember
> which. But Candiani! Yes, sir, she was top-drawer. Now he wanted to
> hear Ernani, which his daughter sang at home to the piano: Ernani, Er-
> nani, involami . . . (Ch. XCII)

To establish his role in the reigning social and literary milieu, Brás
Cubas resorts to a series of dialogues with writers emblematic of the

Western tradition, writers whose works he has thoroughly enjoyed, including Homer, Dante, Molière, and Klopstock. Sometimes the dialogue is mediated through translated or untranslated direct quotes. In other cases the dialogue takes its cue from the quote in a more obvious intertextual relationship.

The blatant borrowings result in a poetics of the novel based upon a rendering of text that is at once immediate and complex. For the full resonance of the verbal play to be realized, the reader must actively engage in a dialogue with the "other." This tactic is essential in establishing the textual parameters within which the meaning of the work is inscribed. The questions of love, power, social relations, and existence are set forth in terms of this narrative symbiosis.

The initial reference to the complex figure of Hamlet is a case in point. Through the insertion of an untranslated quote from English literature the reader is forced to fathom the text through the mediation of Shakespeare.

> That was how I set out for Hamlet's undiscovered country without the anxieties or doubts of the young prince, but, rather slow and lumbering, like someone leaving the spectacle late. Late and bored. (Ch. I)

In the play the character's anxious relationship to death is related to the implacability of the unknown. There is no return possible for he who voyages to the "undiscovered country." In the text under discussion, Brás Cubas plays a different hand. He has already passed over the threshold. He is speaking to us from beyond the grave and is flush with the certainties this state bestows upon him. On the other hand he has neither the pathos nor the princely demeanor of Hamlet. Nor is he young. Rather he is an old rue sated by life and at this point rather indifferent to it.

The differences notwithstanding, it's important to note how the theatrical mode seeps into the text. For instance, through the word *spectacle*, signifying both representation and theatrical show. Then the narrator abandons himself to a delirium in which all of humanity's trials and tribulations are reduced to an amusing if rather monotonous and repetitive entertainment.

The term *spectacle* is apt not only because the theatre is one of the obsessions of our deceased author, but because he is acutely attuned to the levels of dissimulation necessary to thrive in the bourgeois and aristocratic salons of Imperial Brazil.

My brain was a stage on which plays of all kinds were presented: sacred dramas, austere, scrupulous, elegant comedies, wild farces, short skits, buffoonery, pandemonium, sensitive soul. (Ch. XXXIV)

Thus the novel allows for constant theatrical references: Estela Seze-freda, Candiani, *Prometheus Unbound, Norma, Othello, El Cid.* Tartuffe and Figaro also make appearances, characters who skillfully use sub-terfuge to gain financial advantage.

The Influence of France

Let us turn now to the influence exerted by the French. Not only the primacy of its literature, but the vitality of its political and cultural life left an indelible imprint on Brazilian culture. France's artistic renown and intellectual preeminence were firmly established by the seven-teenth century. With the death of Louis XIV, Paris—a burgeoning metropolis with cafes, theatres, and salons where literary reputations could be made or broken—usurped the role the court had once played as cultural arbiter and exerted enormous influence over all European elites. For a picture of France's artistic scope one need only consider the century's literary giants—Corneille, Racine, Boileau, Molière, Bossuet, and La Fontaine (and, later, the Académie Française). The French Revolution fanned the flames of this influence even as it caused a shift in political allegiances. And the ideas forged and tempered in France found a responsive echo in the clamor of liberty spreading throughout the Americas.

Already in the eighteenth century Brazil was turning away from Por-tugal, the European country to which it had the clearest ties. Eschew-ing that cultural and political environment with its waning vitality, Brazil sought its models in a more progressive Europe, assimilating its ideas, debates, and issues. This cross-pollination occurred via Brazilian students educated abroad and through the mediation of Portuguese elites themselves sent to Brazil as colonial administrators or who ac-companied the royal family when it hurriedly moved to Brazil in 1808. In addition, a significant number of French nationals took up residence in Brazil after the fall of Napoleon. As booksellers and entrepreneurs they became the intermediaries between the two cultures.

The principal players were Victor Hugo, Musset, Lamartine, the Du-mas brothers, Zola, and the philosophers Victor Cousin and Auguste

Comte. Paris remained an object of fascination for the Brazilian upper crust. At that time the royal family had many ties with France: Princess Isabel, heir to the throne, was married to the Count D'Eu. The emperor Pedro II exchanged letters with French intellectuals including Gobineau, the exambassador to Brazil, and Victor Hugo himself whom the emperor visited in Paris. Furthermore, since Brazil had never had a colonial relationship with France, there was no vestigial rancor to contend with or unresolved sovereignty issues. A gauge of France's influence on South American cultural and political life in the mid-1800s is expressed by the poet Junqueira Freire:

> After the glorious epoch of our political emancipation, many geniuses emerged, but even today we can not claim complete literary emancipation. Until such a time, we are forced to follow some guiding principle and let that principle be France. For she is the lighthouse which illuminates the entire civilized world. (*Elementos de rhetorica nacional*)

As we have seen, the narrator's domain has been shaped by French elements. In the same way that Brás Cubas has preserved for posterity realities which are typically local—the sweets of the Mothers of Charity, the festivals of independence—he characterizes for us, both as witness and active agent, the elements of Brazil's cultural miscegenation. Let's examine some of the traces this France left in Brazil, without losing sight of the fact that the new fictional parameters demanded that foreign influences be incorporated in original ways.

Love and Illusion

A French quote will offer a window onto the amorous world of Brás Cubas, a world in which tragic emotions have no place. The recurrent underplaying of the theme of love confirms only the cold, static realization that it is impossible to give oneself fully to feeling.

In Chapter VI a vision of Virgília, Brás Cubas' great love, appears to him when he is at death's door. The title of the chapter, a French quote from Corneille's *Le Cid* (*Chimène, qui l'eût dit? Rodrigue, qui l'eût cru?*) is inverted to read "*Rodrigue, qui l'eût cru? Chimène, qui l'eût dit?*"

The significance of the inversion is not readily apparent. After all we're at the beginning of the book and not yet privy to the full details of this passion. What we know is that there is a woman at the funeral who appears to be mourning more intensely than Brás Cubas' own relatives. In the French play Chimène's father strikes Rodrigue's old father, who, unable to parry the attack from the younger man, asks his son for revenge. The son does his father's bidding despite his love for Chimène, obligating her in turn to revenge her own father's death despite her enduring passion for the young man. The quoted verses constitute one of the high points of the play: it is at this juncture with the alexandrine that love and fate are synthesized.

The deceptively vague inverted reference to Corneille is in truth an alteration that has profound bearing on the text. The die have been recast: there are significant shifts in meaning and tone between Corneille's play and Brás Cubas' memoir. Let us see why:

El Cid

He goes to her house
Two noble lovers
The summit of young passion
He kills her father

Honor animates and obsesses her
She wants to kill him, then die herself

Extreme tension in the dialogue
The dialogue turns towards the future

Posthumous Memoirs

She goes to his house
Two bourgeois ex-lovers
Twenty years later, already old
She was the involuntary cause of Brás
Cubas' father's death
Honor doesn't affect them
He is about to die of pneumonia
The dialogue is good-natured
Importance of the past because there is
no future for either one of them

From a pair of Western tradition's most passionate lovers is fashioned this pragmatic duo: Brás Cubas and Virgília. Average through and through, bourgeois, sated, and weary. Corneille has been appropriated and subverted and as parody becomes part of a Brazilian text of the latter half of the nineteenth century.

Love and Ruins

Literary culture helps to shape Virgília as well. Metaphors straight out of French literature define her character. In the beginning the narrator hedges:

> Some nine or ten people had seen me leave, among them three ladies: my sister Sabina, married to Cotrim—their daughter, a lily of the valley . . . Be patient! In just a little while I'll tell you who the third lady was. (Ch. I)

Still without a name, Virgília is soon beholden to French letters, for in his capacity as one beyond the pale of the living, the narrator allows himself a flight of fancy which invokes Chateaubriand:

> And her imagination, like the storks that an illustrious traveler watched taking flight from the Ilissus on their way to African shores without the hindrance of ruins and times—that lady's imagination also flew over the present rubble to the shores of a youthful Africa. (Ch. I)

The reader has no choice but to follow the narrator's circuitous paths with skepticism; at every turn allusions abound as to his aesthetic preoccupations. In Chapter V, for instance, the metaphor distilled straight from Chateaubriand again illuminates the character of Virgília.

> With that reflection I took leave of the woman, I won't say the most discreet, but certainly the most beautiful among her contemporaries, the one whose imagination, like the storks on the Ilissus. (Ch. V)

In addition to the sympathetic rendering of Virgília's beauty and her grief over the death of Brás Cubas, it should also be noted that there are constant references to the passage of time. Essentially time is the leitmotif of the work, from the disenchanted perspective of a narrator, who, from "the other side of the mystery" chronicles the ineluctable deterioration of people, monuments, and institutions. Thus the first mention of Virgília's beauty is nullified by the comment Brás Cubas makes about her apparent decrepitude: "She was fifty-four then, she was a ruin, a splendid ruin . . ." (Ch. V).

Chateaubriand's test (found in the Grecian voyage section in *Itinéraire de Paris à Jérusalem*) also refers to the disenchanted contemplation of ruins. After having visited the Athenian temples, testimony to humanity's past, the French writer entwines observations on culture, transitory and mutable, and nature, permanent and immutable, represented by the eternally youthful storks. The French text prepares the way for a return to the past, a search for youth. Virgília is imagined young, as Brás Cubas remembers her. Yet her youthful beauty is invoked precisely to underscore the "splendid ruin" she, as well as Brás Cubas, has become.

In the context of Chateaubriand's protagonists/ruins, the opening quote from Corneille gains in meaning. It serves simultaneously to minimize and discount conflict and to emphasize—through textural differences such as Brás Cubas' inversion of the quotes—the profound change wrought by the passage of time.

The Poetics of the Legacy

From his privileged position—both materially speaking and literally from beyond the grave—Brás Cubas ironically relates the struggle of a number of characters vying for inheritances, donations, and handouts. This occurs with Sabina, Quincas Borba, Dona Plácida, Dona Eusébia, and even the orator at the cemetery. Additionally, there is Virgília's desire to inherit from Viegas, and the fact that the narrator's own family "begins" with the fortune inherited by Luís Cubas.

Brás Cubas' father wanted to "inherit" from the founder of the city of Santos the prestige associated with the name of the town. Thus the theme of what is handed down from one to another is played out again and again.

But the act of writing involves first and foremost memory, not only of existence itself, but of books and authors. To remember one's lifetime is also to remember what one has read—the legacy of literature— goods that represent a major part of social commerce. There are essentially two types of transmission represented in *The Posthumous Memoirs of Brás Cubas*: texts and material goods. This is what makes up the poetics of the legacy, the integration of the socioeconomic sphere (which affords the characters sufficient leisure to cultivate the arts) and the cultural legacy that devolves from this leisure and which borrows liberally from foreign sources. In this manner plot and bill of lading are integrated into a harmonious whole.

Memory transforms and creates unconscious links as does the narrative. Through the alteration, inversion, and symbolic redeployment of foreign texts, the narrator constantly mediates between the raw material of existence and his writing. Filtered through the utterances of the "other," the legacy and its several modes of remembering is a highly indirect and circuitous route toward the narrative. Plot may be dislocated, but everything is eventually redeemed by the act of writing, the moment when memory transforms itself into text.

The legacy is one of the narrative tricks to distance the reader from the text. Throughout the book we are observed by a narrator who sends us veiled messages by way of this or that quote. The last trick comes at the end: "I haven't transmitted the legacy of our misery to any living creature." In reality, however, the legacy expands beyond its mimetic limits to become a tribute paid to posterity: a novel.

The deceased narrator's use of foreign texts is fascinating. It allows him to deploy his formidable arsenal of erudition and provides a contrast to the humdrum life described in the text. This juxtaposition is crucial because it unveils the relativism of the narrator. It establishes the framework for the play of ambiguity and contradiction and emphasizes the discrepancy between the minutiae of life and the great ideas and ideals embodied in some texts which he also questions with his humor.

The narrator's own relationship to literature undergoes the same process: after an existence animated by literature and his subsequent transformation of reminiscence into a posthumous literary production, he dedicates his work to the worms, a paradox that can only be explained by his melancholy realization of the vanity of all existence. Nevertheless, it is literature that temporarily saves him from dissolution, transforming his work into a legacy for coming generations, and thus assuring the circulation of the written word.

A Strategic Vision of Brazilian Literature

The preceding examples illustrate Machado de Assis' aim in his use of foreign literature: it has helped him depict a panorama in which cosmopolitan and local culture are mixed. As a man of his era, our author couldn't help but be powerfully affected by foreign, and especially French culture. His oeuvre is a testament to the intense interest he had in France's literary and political landscape. His work deserves to the made accessible on the stage of world literature the way French luminaries were made available in Portuguese.

Such an intercultural symbiosis is not merely a result of Machado de Assis' own vision of Brazilian culture. It also reflects the effort of Brazilian literature as a whole since the mid-1800s to reconcile the tension between the local and the universal.

Getting to know the slyly cosmopolitan Brás Cubas enhances our enjoyment of the European legacy, unifying and rationalizing theory and praxis. The new reader will be charmed by this mosaic, featuring not only a character of Imperial Brazil, but the process of his self-representation. The book combines critical vision and fictional dexterity, and is one of the greatest novels of Brazilian letters.

—*Gilberto Pinheiro Passos*
Translated by Barbara Jamison

Printed in the United States
23606LVS00002B/64-93

9 780195 101706